Praise for Francis Ray's bestselling
FOREVER YOURS:

"Francis Ray writes warm, sensual romance that is sure to please readers . . . and touch your heart."

—Jayne Anne Krentz

"Fast-moving, sensual and with dashes of humor, Ray's latest . . . nicely launch[es] the Arabesque line."

—*Library Journal*

"A super story with remarkable characters and snappy dialogue."

—*Rendezvous*

AND for UNDENIABLE:

"Francis Ray's fresh inimitable style of storytelling has assured her the success she deserves and the acclaim she's earned. Readers, run, don't walk to your nearest bookseller and buy this one book."

—*Romantic Times*

"UNDENIABLE . . . is full of riveting drama and spellbinding love."

—*Rendezvous*

ONLY HERS

FRANCIS RAY

PINNACLE BOOKS

KENSINGTON PUBLISHING CORP.

PINNACLE BOOKS are published by

Kensington Publishing Corp.
850 Third Avenue
New York, NY 10022

Pinnacle, the P logo, and Arabesque are Reg. U.S. Pat. & TM Off.

First Pinnacle Books Printing: April, 1996

Printed in the United States of America
10 9 8 7 6 5 4 3 2 1

*To booksellers extraordinaire, Emma Rodgers
and Ashira Tosihwe, co-owners of
Black Images Book Bazaar in
Dallas, Texas. Ladies, you're the best.
Thanks for everything.*

One

"This may be your last chance."

Shannon Johnson heard the ragged voice and barely recognized it as her own. She was closer to the edge than she wanted to admit. But at least she had a chance to keep from completely going over. She owed that to a man who understood her better than her family or James Harper, the man who wanted to marry her.

"Thanks, Wade," she whispered, her throat tight with unshed tears. She had cried enough.

Hands gripped at her sides, she looked out over the flower-strewn meadow, heard the rushing water of a stream edged by towering cypress two hundred feet away, then brought her gaze back to the weathered log cabin to her left.

Arthur Ferguson, Wade's lawyer, had told her the cabin was habitable. The old shack looked as if any strong wind would blow it down. She had heard Texas people were rugged, but she thought this was going a bit far.

Her prominent family in St. Louis would be horrified to think she contemplated, even for a moment, the idea of actually living in such a desolate place. But then, she had horrified her parents a lot.

Only one person in her family had always understood her and now he was gone.

Unclenching her hands with effort, Shannon turned to get a flashlight from the glove compartment of her car.

She wanted to inspect the cabin. Gripping the flashlight, she refused to think it was too late to salvage her life and her career.

But she hadn't wanted to come. That, too, had been forced on her. Two Code Blues and the subsequent loss of both patients in the ICCU unit where she was head nurse had sent her to the nursing lounge in tears. A job she once defied her parents to train for, she now dreaded.

"Go home, Shannon."

Shannon flinched, her eyes snapping shut as she remembered the gentle but firm words of the nursing supervisor who had found her in the lounge fighting tears and an aching emptiness. The underlying reason for the directive—her increasing inability to function effectively since the death of her maternal grandfather from cancer three months previously—had sent her to Texas.

Shannon had seen death many times in her six years of nursing, but it had never taken someone so close to her. Although the specialists had given her grandfather only six months to live after his diagnosis, she had known doctors to be wrong and had desperately clung to that belief. She wasn't prepared for the loss or the overwhelming sense that she, as a medical professional, had failed him.

Care of critical patients only intensified her emotional upheaval. Yet, somehow she knew moving to a less stressful unit wouldn't help. Her grandfather's death had taken its toll. She had lost her professional objectivity. She took things too personally and was preoccupied with her own loss. She wasn't helping those entrusted to her by staying. They deserved and needed the full focus of their caregiver and she could no longer give it to them.

Losing Samuel J. Rhodes had left her floundering and unsure of herself. The worst part was not knowing if she was grieving for him or for herself. She had lost her champion, her confidant, her ally.

Shannon looked at the rough exterior of the cabin and shook her head. "You and I both have seen better days," she muttered.

Without further hesitation she walked to the cabin, opened the stubborn squeaking door, then let the flashlight pierce the dim interior. It was spartan and filthy. A broken, built-in mattressless bed sat on the far side of the room.

Ten feet away an ancient-looking potbellied black stove squatted near a wood-filled apple crate. The only other piece of furniture was an overturned, three-legged wooden chair. Spider webs gleamed in the light; a wasp flew past her. It would require a lot of hard cleaning to make the place livable.

Weariness settled in. Another hope turned to bitter regret. No matter how foolish Wade had sounded, she had prayed that the healing power of his meadow would help her, as he had predicted. She badly needed to feel life instead of the anger and misery she couldn't shake.

She had planned on staying in the cabin and getting her life together again. Now she realized that was no longer possible.

The adrenaline pushing her to make the twelve-hour drive from St. Louis had evaporated. Returning to the car, she opened the trunk and pulled out the quilt given to her by Granddaddy Rhodes. It was the first thing she had grabbed when she decided to come to Jackson Falls. The lovingly hand-stitched squares of cloth was her security blanket. It was always to her grandfather that Shannon had turned when she needed reassurance and guidance.

As the shy, youngest child with two brothers who were as assertive and as brilliant as their parents, she had turned to her grandfather a lot. He had never let her down. Now he was gone and she was lost.

Spreading the quilt beneath the shade of a sprawling

oak tree, she laid down for the first time in over thirty-six hours. A trail of blue clouds sailed past under the guidance of the gentle April wind. Hands pillowed beneath her head, she closed her eyes. Immediately, sleep claimed her.

Matt Taggart couldn't believe a stranger was asleep in his meadow.

Years of checking the Circle T's range had revealed some odd things, but nothing like the scene before him. The ranch was clearly posted, and people in the area knew he didn't make exceptions.

Puzzled by the woman's daring, he let his horse's reins trail loosely between his fingers and leaned over the saddle horn to study his uninvited guest.

Daniel's film crew from Denver wasn't due for another two weeks, so it wasn't likely she was with them. Besides, the Cadillac convertible parked by the cabin had Missouri license plates.

A frown marched across Matt's dark-brown face as his gaze swept from the sports car to the woman with skin the color of toffee. Her long legs were shapely and elegant in khaki shorts. Her hips nicely rounded. From the way her breasts pushed against her thin yellow T-shirt, he suspected they would more than amply fill a man's palm.

His hand tightened on the reins. Brazos brought his sleek head up and stepped sideways. A light touch of a booted heel settled the quarter horse. The corners of Matt's mouth tilted in wry amusement at his quick response to the woman. Must be past time for him to head to Kerrville for some R&R.

Dismounting, he dropped the reins to the ground. Quiet, measured strides quickly carried him to the sleeping woman. Up close, he saw the dark smudges beneath her eyes that the crescent shadow of her lush lashes couldn't hide. He knew those signs. She must have been burning the candle at both ends. Before he quit the rodeo circuit a few years back, he had burned the ends and tried the middle once or twice.

She appeared defenseless, almost fragile, lying there with her bare lips slightly parted, her thick mane of reddish-brown hair swirling in the afternoon breeze.

Studying her from another angle, he tried to see if he recognized her. Her face was exquisite with its high cheekbones hinting at a Native American ancestor somewhere in the family background. Her bow-shaped mouth begged to be kissed. She had a nice nose and her chin had just enough thrust to make it interesting.

He was certain he had never seen this woman before. She wasn't the type a man easily forgot . . . if at all.

Maybe she was the new waitress Moses had mentioned hiring for the Longhorn Restaurant and Bar. In the small ranch town of ten thousand, Moses Dalton owned one of the few businesses that kept growing and hiring.

If she was staying in town that meant she was off limits to him. He had made it a strict policy to steer clear of the local women. He wasn't the staying kind and he didn't want any problems when he moved on. As long as he kept it on the road, he didn't have to worry about causing bad feeling between him and his neighbors and friends or, worse yet, someone trying to push him to the altar.

Since this woman apparently felt enough at ease to fall asleep on his property, it seemed one of his hired hands didn't share Matt's philosophy on local women. Only three of the full-time men were single, but in to-day's society marriage didn't necessarily mean fidelity. It hadn't meant fidelity to Matt's ex-wife. Piercing anger no longer came with that knowledge, just an emptiness he didn't try to fill.

His questioning gaze again settled on the classic lines of the sleeping woman's face. He wondered which one of his men *thought* he had gotten lucky. Experience had taught him beautiful women weren't known for their staying power. For himself, he was too busy trying to make the ranch support itself to cater to a woman's whims no matter how tempting the outer wrapping.

"Hey, lady. Your date's not coming," Matt said. She didn't move, didn't blink. The toe of his scuffed boot nudged the sole of her expensive-looking sandal. No reaction. "Lady, wake up!"

Shannon sat bolt upright at the masculine command. Heavy-lidded eyes widened as they traveled up the long, muscular jeans-clad legs of a powerfully built man. Large hands were braced on a narrow waist. A partially unbuttoned chambray shirt allowed a tempting peek at an impossibly broad chest.

She blinked. No man's chest could be that wide. No man could have a voice that rumbled like distant thunder nor possess velvety black eyes that made her skin tingle. Deciding she was imagining things, Shannon closed her eyes to lie back down on her quilt-covered bed of bluebonnets and buttercups.

"Oh no you don't, lady."

Strong, callused hands circled her upper arms and set her on her feet. The black eyes were even more devastating closer, just like the man. "You're real."

The tall, handsome man laughed, a husky sound that vibrated down her spine. "Too bad you won't be able to find out how real."

"What?"

His sensual mouth quirked beneath his jet-black mustache. "A private joke."

"Oh?" Shannon said, somehow perfectly content to let

him maintain his gentle hold on her arms. He had the most beautiful eyes. All dark and piercing.

"If you keep staring at me like that, I might forget you're off limits," he said, his thumb stroking her skin as his voice stroked her body.

"Off limits?" she repeated, clearly puzzled.

His face hardened. "Forgot the man you came to see already?"

Her confusion increasing with each second, she frowned. "I don't—"

"Save it, lady, I'm not interested. I know it's a long ways from town but Jay and Elliott are busy branding. Cleve has more sense and my other hands are married. So you wasted a trip and I don't like trespassers on my land."

Understanding slowly sank into Shannon's tired brain. "You must be Wade Taggart's nephew, Matt. I'm Shannon Johnson." Both her smile and her hand were ignored.

"Another one."

"Another what?" she asked.

"Another one of Wade's charity cases," Matt answered caustically.

Her chin went up. "I am not."

Heavy brows arched. "Lady, you mean to tell me you didn't come here expecting something from Wade?"

She flushed guiltily. "Yes, but if I could just expl—"

"Save it, lady," he interrupted sharply. "Wade died four months ago, and *I* have no intention of being duped the way he was by every pretty face with a sad story."

Hardcase. The nickname flashed into her mind. During Wade's hospitalization at Memorial Hospital in St. Louis he once told her that was the name some people called his nephew and partner. They didn't think he had any softness in him.

But Shannon had felt the gentleness of his touch, heard the warmth of his laughter. And certainly the nurses at

Memorial wouldn't have been in such a continued frenzy to go out with the Walking Hunk, as they secretly called Matt, if he didn't possess some good qualities. His devastatingly handsome face and strong, lithe, perfect body would only take him so far.

"Mr. Tag—"

"You have two minutes to get off my land," Matt interrupted.

"If you would—"

"You're wasting time."

"You're the one wasting time," Shannon said in a rush. Perhaps she had overestimated the intelligence of the women at Memorial. "This is my land."

Surprise flashed across his dark features, then his face hardened into ruthlessness. "Whatever scam you're trying to run won't work on me."

"Mr. Taggart, if you'll just—"

"Lady, you either put your cute little behind back in your car under your own power or I'll do it for you."

Realizing Matt wasn't going to listen to anything she said, Shannon marched back to her car. So much for hoping they could be friends. She reached through the open window for her purse and withdrew a crumpled white envelope. "I think you better read this."

"Lady—"

"Call me lady in that tone once again and I'll do something we'll both be sorry for." He didn't look the least bit intimidated. Shannon sighed. There probably weren't many things that bothered a man with shoulders as wide as a door. "Please just read the letter."

Taking the envelope, Matt scanned the bold, black letterhead of Ferguson & Ferguson. His body tautened. Blunt-tipped fingers removed the paper inside. Midway down the page a heated expletive singed the air. Razor-sharp eyes stabbed into her.

"You won't get away with this. I'll fight you through every court in the country."

"I hope not, Mr. Taggart. Wade wouldn't have wanted that."

"How in the hell do you know what Wade would have wanted?" he challenged.

Shannon debated only a few moments before she decided to face the issue head on. "I was his nurse when he was hospitalized in St. Louis almost four years ago. We became friends and kept in touch after he was discharged."

Matt's perusal moved with deliberate slowness from her windblown hair down to her toenails polished Racy Red, then lifted to linger for a heart-stopping moment on her breasts before continuing to her eyes. "I don't remember him mentioning you while he was there."

Shannon refused to let his bold stare intimidate her no matter how her heart rate sped up. "I worked the eleven-to-seven shift."

A sardonic smile twisted the sensual fullness of Matt's mouth. "I bet that's not all you did, honey."

"Lady" sounded like an endearment compared to the way Matt sneered "honey."

"Now you've insulted me *and* your uncle. Wade was a fine man and you have no reason to talk that way about either of us."

"Being 'fine' doesn't mean he couldn't be fooled by a woman."

"No doubt not a failing you share," Shannon countered.

He ignored her taunt. "Why did you wait so long? That letter was dated a week after Wade's death."

Shannon looked away from his disturbing gaze and tried to speak around the sudden lump forming in her throat. "P-personal business kept me away."

"I'll bet."

She faced him. "Why are you being so rude?"

Hands on his hips, he glared down at her. "You have the gall to ask me that when you sashay in here and try to take the best grazing section of the ranch? The only one with year-round water? The original homestead site?"

"I had no idea what the land looked like until today. Of course, Mr. Ferguson sent me information on the property, but I don't know anything about ranching. I simply followed his direction and turned off on the first road to the left after entering the gate." She tried to offer a reassuring smile. "Don't worry, I won't be in your way for long. Just act like I'm not here."

"Not likely, lady." He leaned down to within an inch of her face, blocking out everything except his dark look of fury. "This land has been in the Taggart family for four generations. I'll fight you through court and hell for what's mine."

She took a hasty step backward. "I already *have* this land, and if the lawyer's office hadn't been closed because it's Sunday the final papers would have already been signed."

Some of the tension left Matt's face and his shoulders. "Then this farce hasn't been finalized. If it had, though, you'd be landlocked."

Shannon jerked her letter from his hand. She could almost see the wheels turning in Matt's devilish mind. "Only until I tore down the fence bordering the Farm-to-Market Road."

Matt looked thunderstruck. "You do and you'll chase every horse and cow that gets out!"

A tear rolled down Shannon's smooth brown cheek. Everything was going wrong. She hated arguing, she hated crying just as much. Tears implied a lack of control that, until the loss of her grandfather, she had prided herself on maintaining no matter what.

The faster she wiped at the tears, the faster they flowed. Her stomach growled. Watery eyes flew up to meet Matt's, and she turned away in embarrassment. How could her own body betray her like this? Easy. Working sixteen-hour days for weeks, sleeping badly, and eating worse would do it.

"Lady, are you all right?"

"I'm just dandy," Shannon sniffed. "Don't I look dandy?"

No, you don't Matt wanted to say, but he didn't think that would help matters. Tears were the oldest trick in the book used by women, yet somehow his usual immunity wasn't working.

Maybe because she looked so lost. Maybe because ever since his older brother Kane had married Victoria Chandler she had made Matt grudgingly admit that perhaps, just perhaps, there were a few good women left on earth.

Probably it was more the memory of Shannon Johnson asleep in the meadow looking beautiful and innocent. He stiffened. That kind of thinking wasn't going to get his land back. The Circle T was going to remain intact and his alone.

"Look, we need to talk. Where are you staying?"

Shannon couldn't suppress a shudder as she nodded toward the cabin. "I had planned on stay—"

"What!" Matt cried, cutting her off. "No one has slept in there for years. You're liable to wake up kissing a rattler."

Shannon's head snapped up and she stared at the cabin. "I . . . I was in there and I didn't see anything."

"You probably wouldn't until tonight." She swayed on her feet. His hand shot out to steady her.

"Mr. Ferguson said it was habitable," she said softly.

Matt snorted. "After Octavia and a couple of the hands tackled it all day."

"I see. Well that will change now that I'm here." Withdrawing her arm, she stepped away and instantly regretted the loss of the warmth and strength of his large callused hand.

For a split second Matt admired her show of courage and wanted to wipe the frightened look from her sad brown eyes almost as much as he wanted to keep feeling her silken skin. Skin that probably tasted as rich and sweet as its toffee color. He scowled. He must have been out in the sun too long. This woman wanted his *heritage!*

A beeping sound shattered the air. Matt snatched the pager from his belt and read the phone number. "It's almost six. Meet me at the ranch house in an hour so we can talk."

Her stomach growled again. Embarrassment overrode caution. Perhaps he wouldn't seem so overbearing after a meal. "I'll be there."

"Just follow the main road you turned in on and it will take you to the ranch house." The brim of his black Stetson dipped, then he turned away. With every step Matt berated his chivalrous uncle for putting him in a position of going up against a woman who looked as if she was on her last leg. Grabbing the dangling reins of his sorrel stallion, he mounted. Shannon was still staring at the cabin, the letter clutched in her hand.

Matt's eyes turned flint hard. She might be on her last leg, but like a lot of women, Miss Shannon Johnson still had dollar signs before her eyes and in her heart.

Matt's booted heel rapped loudly on the wide wooden front porch of the two-story ranch house. Opening the heavily carved door, he went directly to his office and dialed Arthur Ferguson's home phone number. The soft voice of Arthur's wife greeted him on a recording. Gritting his teeth in frustration, he left an urgent message for the lawyer to call him, then dialed the number on the pager. He and rancher Adam Gordon had talked back and forth so much in the past months that Matt knew the number by heart. The older rancher answered the phone on the second ring.

"Hello, Adam." Matt tried to keep the eagerness out of his voice. "I hope your call means I can buy Sir Galahad." Matt winced every time he said the name, but considering the bull's registered bloodline, it was his due.

"I didn't call to talk business, son."

Matt winced again. Adam had started calling him "son" ever since his daughter Vivian had made her romantic interest in Matt clear. She was a nice kid, but she was just that, a kid. "Oh."

"The wife has decided to give a little party to celebrate Vivian's graduation from junior college. We want you to come."

Matt's grip on the phone tightened. He needed that bull to improve his stock's bloodline but he wasn't going to dance a tune to Vivian's fiddle to get it. "It's hard to believe she's graduating already. Seems I still remember her in plaits."

"Vivian is a woman full grown and knows what she wants."

"I'm sure she does," Matt said, then added to himself, *but it's not going to be me.* "Adam, I hate to push you, but I need a decision on that bull. Getting closer to the time I have to start breeding."

"If Vivian lets us, we'll see if we have time to talk this coming Saturday night. She's so excited and looking forward to seeing you. I don't mind telling you that my little girl has taken quite an interest in you."

Matt's patience reached its limit. "Adam, we've been friends for years, so I'll be up front with you. You know I don't date the local women and, more important, you know why. With my reputation, would you and Peggy really be comfortable with me seeing your daughter?"

Silence stretched across the line for several seconds, then, "A man can change."

"Only if he wants to. If the sale of the bull hinges on my taking Vivian out, I'm withdrawing my offer."

"Now hold on, Matt." Outrage roughened Adam's voice. "You can't think I'd stoop to something that low."

"Ordinarily no, but I think you'd do anything to please Vivian and keep your wife happy," Matt said bluntly. "While I admire you for loving your family, I'm disappointed in you as a friend. You have until tomorrow to give me a decision on the bull or I'll look someplace else."

"Matt—"

"And I won't be able to make it Saturday." Matt dropped the receiver back into its base, then plopped in the chair behind his desk. He desperately needed that bull, but he wasn't going to be used or use a young woman's infatuation and her father's blind love to get the animal.

Adam was a good man, but his only daughter had always been able to wrap him around her little finger. He would bust a gut trying to get Vivian whatever she wanted. All she had to do was point. Apparently, she had pointed at Matt.

He really didn't think the girl wanted *him*. Since his uncle's death, Matt's appeal to the women in the area had increased a hundredfold. He had received more invitations in the past four months than he had in the past four years. Most of the women probably meant well, but he knew being sole owner of the Circle T, the largest ranch in the county, didn't hurt.

But you aren't the sole owner of the Circle T, Matt thought with a grimace. And the blame lay solely at the feet of his soft-hearted uncle.

Wade Taggart had been a robust man with an easygoing manner and a ready smile. A throwback to the bygone days when men protected women, pampered them. He was a sucker for their sob stories. Not even when Matt's wife had turned his life into a nightmare had Wade said one word against her.

Women, in Wade's opinion, were the weaker sex, and if they sometimes acted unladylike, it was their way of surviving. His belief had financed more than one woman out of trouble. No matter how much Matt tried to tell Wade the women were using him, he just smiled and did as he pleased.

Yet, never would Matt have thought Wade capable of giving away a section of their ranch. Wade's ties to the land were as strong and as deep as Matt's. It didn't make sense.

Matt's father, Bill, and his brother Wade were Matt's paternal grandparents' only children. The ranch passed jointly to both brothers. Since Wade was the oldest, when Matt's parents married and moved to Tyler, Texas, Wade stayed on the Circle T and kept the place going.

Ten years ago when Matt's world turned into a living hell, it was to the ranch that he had come to heal. At the time he wasn't fit to be around man nor beast. However, working the land had restored his sanity and given him back a reason for getting up in the morning. The week after the birth of Kane's twins, their father had signed over his share of the Circle T to Matt with Kane's blessing.

Wade had been there. "When my time comes, the Circle T will all be yours."

That was two years ago. What catastrophe in Shannon Johnson's life could have been enough to change Wade's mind? Try as Matt might want to dispute it, somehow he knew her claim was real.

Wade had gone to her rescue.

Matt pushed to his feet. Her story didn't matter. She wasn't getting his land. No woman was ever taking anything else from him again. He had made himself that promise the day his divorce was final, and in the years since, he had yet to break his oath.

But in order to fight Shannon, he had to learn more about her. Inviting her to dinner was the first step. He didn't like subterfuge, but if he had to put on the charm to find out what she was up to, his conscience could take it.

Reaching into one of the desk drawers, Matt pulled out a paperback novel, then strode into the kitchen. He needed the house to himself. Pushing open the swinging door separating the den from the kitchen, he saw Octavia Ralston stirring something with a wooden spoon in an old-fashioned crock bowl. He knew whatever she was making would be mouth-watering.

After burying two husbands, raising six children, and helping to care for twenty grandchildren, Octavia had always said mothering, cooking, and cleaning came naturally. Her gray hair was scraped back from her plump ebony-hued face that was free of makeup, leaving it as open as the owner. At least Matt had thought so until a few days ago.

"Octavia, I need you to leave the house for a couple of hours tonight."

"Why?" The housekeeper and cook for the Taggart household for the past forty years didn't pause as she dumped the soft bread dough onto a floured board.

"I've invited a woman over."

Octavia's speed in turning belied her sixty-odd years and her considerable bulk. "There'll be none of that going on in this house."

Matt returned her stare. "This is business. I've never asked a woman to the ranch. You're the one always inviting them over."

"It's about time you remarried." The housekeeper grabbed the rolling pin.

"At least just stay in your room."

"My TV is on the blink in my room and tonight's the conclusion of that miniseries."

Matt set his teeth. Octavia seldom watched her color TV. She had carried on for weeks to him about the waste after her children had bought it for her for Valentine's Day. She was just being stubborn.

"Strange. All this time I thought you were in your room reading books like these." He pulled the paperback from behind his back.

Wide-eyed, she advanced on him. "Give me that."

"Now, Octavia, don't be so savage," he said, eyeing the rolling pin in her hand. "Or did you get that from . . ." He paused and opened the book. " 'Serena, her black eyes glazed with passion, leaned into Jared's hard—' "

"That's my property," Octavia interrupted sharply. "Where did you get it?"

"In the easy chair." Black eyes twinkled mischievously. "Imagine my surprise when I reached down between the arm of the chair and the cushion for the TV remote I dropped and found a love novel with your name inside."

"Romance novel," she corrected.

Matt grinned. "Pardon me. Romance novel."

She held out her hand. "My book."

"You can have it and I promise to keep quiet about your reading material *if* you'll take the book and stay in your room tonight."

"Never thought you'd hurt a woman of my years."

Matt grunted. "This is the boy you took a broomstick to when I was sixteen, saying you wanted to even the odds."

Octavia smiled, showing strong white teeth. "It did,

too." She took the paperback and pocketed it in her apron. "You win this time, but there's still two or three women I haven't invited back after church for Sunday dinner."

"And while they're here, perhaps they'd like to see what you do when you close your door."

"You're a mean man, Matthew Evans Taggart."

"It's a mean world."

Two

Shannon stopped in the driveway of the rambling two-story white house and gripped the steering wheel. Dread made her tremble. She had to make Matt Taggart accept his uncle's will. As silly and as desperate as it sounded to her own practical mind, she believed Wade's meadow could help her. A legal battle would only delay matters. She only had three weeks of vacation. Every day counted.

She chastised herself for becoming defensive. She should have made Matt understand that she had no intention of keeping the property. Her life was in St. Louis, not on a ranch in Texas. But he had the annoying ability of making her lose her composure.

People usually thought of her as the quiet, sweet Johnson girl. No one she knew would believe she had held her own with a man as commanding as Matt.

"You coming in or what?"

Snatched out of her musing, Shannon glanced around. Matt's handsome brown face was inches from hers. For a split second their gaze met and held. Shannon's stomach muscles tightened. Quickly, she looked away from the magnetic pull of his riveting eyes and grabbed her purse. She must be more stressed out than she imagined. The last thing she needed was another complication in her unsettled life.

As soon as she stood, his gaze moved with maddening slowness from her shoulder-length hair to her sandled feet, then swept upward. The tightness in her stomach moved to her breasts. She fought the urge to hunch her shoulders beneath the same yellow T-shirt she wore earlier. "I . . . I didn't think it wise to change."

"Probably not. You can freshen up inside."

She was encouraged by his offer of hospitality. Perhaps they could come to terms.

Grasping her elbow, he started for the house. "Come on. Dinner is ready."

Shannon faltered on the first step of the wooden porch. "You said one hour. How long before you finish?"

His implacable gaze cut to her upturned face. "Do you think I'd sit down and eat and leave you cooling your heels?"

"I—"

"Don't answer that," he told her and continued up the steps.

Once inside the house Shannon let out a small sound of appreciation. She liked space, hardwood floors, and the durable softness of leather furniture. The front room boasted all three. "It's lovely."

"You expected cow hides and horns?"

Refusing to be baited, Shannon pressed her lips together.

Matt grunted. "Bathroom's on the left of the stairs. I'll be in the kitchen through those swinging doors. It's pot roast." He walked away before she could answer.

Shannon watched his long, measured strides, noticing the grace and ease of his conditioned body, the subtle shift of well-worn supple denim against his muscular legs and tight buttocks. Only after he disappeared through the swinging doors did she realize what she had been doing. Annoyed with herself, she hurried to the bathroom, flicked on the light and splashed water over her flushed cheeks.

She wasn't the type to pant over a man. James politely

referred to her as "restrained." She had always assumed it was because the male body held no mystery for her. Matt had just shot down her theory.

Trembling fingers massaged her temper. *Stress.* Yes, that was the cause of her uncharacteristic behavior, and Matt's distrustful attitude was only making it worse. Confident that she now knew why she was reacting so strangely, she lifted her head, then grimaced at the face staring back at her in the oval mirror.

Gone was the happy, carefree person whose eyes sparkled with laughter and optimism. In her place was a pale shadow with dark smudges beneath somber eyes and lines of strain around a mouth that seldom laughed. If she didn't get Matt to listen to reason, she wasn't sure the image of the vibrant woman she once was would ever return. Snapping out the light, she closed the door and followed Matt's direction to the kitchen.

"Where should I sit?"

Standing at the stove, Matt pointed with a meat fork to a ladder-back chair at the circular oak table. A plate of food was in front. "I can't eat all that," she told him, her gaze on the overflowing plate of roast, new potatoes, carrots, and three steaming biscuits.

Broad shoulders shrugged. "Eat what you can." Bringing his plate from the stove, he sat across from her. "You look like you could use it."

She tucked her head in embarrassment and said grace. She initially picked at the food as she usually did, then found herself actually eating. The roast was delicious. Shannon moaned and closed her eyes in appreciation as she chewed. Swallowing, she flicked her lashes upward. She started to ask if he had cooked the dinner, but froze.

Piercing black eyes watched her intently. "What— what's the matter?" she asked, hating the breathless sound of her voice, hating worse that she was unable to do anything about it.

"You were making moaning sounds."

She flushed. "I'm sorry. I guess I was enjoying the food and got carried away."

His searing gaze flickered to her lips. "So I gathered. Are you always so easily pleased?"

Shannon's grip on her fork tightened. "I enjoy good food, if that's what you mean."

"It's not and we both know it," he said, his voice a lazy wisp of sound that caressed and promised endless pleasure.

Shannon felt flushed. Unsteadily she rose. "Thank you for dinner and good night."

Matt came upright. Unrelenting fingers closed loosely around her wrist. "We haven't had our talk yet."

Shannon felt the heat of his hand, the hypnotic pull of his black eyes. She fought to keep from swaying closer. God, what was the matter with her? "I—I think it's best that I leave."

"Which one of us don't you trust?"

She shied away from the answer to his question. Her chin lifted. "My arm."

For a long moment Matt studied the defiance in her eyes that was in direct contrast to the trembling of her body, the pulse leaping wildly in her delicate wrist. All he had to do was exert the tiniest pressure and she would be in his arms. He was sure of it.

His gaze lifted from her quivering lips to her wide, uncertain eyes. Fear mixed with desire stared back at him. Inexplicably, he felt the twin needs to console and possess. Both were dangerous. A grasping female like Shannon Johnson was the last woman on earth he wanted to become involved with. Long fingers uncurled; he stepped back.

"Ready for dessert?"

Two pairs of startled eyes swung toward the jovial female voice. Octavia stood by the kitchen counter with a lattice-crusted apple pie in her hands. The housekeeper frowned on seeing the barely touched food on Shannon's plate. "Didn't you like my roast?"

Shannon couldn't help from glancing at Matt's emotionless features. "It was very good, but I have to go."

"Nonsense," the robust woman told her. "Matt, sit the young lady back down and I'll put the pie within easy reach. Homemade vanilla ice cream is in the freezer."

Not wanting Matt to touch her again, Shannon quickly sat down on her own, but not before she saw the knowing look in his eyes before he took his own seat.

"Since Matt has forgotten his manners, I'm Octavia Ralston, the housekeeper."

"Shannon Johnson." This time her hand and her smile were accepted and returned.

"You two eat up." Octavia gave Matt a brilliant grin. "Don't forget to put the food up when you do the dishes."

Matt spluttered.

Shannon glanced from Matt's shocked expression to the retreating back of the housekeeper. No sound came from her, but her round shoulders were shaking as if she were laughing.

Shannon's quizzical gaze went back to Matt. He looked ready to take someone's head off. She smiled.

Something had transpired between Octavia and Matt. Shannon hadn't understood exactly what, but apparently Matt had been bested. Whatever the reason, she applauded anyone who could take down her opinionated host. Picking up her fork, she speared a potato and chewed with enthusiasm.

"I see your appetite has returned," Matt said.

"Yes, it has." She cut a sliver of roast. "I like Mrs. Ralston."

"Wouldn't have anything to do with her putting me on dishwashing duty, would it?"

Shannon smiled around a yawn. "I'll help you do the dishes. I haven't enjoyed a meal so much in months."

"I'll do them myself," he grumbled.

"Fine."

Black eyes widened. "You aren't going to argue?"

Shannon took a sip of iced tea before answering. "No."

Matt couldn't believe the whimsical smile on her face. Despite his obvious annoyance, she was fighting to keep from laughing. In his memory no woman had dared laugh in his face. They were too busy trying to get his attention.

He watched as Shannon lost the battle. Brown eyes sparkled. Her obvious weariness seemed to fade as her animated face began to shine with beauty and soft laughter started low in her throat.

"Did you make Wade laugh?" he asked abruptly.

The melodious sound ended as abruptly as it had begun. A shadow crossed her face. "We made each other laugh."

"If he meant that much to you, why didn't you come to his funeral?"

"I wanted to, but I just couldn't leave." Her hand clutched her glass. Her voice lowered. "There was so little time."

"Time for what?"

Her head snapped up. If there had been the least bit of softening in Matt's demeanor, she might have told him about her grandfather. There wasn't.

"Life," she answered, then laid her fork aside and stood. "If you don't mind, I'd like for us to have that talk now. I'm suddenly rather tired."

Matt slowly came to his feet. She was hiding something and he was going to find out what it was. "We'll talk in the den."

Leading the way, Shannon took a seat in a comfortable-looking overstuffed leather chair. Settling back into the welcoming softness, she yawned.

"When did you sleep last?" Matt took a seat across from her and tried not to notice the way her T-shirt clung to the lushness of her breasts.

"In the meadow."

"I mean before that." He shifted uncomfortably in his seat.

She started to shrug and yawned instead. "I got a few hours early Saturday morning after coming off a double shift."

"What!" He came upright in his chair. "You drove all the way here on a few hours of sleep? You could have killed yourself."

Shannon straightened. Her family and James had called her foolish for driving instead of flying; she didn't need Matt adding his two cents' worth. "I'm here to talk about Wade's will, not my work schedule."

Matt's brief nod conceded she was right. It was none of his business what she did . . . unless it involved the meadow. "Why did you wait so long to make your claim?"

"I told you that I was busy taking care of personal business."

"Such as?"

She clamped her hands together. If she tried to discuss the loss of her grandfather with someone as cynical as Matt, she'd fall apart. Talking about Wade was enough of an ordeal. Tears stung the back of her eyes. Yet, to let them fall would only subject her to more of Matt's sarcasm.

"Such as none of your business."

"When you claimed Taggart land you became my business. I can hire someone to find the answers to my questions."

"Then hire someone."

Matt's heavy brow arched. Shannon might be down,

but she was still fighting. "Why did Wade leave you the land? At least you can tell me that."

Shannon leaned wearily back in her chair "Wade was a very perceptive and caring man. Even when he was sick, he thought of others. We used to talk about his meadow. He called it a place of sunshine. After he was discharged from the hospital he invited me on several occasions to visit, but there never seemed to be enough time." Regret rang in her soft voice. She swallowed.

"About a . . . a month before he died, he called and we talked. I . . . I was going through a difficult time and he said I needed his meadow."

"Why did Wade think you needed his meadow? Had some man dumped you?"

"No, but a woman obviously dumped you." Matt's jaw clenched. Shannon shrank from her own cruelty. It wasn't like her to taunt someone, no matter the provocation.

Trembling fingers rubbed her pounding forehead. "I'm sorry." Wearily she pushed to her feet. "Thanks for dinner. It's time I started back."

Matt stood. "Back where? You're so tired you can hardly stand."

"Thank you for your concern, but I can take care of myself. Frankly I haven't been sleeping well lately," she confessed. "I didn't have any trouble staying awake until I reached the meadow. Now that I'm here, I can't seem to keep my eyes open."

Matt snorted in derision. "I guess you're going to tell me Wade left you the meadow as a sleep aid."

"I wouldn't dare tell anyone as judgmental and pig-headed as you anything."

Eyes narrowed, Matt glared down at her. "I don't like being called names."

"Neither do I, but that hasn't seemed to stop you."

"I never called you anything."

Eyes flaring, Shannon advanced on him. "Not outright, but you have a biting way of saying an innocent-sounding word and making the person feel like an inchworm."

"Lady—"

"Don't you ever call me lady again!" she yelled, so furious with him that she jabbed her index finger against his unyielding chest.

Matt wondered where this fiery woman had come from. Then his thoughts centered on something else, on the softness of her lower body pressed enticingly against his. Desire struck him low and fast. "Damn."

Shannon realized two things at once: that her thighs were pressed intimately against Matt's and that her body was enjoying every titillating second. She stumbled backward. The meadow might be helping her rest, but it was also turning her into an oversexed, argumentative shrew.

James Harper, the brilliant lawyer who wanted to marry her, the man she had known and respected for two years, had never made her body react this way. He had never made her want like this. He also had never made her lose her temper.

Of all the etiquette her mother had instilled in Shannon, the one lesson she never forgot was that no matter the situation or the provocation, she must always remain a lady.

Then, too, her grandfather had always maintained that being in control of your emotions had little to do with breeding and everything to do with intelligence. No one in her family shouted . . . except in court.

Even when her parents were at their steam-rolling worst, everyone remained polite. Whatever the situation, the Johnsons were always well bred.

"I . . . I don't usually act this way," Shannon excused. "Must be the meadow."

Shannon didn't know if Matt was trying for humor or

sarcasm. She decided she was too tired to care. "Good night and thank you again for dinner."

"I asked you before, where do you think you're going?"

"To find a comfortable bed."

"You're not leaving this house." Her mouth gaped. His thinned. "Don't flatter yourself. Octavia sleeps here."

"Thank you, but—"

Matt talked over her protest. "Jackson Falls is twelve miles from here on some of the most winding two-lane roads in the county. There is no sense in putting yourself, much less someone else, in danger."

Her chin lifted. "Thank you for the offer, but I can manage. If I can't, I'll pull over and sleep in the car." Without another word she headed for the door, well aware that Matt followed behind her. She quelled the urge to run down the steps.

"You aren't going to let her go, are you?" Octavia asked from directly behind Matt. "Sleeping in her car is ridiculous and dangerous, especially when we have three empty bedrooms upstairs. The poor thing is so tired she can hardly think straight."

Matt wasn't surprised by Octavia's appearance. Keeping anything from her was like trying to hold a greased pig, frustrating and almost impossible. "What do you want me to do? Drag her back by her hair?"

The housekeeper sniffed. "All I know is that any man worth his salt—"

Matt turned. Something about the look in his eyes stopped Octavia from completing what she had been about to say. She started back toward the kitchen. "I guess I better get to those dishes."

Shannon's car engine and her headlights came to life the same instant.

"Stubborn woman," Matt muttered. He strode from

the house and didn't stop until he stood directly in the path of the car. Tires screeched.

Shannon jumped out of the car, her voice and her body trembling. "W-what do you think you're doing? I could have killed you."

Ignoring her, Matt reached into the car, cut the engine, then removed the keys from the ignition. Opening the trunk, he grabbed her two pieces of Louis Vuitton luggage and slammed the lid.

She was right behind him. "Put those back."

"I'll be happy to in the morning. Now let's go inside."

Shannon moved away from his outstretched hand. "Why?"

"You're in no shape to drive into town, and it's too dangerous for you to sleep in the car."

"Not good enough. You've made it painfully obvious that you don't trust me or want me as a partner."

"That's right, I don't." Surprise widened her eyes. "But regardless of how I feel about you personally, I'd be less than a man if I didn't offer you a place to spend the night."

She folded her arms. "I'm not giving up my claim to the land."

"I didn't think you were and, for the record, I still plan to fight you, but not tonight, not when you're about to collapse."

Shannon wanted to argue, but she knew he was right. Matt looked like the type of man who was seldom wrong. He'd make a loyal friend or a bitter enemy.

She studied him a long time, measuring the man against his words and knew he'd keep his word, he'd wait until she was stronger. Then watch out. Opening the front door of the car, she drew out the quilt.

They both were silent as they reentered the house and walked up the stairs. Opening the last door on the right side of the wide hallway, he flipped on the light, then set her cases down. "Bathroom through that door. Sleep as long as you like." He turned to leave.

"Mr. Taggart?"

Knob in hand, he glanced over his shoulder. "Yes?"

"Thank you, but I still think my staying here is a mistake."

"Won't be the first for either of us, now will it." The door closed.

Clutching the quilt closer to her chest, Shannon sagged on the bed. "No, it won't be my first, but something tells me it might be my worst."

The blinding rays of the sun on Shannon's face snatched her from sleep. Panic seized her. She had to be on the floor at 6:45 A.M. Throwing off the quilt, she jumped from bed. Halfway across the room the sight of a double dresser instead of an armoire stopped her in mid-stride.

Slowly, then with increasing speed she remembered where she was and why. If she didn't get herself together, there would be no job to be late for ever again.

The prospect of leaving nursing and becoming a wife to James would please him and her parents, but not her, and certainly not her grandfather if he were alive. He was the only one in the family who encouraged her to pursue a career in nursing instead of going to law school.

When she held firm in her decision to become a nurse after graduating from high school, her family had urged her to attend medical school instead. If she was set on the medical profession then aim for a specialist. She had expected as much from her authoritarian parents yet they only wanted what they thought was best for her.

Yet, even after obtaining her degree in nursing her parents still harbored the hope that she might eventually go to law school and join the family practice. She had the brains and the tenacity; they thought hardness could be developed. She knew differently. She just didn't have the toughness she saw in James, her parents, and her brothers. They delighted in stirring things up and going for the jugular vein; she liked to soothe and comfort.

Or at least she had until she met Matt Taggart. Well, perhaps today would be different.

Looking around the room, she saw her suitcase. After Matt had left last night she had showered, then fallen into bed. She was asleep by the time her head hit the pillow. Opening the case, she picked up a pair of white shorts only to put them back, instead choosing slacks and a turquoise blouse. There was no sense tempting trouble. After she was dressed, she'd find Matt, thank him, then drive into town and get a room.

Not finding anyone downstairs, she set her luggage by the front door and went into the kitchen. A woman sat at the table, her face hidden by an open paperback. Its cover in vivid hues of mauve and gold showed a man and a woman in passionate embrace.

"Good afternoon."

The book jerked. Octavia, her eyes wide, appeared around the side. Scrambling up from the chair, she quickly put a dish towel on top of the book. "Ah, good afternoon, Miss Johnson."

Letting the swinging door close behind her, Shannon smiled and walked farther into the room. "Please call me Shannon. I'm sorry. I didn't mean to startle you, but you were so engrossed in your book."

The housekeeper tucked her head in obvious embarrassment.

"From the cover it looked good. One of the things I missed most when working long hours was not being able to curl up with a good romance book."

Astonishment lifted Octavia's head and widened her brown eyes. "You read them, too?"

"Used to. Every chance I got."

A wide grin spread across the older woman's charcoal face. "I knew there was something about you that I liked the second I saw you." Still smiling, she opened the refrigerator door and took out a plate of fried chicken and potato salad. "It's almost one. You must be starved. Sit down and eat."

"I really must be going," Shannon said, but her eyes were on the golden-brown chicken.

"Can't," Octavia announced, and set a glass of iced tea beside the place setting for one. "Matt said for you to wait until he got back. Usually once he eats breakfast I don't see him until late in the evening, but today he's been back twice to see if you were awake."

"Why didn't he have you wake me up?" Shannon asked. "I don't remember the last time I slept this late. I wouldn't have minded."

Octavia chuckled, a deep sound that shook her heavy body. "That may be, but he almost took my head off when he came back the last time around twelve and found me vacuuming. Told me to stop making so much noise because you needed your sleep."

Uncomfortable and oddly pleased, Shannon addressed the one safe issue. "I'm sorry I interrupted your cleaning."

"Don't be. As you can see, I made good use of the time. Anyway, having you in the house is good for Matt. Makes him remember his manners. Does my heart good to see that woman didn't kill all of his protective instinct toward females." Octavia pointed toward the ladder-back chair. "Now sit down and eat, so we can discuss books."

Shannon sat and half listened to the housekeeper discuss her favorite romance novels, but what Shannon really wanted to discuss was who "that woman" was and what had she done to Matt.

Three

Two hours later Shannon sat on the bank of a stock pond beneath the shade of a willow tree with a book dangling from her fingertips. A yard from her canvas-covered feet lay the end of her cane fishing pole, the red-and-white plastic cork barely moving in the tranquil water. Unfortunately, she wasn't as peaceful.

She would have preferred going in search of Wade's lawyer rather than dealing with the unsettling task of meeting Matt again. She was, if only temporarily, going to take his land away from him. And he was going to fight her with everything within him.

Peace was what she had come for and that was exactly what she had yet to obtain. Instead of leaving as she'd wanted, she'd let Octavia bamboozle her into going fishing.

After lunch and still no Matt, the housekeeper had thwarted all plans of Shannon leaving. Before she knew how it happened, the jovial Octavia had thrown some chocolate-chip cookies, a thermos of lemonade, and a paperback into a canvas tote, then led her outside. Several fishing poles leaned neatly beneath the overhang of the white house.

"Pick one."

When Shannon simply stared at the housekeeper, the older woman snatched the one nearest her, then shoved the eight-foot-long pole and a plastic bag of bait into

Shannon's hand and pointed toward a clump of trees twenty-five yards away.

"Fishing is the best remedy for what ails you," Octavia said before she disappeared into the house. The banging of the screen door jarred Shannon out of her passivity.

She had reached the steps before she realized the woman was only being kind. More than once during their conversation Shannon had drifted into her own thoughts. Perhaps fishing wasn't such a bad idea after all.

Finding a shady spot, Shannon had baited her hook and prepared to do something she had never done in summer camp: catch a fish. However, the fish weren't cooperating. She picked up her book, then decided she'd rather just enjoy the countryside.

The meadow might have been Wade's favorite place, but the entire ranch, with its budding green grass, wide-limbed trees and scattering of rainbow-hued flowers, was just as peaceful. As long as Matt wasn't nearby.

Shannon winced at her unfair thought. The man was only trying to protect his heritage. In a way, she respected him for his tenacity, but not his attitude. If he'd stop being so judgmental, perhaps she could reassure him.

The fishing line moved so only the top half of the white cork showed. The cork dipped once, twice. Instantly Shannon forgot about her reluctant partner. Excitement bubbled within her as she scrambled to pick up the fishing pole. The cork disappeared completely beneath the water's surface. Two-handed, she jerked with all her strength. Line, cork, and fish came out of the water.

The fish kept going.

She sighed deeply. Even fishing as a child she had always pulled too hard. Usually the hook detached itself from the fish's mouth before it left the water. At least this time it had held long enough for her to finally get a fish on the bank. Dropping the pole, she went in search of her catch.

Several feet away in the grassy area, a grayish-brown bird with a black-striped chest flew into the air only to land again, walk a few feet, then fall flat on the ground making pitiful sounds. Shannon rushed toward the bird to help, but it got up dragging both wings on the ground.

Moving cautiously, she approached slower. Yet, again the bird moved farther away, gasped, then rolled over as if in terrible agony. Shannon saw a red spot.

"Oh, goodness. You're bleeding." She took another step. "Easy now. I won't harm you."

Out of nowhere another bird flew over Shannon's head screaming protest. She glanced at the bird in the air, then back at the bird on the ground. "I won't hurt your mate, but he or she needs help."

"It's a she and she's no more hurt than I am."

Shannon swung around. Matt, wearing a blue plaid shirt and jeans, stood a few feet away. He looked tall, handsome, intimidating. Her throat dried. No man should affect a woman that way. "I saw blood."

"What you saw was her rump. She's trying to lure you away from her nest." He inclined his black Stetson toward the squawking bird flying above them. "The male is getting into the act, too. Killdeer can put on quite an act when it comes to protecting their nest or their young."

"I certainly feel like an idiot."

"You shouldn't. Not many people care enough to try and help an injured bird, especially after the male gets into the act." He gave her a long, level look. "Were you that concerned and attentive with Wade while he was your patient?"

"I tried to be," she said softly, hoping this could be the turning point in their relationship. "Patients in ICCU often need healing in spirit as much as in body. Wade was an exception. It didn't matter that he was seventy-five years old with internal injuries and two broken legs from his automobile accident, he never doubted he'd walk out of the hospital and come home to the ranch."

The corner of Matt's mouth lifted in a fleeting attempt at smiling. "The physical therapist said she never had seen anyone more determined to not only walk, but run. He never did manage to run, but he could do a mean skip and a hop with his cane."

"He told me he let his horse Paintbrush do the running for him."

"He did. Every morning the two of them would head out and usually end up at the meadow." Matt shook his head. "No matter how I objected about him going alone, he went anyway. Turned up his nose if I mentioned me or one of the hands driving him."

"Why did you want someone with him?"

"Glaucoma," Matt answered succinctly. "Doctors found out early last year, but it was too late to be treated. Got so bad Wade could barely see his hand in front of his face. I understood riding Paintbrush gave him back his independence, but it was too dangerous for Wade to wander over a thousand acres by himself."

"Knowing that, you let him go anyway?" Shannon asked in disbelief.

"I had to."

"But—"

"Taking away Paintbrush or not helping Wade find his way to the barn would have been the easy way out for me, but not for Wade. He would have felt helpless, less than a man." Matt tugged on his hat. "So I hired someone to watch him from a distance. I couldn't take his pride away from him. He had lost too much already."

A wave of sorrow and regret swept through Shannon. One of the most heart-wrenching decisions a family member had to make was knowing when to set your own wants aside and do what the patient needed. "You did what was right."

"Yeah."

The one clipped word from Matt told her he didn't think it had been enough. She knew exactly how he felt. All her specialized training hadn't helped her grandfather. Her hand fisted to keep from placing it on Matt's tense shoulders and comforting him. "In all the times we talked, he never mentioned his failing vision."

"Wade wasn't the type to lay his problems on someone else; he was more apt to take on another person's problems. He never complained about the hand life dealt him. Only said that a man ought to be willing to take the bad times with the good." Matt glanced away, his voice gruff. "He was a hell of a man."

"Yes, just like Granddaddy," she mumbled. Her throat tight, she turned away and almost stepped on her escaped, gasping perch. Carefully, she picked up the foot-long fish and carried it back to the bank. Slipping the fish into the water, she picked up the fishing pole and the rest of her things, then started back to the house.

"He was a keeper. Why did you throw him back?"

She kept walking. "Life is precious in any form."

"That didn't stop you from eating that beef last night."

So the truce was over. "I didn't have to see it before it died."

"So it's all right as long as you don't have to dirty your own hands," Matt said, catching up with her. "I'm surprised you didn't send someone else to claim my land."

The unfairness of his taunt swung her around. The rebuttal sprang to her lips, but somehow she managed to swallow the words. "People in St. Louis consider me a nice, decent person. Why can't you?"

"Try taking one hundred acres of prime grazing land

or, in your case, riverfront property, from one of them and see how long that opinion lasts."

He was right. Again. Her shoulders slumped. "Can't you understand? I had to come."

A callused thumb kicked his Stetson back on his head. "How could I have forgotten? As I said, it's your own personal sleep aid."

Shannon resisted the urge to bop him on the head with the canvas bag in her hand. "You are making it very difficult for me to like you."

Matt leaned down until their noses were an inch apart. Shannon quelled the impulse to lean away. "You didn't seem to have any difficulty liking me last night in the kitchen."

Face flushed, Shannon stumbled backward. Her canvas shoes caught in the underbrush. With a startled cry, she felt herself falling. Matt's hand shot out and pulled her upright against his hard chest, his other hand tunneling through her heavy mass of hair, his fingers warm and unsettling against her scalp. Her heart pounding, she stared up into glittering black eyes.

"Did you?" he asked, his voice a husky whisper of veiled hunger.

No words came. She was too busy feeling the muscular body pressed against hers. Sensations swept through her. Her mind shut down except for the narrow perimeter of the sensual outline of Matt's lips.

Would his lips be as abrasive as his taunt or as gentle as his hands holding her? Would they take or give? Would his mustache be soft or prickly? Unconsciously digging her toes into the grass, she lifted herself upward toward temptation and the answer to her question. Her eyelids drifted shut.

Trembling lips barely touched something warm and soft and tantalizing before she was snatched away. Her eyes opened. Matt glared down at her.

Comprehension of what she had done hit her like a fist. Heat flooded her face. She had acted on impulse, a sexual one at that. If she could bottle the meadow, she could make a lot of people happy. Apparently Matt, who was holding her at arm's length, would not be one of them.

"I'm all right. You can let me go," she offered, pleased that her voice didn't sound as shaky as her legs felt.

He continued to stare down at her, his stillness as unnerving as his tight face, the strange light glittering in his dark eyes. He seemed to be wrestling with his own emotions. She couldn't blame him. He probably wasn't sure what she was all right from, nearly falling or throwing herself at him. Slowly, he unclamped his hands from her upper arms and bent over.

Her face heated again as he picked up her fishing pole and canvas bag, then started toward the house. She hadn't even realized she had dropped them. Trying to ignore her trembling legs, Shannon fell into step behind him.

None of her mother's etiquette lessons had covered the proper method for recovering graciously from throwing yourself at a man who obviously didn't want you. From the peculiar way Matt acted afterward, he had only intended to annoy her.

Instead of being adept enough to read him correctly or strong enough to resist him, she had acted like a love-starved bimbo. If he hadn't pushed her away . . . She bit her lower lip and refused to let her mind go any further. One thing was certain, initiating the kiss had only given more credence to Matt's mistaken belief about her. There was only one way to let him know he was wrong.

"You can have it back as soon as I'm finished," she offered.

Stopping abruptly, Matt swung around. "What did you say?"

Shannon pulled up short to keep from walking into

him. "I—I never planned on keeping the land your uncle left me. I decided when Mr. Ferguson first told me about the meadow that it wouldn't be right for me to accept. Nothing has changed my mind. I only plan on being here three weeks."

His dark brow furrowed. "If that's so, why haven't you mentioned it before now?"

"Because you aren't the nicest person to get along with."

Unlike the last time she had given a similar assessment of his character, Matt appeared undisturbed. "What do you plan to do in that time?"

"Live on the land."

"So you're telling me you just want to live in a run-down cabin for three weeks and then you'll sign over the place to me?"

"Yes."

"I wasn't born yesterday. Once you get the land, there'll be nothing I can do to stop you from selling or leasing the property."

"You have my word."

"Your word, huh? What if I promised you that if you renounce your claim to the meadow in writing, I'll let you stay for as long as you want."

She answered immediately. "I wouldn't believe you."

Matt nodded as if that was the answer he expected. "Neither one of us trusts the other, so it looks like we're at an impasse." He grasped her by the elbow and headed for the house at a faster pace. "Come on, Ferguson is waiting to see us."

She practically ran to keep up with his long-legged stride. "Us? When did he call?"

"About twenty minutes ago."

Her eyebrows furrowed. "But how did he know I was here?"

"I told him," Matt said.

She glanced up at the hard line of Matt's jaw. Something wasn't right. "Exactly when did you tell him?"

"Yesterday" came the flat reply.

She mentally called herself a naive fool for thinking for one second the stern-faced man dragging her back along a narrow path was kind. Arrogant, yes. Devious, positively. But kind, never.

"So that's the real reason you didn't want Octavia to disturb me. You weren't as concerned with my rest as my not seeing Arthur Ferguson and signing the final papers before you saw him. For a little while this afternoon I thought I might have misjudged you."

Apparently unconcerned by her opinion of him, he kept walking until he reached the side of the house where the fishing poles were kept. Without a glance in her direction, he replaced the gear, then dropped the canvas bag on the back porch steps.

Incensed at being ignored and duped, she put her hands on her hips and stepped in front of him. "It appears I was wrong."

"I never implied any different," he finally replied. Walking around her, he went to the front of the house where a dusty black truck was parked and opened the passenger door. "Get in."

Shannon folded her arms across her chest. "I prefer to drive my own car."

The door slammed shut. "Suit yourself, but you better be in Ferguson's office in thirty minutes."

Outraged, she snatched her arms to her sides. "I can't possibly get cleaned up and drive to town in that short a time."

"Look, la—*Miss*. I have a ranch to run in case you haven't noticed. I don't have time to sleep half the day and fish the other half." Brushing by her, Matt went around the end of the truck and got in.

She was right on his heels. "Sometimes I can't believe Wade was related to you."

"Sometimes neither could he." He started the motor and drove off leaving her staring after him.

"Where is she?" Matt tossed over his shoulder as his booted foot struck the hardwood floor of Arthur Ferguson's office. "I know she's anxious to stake her claim."

Watching Matt over tented fingers pressed against his beaklike nose, Ferguson continued to rock back and forth in his chair behind his desk. "You said she had to get dressed."

From beneath thick black lashes Matt shot Arthur a quelling glance. "Might have known you'd make excuses for her."

The lawyer's pensive expression never altered. "I'm merely making an observation. Like most women she probably just wants to make a favorable impression."

"She'd look good in a feed sack and she knows it," Matt blurted in rising irritation. "She just wants to annoy me."

Ferguson stopped in midrock backward and sat up straighter in his chair. His vague gaze of a moment ago was replaced by one of keen speculation. "Ms. Johnson sounds more interesting by the moment."

"Why?"

"In the years that I've known you since you came to live with Wade, I've never heard you compliment a woman or known you to let one take more than a fleeting thought in your mind. This one has done both."

"This one is trying to steal my heritage," Matt told him.

"I wouldn't jump to such a conclusion until you have all the facts, Matt," Ferguson said, and went back to rocking, all the time watching Matt as if seeking the answer to some difficult puzzle. "This is not her fault."

"Whose is it then? I need every cent to keep the ranch running until the beef can be sold in two months. I'm not paying off some little gold digger. The only thing I don't understand is why my uncle didn't want the bequest known to me until she and I were together."

"I'm sure he had good reasons."

Matt snatched aside the gauzy curtain on the office window and looked outside. "Yeah, I'll bet. I don't like the idea of meeting his lady friend this way."

A frown wrinkled Ferguson's deep-brown forehead. "There's no reason for that kind of talk. Wade Taggart was an honorable man."

"He was a man," Matt said flatly, remembering his own body's reaction to Shannon. Explosive.

When he'd baited her near the stock tank he had expected her to go prim and proper and indignant on him. Instead, she had looked at his mouth with a curious longing in her bottomless brown eyes. He felt himself falling in their glittering depth with nothing to grasp except her. A mistake. Her smooth, satiny skin was even more of a lure. Desire coiled through him as he watched her lips soften, part. Watched her long lashes flicker, then close.

He could have stopped what happened next, but he found himself as curious about her taste as she apparently was about his. It was a mistake. She tasted like his dream. A dream he was unaware of until Shannon's lips had touched his and made him want like nothing he had ever experienced. But life had taught him wanting wasn't enough and dreams had a way of turning into a living nightmare.

It had taken considerable willpower to push her away. Seeing the unbanked passion in her face, he had been tempted to damn the consequences and kiss her as her mouth and body begged to be kissed. Deep and hungry and forever. Instead, he had walked away because one kiss would never be enough with Shannon.

But the familiar heat in his loins didn't go away. Taking a deep breath, he continued to stare out the window. If he had to fight his own hunger, how could he have expected Wade to have resisted a woman whose sensuality was as much a part of her as her pretense of innocence and kindness?

His gullible uncle hadn't stood a chance against a grasping, seductive woman like Shannon Johnson. But this time she wasn't up against a man who would gladly give his last cent to any woman in need.

During the time his uncle was in the hospital, Shannon must have discovered Wade's weakness for helping women and used it to her advantage. The only thing Matt couldn't figure out was why she had taken so long to try to collect.

Scanning the two-lane street for her car, he finally spotted her convertible. The dark-blue Allante pulled into the space across the street from the law office. He glanced at his watch. 4:10 P.M. Fifteen minutes late.

The car door swung open. A pair of long, shapely traffic-stopping legs swung into view. Three-inch pale-yellow heels met the street seconds before Shannon stood and turned to face him.

Air hissed through Matt's clenched teeth. Involuntarily his hand fisted in the curtain. He damned Shannon Johnson as his body absorbed the full impact of her beauty.

Dressed to the hilt in a designer, figure-flattering pale-yellow suit, she looked elegant and beautiful and sexy. Barely four inches of material separated the hem of her skirt from the hem of the midthigh sculptured jacket. Without a woman's usual self-conscious swipe at her hair or her clothes, she headed for the street crossing.

Head high, she didn't appear to notice the people

around her slowing down for a good second look. The women might be scoping out the clothes or the hairstyle, but Matt knew very well why the men were practically drooling. The same reason he was having trouble taking his eyes off her. She was a walking fantasy.

Releasing the curtain, he turned away. "Maybe I should be thankful Wade only gave her the meadow," he muttered.

"What was that?" Ferguson inquired.

"Shannon Johnson just arrived."

A knock sounded on the door, then a middle-aged woman entered. "Ms. Johnson is here."

"Show her in, Helen," the lawyer told his secretary and stood, straightening the slightly wrinkled gray suit jacket.

Shannon entered the office with a smile on her face and a subtle scent of an exotic floral perfume. Diamonds winked in her ears. Matt watched Ferguson's lower jaw become unhinged and knew Shannon had just scored points.

"Ms. Johnson, I'm glad you finally decided to come," Ferguson said.

"Thank you, Mr. Ferguson. I just wish it didn't have to be under these circumstances," she said softly.

Matt snorted. Her gaze sought him out. If he didn't know better he would have thought the sadness in her eyes was genuine.

The lawyer cleared his throat in the ensuing silence. "I believe you two are already acquainted."

"Yes, we are." Shannon gave her attention back to the lawyer. "I hope I didn't keep you waiting too long."

"Not at all." Ferguson patted the soft hand in his he had yet to relinquish. "Please sit down. Would you like something to drink? Tea? Coffee?"

"No, thank you." Taking the indicated chair in front of the antique wooden desk, she folded her hands over her small handbag. "I'd like to get this over as soon as possible."

"I told you she was anxious, Arthur." Matt strode across the small office and placed both hands on the arms of her seat. "What's the matter? Your last man woke up and now you need help in keeping yourself in the style you're accustomed to? On your salary you couldn't afford those clothes, the diamonds, and certainly not the Cadillac."

Her harsh intake of breath cut through the air.

"Matt, Ms. Johnson has been through enough in the past months without your adding to it," Arthur defended.

Straightening, Matt swung to the lawyer. "How would you know what she's been through?"

"I—"

"We're here to hear what Wade wanted, nothing more," Shannon interrupted, cutting off Ferguson.

The lawyer looked for a moment as if he wanted to say something, but at the almost imperceptible shake of Shannon's head, he clamped his lips shut. Going behind his desk, he took a seat, opened his desk drawer, then took out a heavy brown folder.

Their silent communication only gave more credence to Matt's belief that Shannon used her beauty and her aura of sadness to make fools of men. He wasn't going to be one of them.

"You're something else," he said, his eyes hard. "I bet your family is real proud of the way you turned out."

Shannon flinched.

Score a point for me, Matt thought. Then she lifted her tear-brimmed eyes to his. Misery stared back at him and he felt as though he had kicked a defenseless animal.

Calling himself a fool for falling for her act, he walked back to the window and leaned against the wall. "You have the floor, Arthur. But whatever happens, no one is going to get a square inch of Taggart land without a fight."

Ferguson paused in removing the legal document from the folder. "You haven't heard the will yet. On what grounds?"

"I think that's obvious."

Shannon finally looked at Matt. "Wade loved you like a son. Too bad you couldn't respect him like a father."

Matt came away from the wall in one fluid motion and crossed the room. Instead of cringing as he expected, Shannon jutted out her chin. The show of courage on her beautiful face stopped him more effectively than Ferguson's frantic voice.

"Matt, sit down," the lawyer ordered. "I know you don't like what Wade did, but he had his reasons. If you can't understand them, at least respect him enough to have his last wishes heard. Give him the same love and respect he gave you."

"It's not Wade I don't respect," Matt said, his meaning bitingly clear.

"Then we'll proceed as soon as you take a seat."

Four

"I don't care if you trust me or not," Shannon said with heat. "I do care that you keep going on as if Wade couldn't come out of the rain. He was one of the most intelligent men I've known. He was also one of the kindest. If you want to dislike me that's your privilege, but don't use Wade as an excuse."

His gaze drilled into Shannon's irate face. She returned the glare full measure. He *did* want to dislike her and he wasn't sure if the reason had to do with her wanting his heritage or because, despite his best efforts, he wanted *her*.

For the first time since his ex-wife taught him the bitterness of deceit, Matt was having a tough time suppressing his desire for a woman. He sat down.

Arthur Ferguson let out a tension-filled breath and looked from Shannon's tense body to Matt's. Lowering his gaze, he began to read Wade Taggart's Last Will and Testament.

Finished, he laid the papers aside. There were no surprises. Everything had been left to Matt except the original Taggart homesite of one hundred acres.

"How did you get him to turn his back on his family?" Matt asked.

This time he was the one who was ignored. "Please show me where I sign."

"Get ready for the fight of your life." Matt stood.

"You wouldn't let me have a moment of peace, would you?"

"No," he promised harshly.

"Just as I thought." She turned to the watchful lawyer. "After I sign, perhaps you can tell me where the nearest realtor's office is located."

"You're not going to sell my heritage," Matt thundered.

Surprise widened the lawyer's eyes. "Ms. Johnson, Wade wanted you to live on the property, not sell the land he loved. Perhaps I should have given you both these letters sooner, but Wade had instructed me not to hand them to you until after the will was read." Removing two letters from the folder, Ferguson rounded the desk and handed them out. "Because of his failing eyesight I offered to write them for him, but he wanted to do it himself. Not because of pride, but because he said the letters were too personal."

Shannon and Matt glanced at each other, then opened and began reading their letters.

Dear Shannon,

Life must be riding you pretty hard about now. The meadow will heal you. You did all you could for your grandfather. He was a lucky man to have had you. You may not believe it, but I felt just as lucky to have had Matt. Would you believe he thought he could hire Johnny Sanders to spy on me while I rode Paintbrush and expected me not to know it? Shows how gullible young people think their elders are. Many a day Paintbrush and I gave Johnny a scare or two. I didn't mind the watchdog because I knew it would keep Matt from worrying and it proved he wasn't as hard as some people thought.

That boy has had to get over a lot of heartache. At first, I had my doubts. But after watching him worry and fuss over me and all his shenanigans with Octavia, I know that other woman didn't tear the heart out of him, she just badly bruised it.

So while you're here don't mind Matt if he gets testy at times. Beneath that gruffness he's a good man. The roughest part in going is knowing he's still hurting because of that woman. He needs healing, too, just like you. I pray you can help heal each other.

Wade

Dear Matt,

Don't you make Shannon cry! If you do I'll get a pass from heaven and come after you. She needs all the help she can get.

When I woke up after that car in St. Louis piled into mine, the first thing I saw was Shannon's beautiful face. I thought I was seeing an angel. During the weeks I was in that hospital bed fighting depression, pain, and my fear of never walking again, I came to rely on her. With a gentle touch, a reassuring word, she helped me remember I wasn't alone. You and the family were my strength by day, but Shannon was my own special angel at night.

She is one of a kind. Do anything to make life worse for her and when I return, we're going behind the barn again. I can still best you and don't you forget it. So cut her some slack.

I know you're probably angry and hurt because I left her the meadow, but I owe her among other things. One day I hope you'll understand and forgive me. I loved you like a son and I came to think I was a pretty close second to your daddy. I'm counting on you to do what's right, but if you don't, remember I'm watching.

Wade

How long must it have taken you to write the letter,
Matt thought. He shook his dark head in admiration and
love. Wade was a tenacious fighter in more ways than
one. Matt's mouth tilted slightly at the corners at the
warm memories his uncle's letter evoked. When he
glanced at Shannon, his blossoming smile vanished.

She looked utterly devastated. Her expression reminded
him too much of himself when, ten years ago, Kane had
brought a reluctant and angry Matt to Wade's ranch.

Matt had initially stayed because of his mother's tears,
but it was his uncle's prodding and the land that helped
Matt forget his wife's infidelity and turn his life around.

The painstakingly written letter clutched in her hand,
Shannon recalled the peaceful expression on Wade's face,
the wistfulness in his voice when he talked of his
meadow. He called it a place touched by the smile of
God. No, Wade wouldn't have wanted her to sell the
land. Nor would he have been pleased to know she had
taunted Matt with the possibility.

Wade thought she and Matt might help each other.
That was impossible. Healing took time and trust, and
Matt wasn't going to give her either.

Unsteadily, she pushed to her feet. "I'd like to think
things over before I sign. I'll let you know my decision
before I return to St. Louis." She turned to Matt. "In . . .
in my letter Wade speaks fondly of you. Remember him
the same way. He wasn't trying to take from you as much
as he was trying to help me."

His continued silence hurt as much as the censure in
his unrelenting face. She needed someone to recall the
good memories instead of the sad ones. After reading
Wade's letter, a part of her wished it could be Matt.

Sadness weighing heavily on her shoulders, she extended her hand to the lawyer. "Good day, Mr. Ferguson, and thank you for all your help."

"If there is anything I can do, please don't hesitate to call," Mr. Ferguson said. "Wade was more than a client, he was a close friend."

Shaking the lawyer's hand, she left very much aware of Matt's continued silence and the growing sadness within her.

"Where is she?" Octavia asked as soon as Matt walked through the front door of the ranch house.

"She who?" Matt never slackened his stride.

"Don't get funny with me, Matt Taggart," Octavia told him. "Shannon Johnson, that's who."

Matt flipped through the mail in his hand. "How should I know?"

"You had an appointment with her at Ferguson's office. I know you didn't expect Wade to leave her the meadow," she said, "but I guess he had his reasons."

"So I gathered, but there has got to be more to it than his letter explained. It also doesn't explain why the woman he left it to is ready to take my head off one minute and then before I can blink, she's trying to comfort me," Matt railed.

His mood had grown darker since he saw Shannon fighting tears. She hadn't acted the way he expected. Why hadn't she signed the papers in the lawyer's office? Why wait?

Suspicion narrowed the housekeeper's eyes. "What did you do to her?"

"Nothing." Matt barely kept from growling the word. Tossing the letters and magazines on his desk in his study, he retraced his steps to the front door. He hadn't felt so on edge since Kane dumped him at the Circle T. Octavia's nagging wasn't helping.

"She doesn't know anyone else here, where would she go?"

Matt spun around. "How would I know? She's probably someplace trying to con some man and make a fast buck."

Octavia opened her mouth, saw Matt's scowl deepen and said, "My arthritis is acting up. I won't be able to fix supper tonight or breakfast tomorrow."

"Fine." Jerking open the heavy front door, he headed for the barn. Whenever the housekeeper wanted him to know she was really upset with him, her "arthritis" acted up and she went on a work strike. In reality, she was as limber and as spry as a woman half her age. Let her get an attitude. He could fix his own supper. Shannon Johnson was no concern of his.

"I came to say good-bye, Wade, and to thank you," Shannon whispered as she stood amidst an array of wild-flowers in the meadow. "I wish things could have ended differently."

She swallowed. The lump in her throat refused to budge. She hadn't ached this much since the day she lost her grandfather. Then, as now, she felt adrift, lost. Her family and friends hadn't been able to help, nothing had, and now she wasn't sure what would.

Hands clenched, she took one last look at the rustic cabin and walked to her car. Matt didn't want her around, and pushing the issue would solve nothing. She didn't have the time or the heart for a nasty court battle. And it would get nasty.

Matt might not be aware of it, but once he began pro-ceedings to contest Wade's will, their private disagree-ment would become public knowledge. Both the Taggart and Johnson families were too well known and too prominent for the story not to grab attention.

News that Wade had left his former nurse, a single

younger woman, a valuable section of his ranch and that his nephew was hotly contesting the will would send the media into a frenzy. Unfortunately some people were as suspicious as Matt and they would think the worst about her friendship with Wade. Wade's reputation would suffer, and the man who Wade had asked her to help would have another reason to mistrust women.

A horse neighed. Automatically she turned in the direction the sound had come from. Her heart stopped, then redoubled its beat. Matt, his signature black Stetson pulled low, sat on a horse fifty yards away watching her.

She'd know those broad shoulders and muscular build anywhere. She didn't have to see his face to know it was unrelenting in its disapproval. Whoever the woman was in his past, she had done more than "bruise his heart," as Wade had put it. She had wounded his soul.

Fumbling fingers opened her car door. Within seconds she was heading back down the road. Cowardly as it was, she didn't want another confrontation with Matt. Thank goodness she had put her bags in her car before she drove to the lawyer's office. She had intended to say good-bye to Octavia and thank her in person for making her feel welcome. A letter would have to suffice.

Glancing in her rearview mirror, she saw that Matt remained unmoved on his stallion. At least she hadn't had to suffer the humiliation of falling apart in front of him. She just wished she knew where she went from here.

One arm draped over the open door of the refrigerator, Matt studied the well-stocked interior. Bone-weary, he couldn't decide if a hot shower or hot food called to him more. Every muscle in his body ached, but he hadn't eaten anything since breakfast and it was past nine at night.

Questing fingers lifted the corner of a foil-sealed glass dish. Roast beef. Recovering Sunday's leftover, he picked up a quart-size plastic-covered bowl.

"I need you to take me into town," Octavia said from behind him. "My grandson has my car."

Having heard the housekeeper's heavy treads on the linoleum floor, Matt didn't even glance around. Instead, he tilted the clear container in his hand, recognized sliced canned peaches.

"It's important," Octavia continued, her voice strained.

"Riding in my truck might aggravate your arthritis."

"Shannon is in room twelve of the Paradise" came the tight-lipped reply.

His hand paused inches from the meat drawer. Broad shoulders tensed. The Paradise, known around town as the "no-tell-motel," had rates that were hourly and cheap. It was just the kind of place his ex-wife had frequented with men who could buy her the things Matt couldn't. So he had been right about Shannon after all. Something in his gut twisted.

He opened the meat drawer, then shoved it shut with more force than necessary. If his life had depended on the answer, he couldn't have named one item inside.

"I just knew something was wrong. She wouldn't have left without saying good-bye," Octavia reasoned. "So I called every motel in the vicinity until I located her at one I wouldn't let my dog stay in. That decent, caring woman I talked to this morning wouldn't go near such a place unless she had no choice."

"Have you talked to her?"

"The phone wasn't working in her room, so they couldn't connect me. But I know I'm right."

"I see." Absently, he moved a jar of jelly to one side. "Shannon didn't look like the type of woman to let herself get into a financial pinch."

"Looks can be deceiving." Octavia came around to

the front of the refrigerator door and spoke to Matt's unyielding profile. "That young woman is here because your uncle left her Taggart property. That makes her partially your responsibility. You know what kind of place the Paradise is. What if some no-good man sees her and doesn't understand the word no?"

Matt's long fingers gripped the corner of the refrigerator tighter, but otherwise he didn't move. Shannon might have suckered his uncle and Octavia, but she wasn't adding his name to her list.

"Besides," the housekeeper continued, "since she has a claim on the meadow, it seems to me it would be in your best interest to keep an eye on her rather than letting her do God knows what with the property."

Finally, she had said something that got Matt's attention. He gave up all pretense of searching for something to eat and faced the housekeeper. Lines furrowed her forehead and crinkled the corners of her eyes. Obviously she was worried, and now he was, too. Not about Shannon, but about her future plans for the land.

That afternoon when he had seen Shannon near the cabin, he had been too angry to approach her. The thought that she had legal claim to the meadow and that he might have to pay her to get it back burned his insides like acid. After all these years, this woman was going to make him break a promise he'd made to himself because of another woman's deceit.

"She isn't going anyplace until she signs over all rights to the meadow to me." Slamming the refrigerator door closed, he headed for the front door.

"Now you're talking," Octavia encouraged, a pleased smile on her ebony face.

A mile from the motel Matt saw Shannon's car on the shoulder of the road. Since the car appeared undamaged, he reasoned it must be a mechanical problem. Recalling the last time he had seen her, how her miniskirt displayed her long, elegant legs, how her thick hair swirled wildly around her beautiful face, a face that sadness only made more compelling, he didn't imagine it was long before some man had stopped.

And now she was registered at the Paradise.

His grip on the steering wheel tightened. Her name might be the only one registered, but that didn't mean she was alone. The rage that splintered through him caught him off guard.

Loyalty and fidelity were two things he didn't expect from beautiful women like Shannon. His wife's had lasted only as long as he finished in the top money roping calves in the rodeo. But the more they argued over her spending habits and her refusal to travel with him on the circuit, the worse his concentration became, the more he lost.

By the time their nine-month marriage was over, he had gone from being ranked tenth in the country with a good chance at winning the National Calf Roping title to being unranked. At twenty-four he was a has-been and he owed it all to his stupidity and a greedy, unscrupulous woman. He had confused lust with love and paid the price.

So why did the confirmation that Shannon was exactly the same way anger him? He didn't look for an answer, he simply pressed his booted foot on the accelerator. The speedometer needle rocked to the right.

The purple-and-green neon-lit palm tree over the name Paradise winked on and off in subtle invitation and underlying promise of discretion and pleasure. The overgrown shrubbery, dingy windows, and cars of assorted ages and models told their own story of those whose carnal desires outweighed any other consideration. At least, on this night.

Matt passed the front office without slowing. His headlights on bright, he turned in a wide, searching arc in the one-story motel court. Number twelve was at the farthest end. An old dented Buick was parked at an angle in front, as if the occupants had been anxious to get inside.

Coming to a gravel-spitting stop, Matt jumped out of the vehicle. A heavy fist pounded on the door. "Open up!" A choked cry came from behind the peeling pink wood.

"Shannon! Shannon!"

Frantically, he twisted the knob. He stepped back with every intention of breaking the door down when he heard what sounded like his name and furniture being moved. Seconds later the door swung open. He only had a moment to glimpse Shannon's tear-stained face before she launched herself against him, her arms going around his neck.

"I—I thought you were that man who was bothering me earlier. Oh, Matt. I was so scared," she cried, her cheek pressed against his chest.

Something in his gut clenched again. His arms clutched around her shivering body drawing her closer. What if it hadn't been him? Fury at the unknown man— and himself—whipped through him.

For the first time in his memory, he didn't think right or wrong, he didn't weigh the cost. He simply held her. "It's all right, Shannon. I'm here."

Her grip tightened as she tried to burrow closer. Her voice quivered. "I . . . I was so scared."

"It's over. I'm here now." One hand slid down the smooth curve of her back, the other one tunneled through her hair. He soothed her with his voice, the steady rhythm of his hand.

The angry voices of a man and woman erupted in the courtyard. "I need to close the door, Shannon."

She tensed. "D-don't leave me."

"I'm not." Curving one arm around her small waist, he anchored her against his chest, moved just enough to reach the door, then slammed it shut. The instant the door closed, she released a tension-filled sigh. Her warm breath raked delicately over the side of his neck, the bare skin beneath his partially opened shirt.

Reluctantly, he set her on her feet, but kept her within the confines of his arms. "You feel better?"

She nodded, still not releasing her hold or moving away from him. With the full length of her body flush against his, he felt the lush imprint of each soft curve, the generous fullness of her breasts, inhaled the alluring fragrance of her perfume. Desire tore through him, but he ruthlessly controlled it.

Wrong time, wrong place, wrong woman.

The problem was she felt so right in his arms.

"No one is going to hurt you," he assured her.

"I—I knew that once I saw you."

Her words shouldn't have caused the strange feeling in his chest, but they did, and at the moment, there was nothing he could do about it except remember vulnerable women said things they often didn't mean. "When you feel better we're leaving."

A shiver ripped through her. "This was the only place I could afford after I couldn't find the rest of my money or my credit card," Shannon explained.

Every nerve in Matt's body went on alert. His hand in the small of her back paused. "You lost your money?"

"At first I thought I did. But after going over it again and again, I think I must have left the rest of my money and the one credit card I always carry on trips at home on my dresser." Sadness darkened her amber-brown eyes as she looked up at him. "I was in such a hurry to leave."

"To see the meadow," he said, ice sliding into his voice.

She nodded and lowered her head to his chest. "Everyone I called back home tonight was out. I just sat by the pay phone at the store and kept calling my family and friends in St. Louis with my calling card even though I had left a message on all their answering machines. Then it got dark and the store closed. There wasn't another place in town open for anyone to wire money to."

She took a deep, shuddering breath before continuing. "I thought about staying in the car, but after it got dark some men in a beat-up old truck kept cruising by. I had already asked the lady working in the store about the cheapest place in town to stay and she told me the Paradise. I should have suspected something from the surly way she answered my question."

"Why didn't you call Arthur Ferguson?"

"I tried. His office was closed and I got another answering machine at his house. So I decided to come here. Knowing how my family and friends would worry, I called everyone back before I left the store and told them I had run into an old friend."

"That was very considerate of you," said Matt coldly, his eyes narrow slits.

The terseness in Matt's voice finally penetrated Shannon's fear. Leaning back, she looked up into his starkly handsome face. His body against hers was as devoid of comfort as the emotionless black eyes that stared accusingly back at her.

"W-what's wrong?"

Matt studied the beautiful tear-stained face. If he didn't know better, he might think the puzzlement she showed was genuine. She had almost fooled him. Greedy like his ex-wife and a lot of other women he had known.

If she thought he was going to put her up at one of the hotels on the interstate, she had picked the wrong man to con. It was a good thing it suited his plans for him to be able to watch her or he'd leave her here with the roaches.

"Get your things," he ordered.

The stiffness of Matt's voice caused Shannon to hesitate for a moment before she rushed to get her overnight case and her purse from atop a rickety table. She didn't know what had gotten into him, but if he was taking her out of the Paradise that was all that mattered. The place made her skin crawl. "I'm ready."

"I see you didn't bother to unpack."

"I don't think a rat would stay in this place," Shannon said with feeling.

Matt glanced around the dingy room, the cobwebs on the one light fixture in the ceiling, the faded and chipped Mediterranean decor, then at the sizable diamonds in her ears. "Not what you're used to, huh?"

"No woman should have to get used to this."

"You'd be surprised at the number of women who like sleeping in low places." Taking her case, he grasped her by the arm and led her outside to his truck.

Unworried about decorum, Shannon pulled up her short skirt and climbed ungracefully inside as soon as he opened her door. Seated, she glanced at Matt's stiff profile as he slid in behind the wheel and wished the caring man who held her earlier would return.

She had told him the truth when she'd said she knew she was safe as soon as she saw him. He might make her angrier than she ever thought possible, but she couldn't deny he was the one person she had prayed would come and find her. And when he had held her in the shelter of his strong arms and soothed her with his deep voice, she had felt as if nothing could harm her.

At least she now knew Wade was right, that somewhere beneath Matt's cold exterior he had a heart. She hadn't missed his remark about a woman sleeping in low places. Had the woman Wade mentioned in his letter cheated on Matt? Was that why he distrusted women?

Absently, she wondered what kind of woman had taken away his ability to trust and what kind of woman it would take to restore his faith in a woman and make him smile. The sudden urge to be that woman jerked her back to reality almost as strongly as seeing them pass the motel's office without slowing.

"Stop!"

Tires screeched on gravel. "You forget something?"

"To check out." She held up the key. "I have to turn this in."

"If you think you'll get a refund, forget it."

"I don't, but I don't want anything to remind me of the last two hours." She opened the door, looked at the naked light bulb at the front door of the office, then back at Matt. Her voice hesitant, she asked, "You'll wait here, won't you?"

"I'll wait."

Offering a smile of gratitude, Shannon got out of the truck and went into the dingy office. The sight of the thin, unshaven man behind the counter caused her to shudder. She had been mentally groped by men before, but never had she wanted to rush home and take a scalding bath.

"I'm checking out."

Hands under his armpits, his back propped against the doorframe of a connecting room of the office, he slowly turned toward her. As when she had registered, his gaze dropped to her breasts and stayed there. His tongue ran across his narrow lower lip.

Shannon barely kept her disgust from showing. She wouldn't give him the satisfaction. The key landed with a soft thunk on the counter. "I'd like a receipt."

His gaze lifted. "Didn't take you long to get a better offer."

"The receipt."

Dragging his hands from beneath his arms, he went behind the counter and moved a sheet of paper. "Can't seem to find the receipt book. Wanna come behind the counter and help me look?"

"Not if my life depended on it."

"I'll just see about that," he snarled and started around the counter.

Shannon spun for the door. She heard a curse, then the distinctive clang of a phone hitting the floor. She looked over her shoulder. Not seeing anyone, she cautiously peeped over the four-foot wooden countertop. The clerk was sprawled on the cluttered floor, the phone cord tangled around his bony legs.

"Saved by Ma Bell," she said, and began to laugh.

The door behind her opened and she turned. Matt filled the doorway, his face harsh and relentless. "Having fun?"

"Hardly. The clerk appears to be having some difficulty finding a receipt book," she told him.

There was another clank behind the counter, then a string of curse words. "When I catch that bi—" A head shot over the counter and looked straight into Matt's dark, forbidding face. The man stumbled backward, tripped over the phone for the second time and went down.

Shannon laughed again. Catching her sides, she glanced up at Matt. Laughter abruptly ceased. She well understood the clerk's fright. Matt looked as if he could strangle her. She couldn't imagine what she had done this time to annoy him.

"Do you need help in writing that receipt?" Matt asked, his voice tight and clipped.

"No . . . no, sir" came the hasty reply.

Her eyes widened. Her gaze went to Matt. The pimply-faced, surly young man probably hadn't said "sir" in his life. At least it was nice to know she wasn't the only person intimidated by Matt.

True to the clerk's words, his head came back up this time with a body and a receipt shaking in his grubby hand. "Nice having you, Ms. Johnson."

Matt snatched the receipt with one hand and Shannon with the other. He didn't stop until he practically tossed her into the passenger seat of his truck. This time when he took off she had no intention of saying anything. Just breathing appeared to upset her reluctant rescuer. With no money she was at his mercy. She shivered. Not a comforting thought.

Five

Less than five minutes later Shannon realized she wasn't going to be able to keep her promise of not speaking to Matt. A small groan slipped past her lips as he slowed his truck and pulled off the highway behind her Allante. She had hoped he had forgotten about her car. The way her life was going she should have known that wouldn't happen.

Cutting the engine, he twisted in the seat toward her. "Which light came on?"

"Light?" Long, sooty lashes veiled her eyes.

Beneath his mustache sensual lips thinned in annoyance. "The red warning light in the dash."

"Oh." She twisted uneasily in her seat. She had known exactly what he had meant. Stalling wasn't something she usually did, but she had never been up against anyone who inspired such conflicting emotions within her.

Matt could be as compelling as he was annoying. For the last five minutes he was definitely the latter. "It's late. I'll just have the car taken care of in the morning."

He grunted. "The same way you took care of your sleeping arrangements?"

Bristling, she faced him. "I did the best I could with the money I had."

"If you couldn't afford a decent hotel, how are you going to get the car repaired?" he asked tightly.

"I'll manage." She resumed staring straight ahead. "I really thank you, but can we please just go."

"Give me the key."

Her head snapped around. Matt's face was determined, inflexible. He wasn't leaving until he checked her car. He held his hand out palm up. He wasn't the type to wait long.

"What difference does it make?"

"Jackson Falls may be a small town, but we still have car thieves. Your Cadillac would be too good to resist if one of them came across it," Matt explained impatiently. "You need your car to get home."

She looked into his resolute face. It didn't take a genius to decipher his words. He planned on her leaving soon and he wanted to make sure she had a way of doing so. He might have rescued her, but he still didn't trust her.

For a short time at the motel she had dared to hope things might be different between them. Another regret to add to her growing list. Opening her purse, she located the keys and dropped them into Matt's palm.

"Stay in the truck."

Shannon knew it was useless to continue with the charade. So what if he yelled at her again. She could take more of his condemnation, couldn't she? "It's out of gas."

Matt's muscular body paused halfway out of the cab. He sat back in the seat and just looked at her for a long moment.

Shannon found herself fidgeting and instantly stilled the nervous motion. She was stronger than this. "I discovered I was almost broke when I went into the service station to buy gas. Finding someplace where money could be wired to me took precedence. Then by the time I realized I wasn't going to be able to contact anyone, finding a safe place to stay seemed more important than the possibility of walking."

Her nose wrinkled in disgust. "At least I thought it was safe."

A flicker of something crossed his face so swiftly she couldn't read it in the dim cab. "You make a habit of running around on fumes?"

"Oh, no. In fact it's just the opposite since I work at night," she explained. "It's just that everything has been so hectic here. I didn't think about gas until it was too late."

Straightening, Matt started the engine and pulled back on the highway. On the interstate, he pulled under one of the eight bays of a brightly lit gas station.

"Thank you. I'll pay you back," Shannon told him as he got out of the truck.

"You can count on it," he promised harshly.

The door closed. Despite temperature in the upper seventies, Shannon shivered. She was safe and that was all that mattered. Matt's poor opinion of her shouldn't be important, yet somehow it was.

Octavia met Matt and Shannon at the front door of the ranch house with a nod of approval for Matt and a hug for Shannon. "You look tired, child. Go on up to your room and I'll bring a tray."

"Won't climbing the stairs be difficult with your 'arthritis'?" Matt asked.

"Nope," Octavia answered with a sassy smile and headed for the kitchen. "It's in remission."

Matt's grip on Shannon's luggage tightened. He was afraid this might happen. Octavia had accepted Shannon as one of her charges, which meant no matter what Shannon did or said Octavia would staunchly stand by her.

The woman didn't give her friendship lightly, but once given it was irrevocable.

The moment Matt heard the words "child" and "her room," he knew Shannon had gained an ally. Shannon had managed to work her magic on the housekeeper, just as she had on Wade, just as she had tried to do on Matt himself.

"She did it to you again, didn't she?"

Matt glanced at Shannon. She was smiling. Again he experienced the almost imperceptible softening. "Did what?" he finally asked.

Her smile wobbled. "Got to you somehow. You had the same expression on your face last night."

"And that was?"

"A mixture of admiration and pique."

Grunting, Matt started up the stairs. Her intelligent brown eyes saw too much. "Men don't have pique. If we're angry we show it."

"Tell me something I don't know," she mumbled.

Matt heard the softly spoken words and decided to ignore them. It was just as well that he was immune to her. He hadn't realized it before, but he admired a spirited woman. Too bad she wasn't honest as well.

Shannon stepped inside the room and experienced an unexpected sense of peace. The homey room filled with heavy maple furniture and scattered rugs on the hardwood floor was nothing like her own Italian decor, yet somehow it felt right. She felt right being here.

She turned with a smile. "I can't thank you enough."

"Thank Octavia." He closed the door and placed her luggage by the dresser. "She's the one who called all the hotels until she found you."

"But you came for me." The breathlessness of her voice surprised and annoyed her. Matt might be one of the handsomest men she had ever met, but he was also one of the most unpredictable.

"I had my reasons."

"Whatever they were, I'm grateful." He looked stern, untouchable. The peace she had found began to fade. She knew the unbending man in front of her was responsible for that. His opinion of her mattered. She wanted the caring man to return and hold her one last time.

On impulse, she pressed a light kiss against his cheek. The sudden stillness of his body told her she had made a mistake. Eyes wide with apprehension and embarrassment, she took a step backward.

Something about Matt's entire demeanor changed, grew more calculated. Unsure of how to deal with this new aspect of an already unpredictable man, she decided to put more space between them. "I . . . er . . . good night."

Matt matched her step for step, his avid gaze watching her every movement. "How grateful?"

His husky voice vibrated down her spine. It was at once a lure and a challenge. "I don't understand."

Matt took another step. The heat of their bodies mingled. Shannon's lungs seemed to be fighting to suck enough air into them. And with each attempt her breasts came uncomfortably close to brushing against Matt's shirtfront.

Her foot eased back and struck a low cedar chest at the foot of the bed. She was trapped.

"I think you do, Shannon."

The sound of her name affected her almost as much as the pad of his thumb grazing across her lower lip. She had heard him say her name at the motel, but at the time she had been too frightened for it to register. Now she was too aware of him not to notice. Heat pooled in the center of her body. Desire made her legs weak.

"I think you understand very well. You need a place to stay and a man in your bed." The long, lean fingers of his other hand trailed along the collar of her suit. "I can give you both."

The blatant insult cleared the sensual haze from one heartbeat to the next. For a moment she was too surprised and too hurt to speak, and when she did it was barely above a shocked whisper. "You think I'd sleep with you for a place to stay?"

"We won't be sleeping," Matt told her bluntly. "You should have waited a little longer to tell me about your missing money and credit card."

Understanding hit, and with it came the bitter knowledge of what kind of woman Matt thought she was, and despite that knowledge, even now she couldn't keep her body from shivering from his touch. "Take your hand off me."

"There's no reason to keep—"

He was talking to air because Shannon had ducked beneath his arms and headed for her luggage. She reached them within seconds.

"Where the hell do you think you're going?" He stepped in front of her.

"Since I won't pay your price, why should you care?"

Surprise at Shannon's seemingly displaced anger made Matt's brow arch. In spite of himself he watched in reluctant fascination as her flushed cheeks and jutted chin made her face even more striking. "It's a little late to be playing the shocked innocent."

"I guess the same could be said of you playing the gentleman." She gritted a false smile. "Looks like we both guessed wrong."

"What did you expect?" he practically snarled. "You were all over me."

"Tenderness," she told him, her voice strained. "A hint of kindness. Foolish of me, wasn't it." Her chin lifted. "Please move."

He didn't budge. "So now I'm supposed to believe

you're going to walk twelve miles back to town and sleep in your car over a harmless pass."

Shannon remained silent and stared at the door over his wide shoulders.

Her silence infuriated him. She was the one who had started this. "I don't force women. There's a lock on your door. Use it if you want, but I won't beg you to stay."

Placing her overnight case under her arm, she secured her hold on the larger suitcase and stepped around a grim-faced Matt. Opening the door, she started through it only to come to an abrupt halt. Octavia, a tray of food in her hands, blocked the way.

"Thanks, child." The heavy woman frowned. "Why are you still holding your suitcase? Matt, where's all that training your mother and I tried to give you? Take her things," Octavia instructed as she placed the tray on the dresser.

Taking a step away from Matt's outstretched hands, Shannon said, "I can't stay."

"Why?" the housekeeper asked, clearly puzzled.

Shannon glared at Matt. His jaw tight, he looked away. At least he wasn't without some shame. Yet, there was no reason to embarrass Octavia. "I don't have any money."

"I knew there was a reason for you staying at that place," Octavia said with conviction. "Don't worry about a thing. You don't need money to stay here. Besides, since Matt's cattle have been grazing in *your* meadow, he's the one who should be paying you."

"Anytime Shannon wants to pay her share of the taxes on this place, I'll be happy to pay her a grazing fee." Matt stalked from the room and shut the door on the silent women.

* * *

After Matt's late supper and a bath, sleep still eluded him. The letter on the nightstand from Wade wouldn't let him. There was no way in hell his uncle or any of the Taggart men would have approved of the way he had treated Shannon.

No matter what she was, he shouldn't have stooped to her level. He didn't threaten women. He had no intention of making his suggestion a reality. He had just wanted her to know she couldn't keep pushing her lush little body against his and not expect any consequences. He was an all too human male.

She evoked needs in him that made a mockery of common sense. He didn't trust her, but for the first time since his divorce ten years ago, his mind and his body weren't in complete accord in dealing with a woman. Shannon tested his control and tried his patience with every glance, every touch, every enticing sway of her shapely hips.

No matter what he thought of Shannon, his uncle had thought well enough of her to leave her his favorite place, the place of the Taggart original homestead. Matt's anger had cooled down enough to realize there had been nothing romantic between the two, but that still left a lot of questions. There was more to it than just Wade owing her.

Apparently Arthur Ferguson was privy to Shannon's past and Matt was almost positive Octavia was, too. She wasn't surprised by Wade's will and what's more, she had never taken to a woman the way she had to Shannon. He was flying blind on this one and making mistakes.

He couldn't forget the hurt look on Shannon's face when he made his crude suggestion. It was too much of a contrast with the aroused look of moments before. Somehow he had badly misjudged things. Anger assaulted him again at life for pitting him against a woman beautiful enough to make his body clench each time he looked at her and mysterious enough to doubt himself.

But she wasn't taking his heritage. He'd help her get back on her feet and then she was leaving . . . after she signed over her claim to his land. Yet somehow he had to accomplish the first goal in such a way as to help him accomplish the second and most important objective.

The idea came out of nowhere. Shannon probably only thought of the monetary gain in owning part of a ranch, not the hard work it took to keep it in the black. Obviously she lived well above what her nursing salary provided.

It stood to reason someone else was paying the price for her expensive tastes. This time she was going to work for what she wanted. She was about to find out firsthand the back-breaking work it took to make the ranch run smoothly and return a profit.

Within a week, she'd be begging to go home. He had already broken his golden rule and bought her gas, he might as well give her enough money to get to St. Louis . . . after she signed over the meadow. Without another moment's hesitation, he went to Shannon's room and knocked.

Opening the door at her assent, he saw her sitting on the side of the bed, her back to him. "You needn't have bothered coming for the tray, Octavia. You've done too much already." Rising, she turned toward him. The weak smile on her face froze, her body went rigid.

Matt accepted the accusations in her wary eyes and the bitter taste of self-disgust in his mouth as partly his due. The other part was hers. "Next time don't send out signals unless you're willing to back them up."

Shannon flushed guiltily and glanced away. In the aftermath of their argument, she had time to think about what she had done and realize she shared a large part of the blame. Matt knew nothing about her except she was trying to take his heritage . . . not a very good character reference.

At least he had been honest enough to tell her beforehand what he thought of her instead of *afterward*. Her cheeks heated. She wasn't sure what the afterward would have been, but there definitely would have been one if he had returned her kiss. Twice, by the stock tank and in this very bedroom, he had showed more restraint than she had. He hadn't taken advantage of her.

Finally, she nodded. Matt wasn't as dangerous to her as she was to herself.

Callused fingers brushed across his hair. She should give up nursing and go into acting. Averted eyes, trembling lips, slumped shoulders . . . she really had mastered the art of appearing the uncertain, sexually awakening virgin. If Shannon was a virgin, he was from outer space.

"We need to talk about the meadow."

Her head came up. "Yes."

He wasn't surprised he had gotten her attention. "The meadow as I told you has the only year-round water on the thousand acres of the Circle T. Yes, the cattle graze there, but if it wasn't for the alfalfa hay that is bailed in another section of the ranch for winter feed, the ranch couldn't sustain the large number of cattle we run.

"Since nothing in the meadow is sold, the profits from the ranch have to supplement this house, the wages for the hands, and all the other things needed to make the ranch solvent, including the meadow."

"I see."

"I hope you do. The ranch and the meadow are interchangeable. One can't prosper without the other."

"You're asking me to sign over the meadow?" she asked, aware of the slight tremor in her voice.

"I'm asking you how badly do you want the land? Bad enough to sweat and get your hands dirty?" Seeing her stricken face, he rushed on. "After breakfast would you be willing to work for the land you want to claim?"

Shannon watched in stunned amazement as Matt slammed out of her room. Gradually what he had said began to sink into her tired brain. She had just been issued a challenge. Living in St. Louis all her life, she knew nothing about a ranch. She could only ride a horse because her mother insisted she have riding lessons as a child.

Work in Matt's mind was probably the grungiest, dirtiest job he could find. She'd be crazy to take him up on his challenge. She should call her parents in the morning and have them wire her her money and leave.

Then what?

Shannon sat back down on her bed. If she ran this time, how long before she ran away from another problem? She had run away from her grandfather's death, her profession, her family, and the man who wanted to marry her. Her head lifted, her shoulders straightened. She wasn't running a step farther. She was accepting Matt's challenge.

She'd be less than a Johnson if she didn't beat him at his own game. A slow calculating smile tilted the corners of her mouth in anticipation of the coming battle. Apparently she had more of her parents' tenacity than she thought. She was going to make Matt Taggart take back every insult he had ever flung at her.

The arrogant, distrustful scoundrel didn't believe she had left her money and credit card at home. At the time she hadn't wanted to believe it either as she had frantically searched through her wallet, her purse, and her suitcase.

Recalling her haste to leave her parents' home, she remembered cleaning out her wallet, laying the one all-purpose credit card she always took on trips and the green-and-white bank envelope with five hundred dollars on top of her dresser. And that's where she had left them.

So, she had run out of gas getting to the only place in town she could get a room for the twenty-five dollars and odd cents she had left. One look at the run-down motel, the slovenly clerk, and she knew what type of place the Paradise was.

Matt might have rescued her, but obviously he had not reversed his opinion of her.

There was something about his handsome, unsmiling face that called to her. She wanted to see him smile. To see him look at her with something other than mistrust in his piercing black eyes.

She couldn't possibly accept James Harper's marriage proposal. Not when Matt affected her so.

The two men were alike in so many ways, yet so totally different. James was charming, gracious, and witty; Matt snarled and sniped. Both were handsome, aggressive, and reveled in taking charge.

James usually planned the evening for them. It was "I have tickets for" or "we're invited to." To give James credit, he did ask for her preference early in their relationship, but since she didn't have any interest in most of the social whirl of see-and-be-seen, he usually ended up making the decision anyway.

As he explained once, it was important to his career as a lawyer that he be visible, and since he was going to have to make the decision anyway, why go through the motions of asking her. If his take-charge attitude irritated her sometimes, it wasn't enough for her to make an issue of it.

She didn't like arguments. In fact, she usually went out of her way to avoid them. It was the one flaw in her character Granddaddy Rhodes regretted not being able to change.

With the exception of Granddaddy Rhodes, the rest of

her family adored James. Not one of them was going to like the decision she was about to make, but she had made unpopular decisions before. Granddaddy Rhodes was always there to back her up before. Sadness slumped her shoulders. He had always been there for her, with a smile of approval and love.

The two of them had always been closer than he was to her brothers. Her mother often said it was because both Shannon and her grandfather had stars in their eyes. Coming from a family of practical, hard-nosed lawyers, her success in nursing and Granddaddy Rhodes's in real-estate speculation was something talked about frequently, and always with wonder.

Now those same stars in her eyes had gotten her in trouble with her reluctant partner. In the future she'd have to remember to keep her lips clamped together and her hands in her pockets around Matt.

Walking over to the dresser, she picked up the roast beef sandwich Octavia had brought and took a small bite. Her appetite had returned. Of course Matt expected her to fail. He wasn't the type of man who liked to lose. She knew that from his reaction when Octavia bested him.

Well, he shouldn't issue challenges because he was in for the surprise of his life. Obviously he didn't know the long, grueling hours nurses worked bending, lifting, stooping. This time he was going to lose. She took another bite of the sandwich and smiled despite her full mouth.

Six

"Shannon dear, are you sure you're all right?" asked George Johnson.

"Perhaps you should come home," Henrietta Johnson added.

Seated in a chair in the den, Shannon almost regretted calling her parents tonight instead of waiting until morning to reassure them. They had put her on the speaker phone in their bedroom and she could just imagine them pacing the floor, each ready to fire questions at her as if she were on the witness stand.

"I'm fine and I'm not coming home," she finally said. "I'm old enough to take care of myself."

The minute the words were out of her mouth she knew she had made a mistake. Her parents were too sharp to miss an opportunity to come back at her.

She was right.

"Leaving your money and credit card is hardly responsible," they parroted.

Shannon slouched lower in her seat. She had debated whether or not to mention the money and credit card, then decided she had no choice if Melanie, her best friend, was going to pick them up in the morning from Shannon's parents and send them to her by overnight mail.

"Mother, Daddy. I'm with friends, I've just eaten and I'm about to go up to my room and go to sleep."

"What's the name and phone number of these friends?" her father asked.

"Where do we send the money? You know how I feel about that," Henrietta said almost frantically. "I shudder each time I think of what might have happened."

Shannon smiled. Despite everything, she never doubted her parents' love. They might disapprove of her actions at times, but their love was constant. Her father as usual wanted to know the who and the what, but her mother, her mother believed a woman should never be at the mercy of fate or a man. No matter how nice or upstanding her date, Shannon always had a quarter in her shoe and a twenty-dollar bill pinned to her bra when she went out in high school.

"I love you both."

"You know we love you, too, baby," answered her mother. "So does James."

Shannon straightened in her chair. "Mother, I don't want to go into that now."

"Of course," her father placated. "Just give me the name and phone number of these friends who helped you and we'll wire you some money. There's no need to bother Melanie."

"Nice try, Dad. You'd also call me every day." She continued to talk over their protests. "You mean well, but this is my life and at the moment I need to take a good long look at it. If I get into something I can't handle, I promise, you'll be the first to know."

"But, baby—"

"Shan—"

"Please give the money and credit card to Melanie when she comes by in the morning and don't badger her with too many questions. I love you." She hung up the phone, then leaned back in the chair and stretched out her legs. Her parents were probably dialing her brothers' phone numbers now. They'd hook up a three-way and discuss her life. As always, they thought they knew what was best for her.

Their answer to her emotional upheaval since her grandfather's death was for her to quit nursing, accept James's marriage proposal, become a social butterfly and have two beautiful, well-mannered grandchildren. The idea had even less appeal now than it did when he first proposed six weeks ago.

James was nice, but he didn't excite her like—

"What are you doing downstairs?"

Shannon jumped up from her chair. As if she had conjured him up, Matt stood in the den. Bare-chested, jeans unsnapped and perched on his hips, he looked tempting. Muscles rippled as he braced his hands on his waist. The man had one fine body.

"I asked you a question." His eyes were hooded, but there was a hint of something in them that made her heart race.

She tried to work up some moisture in her mouth so she could speak. "Using the phone." She held up her calling card. "I hope you don't mind."

A dark brow arched. "Reassuring everyone again."

She smiled. "That's right. Sorry if I disturbed you."

"If you're finished, I'd like to get some sleep. *I* have to work."

Shannon continued smiling despite the barb. "Good night." She brushed past him and went up the stairs. If she could control her attraction to Matt, it was going to be a pleasure to teach him a lesson.

"Shannon. What are you doing here?"

Heavy-eyed with sleep, Shannon lifted her head and greeted the housekeeper around a yawn. "Good morning, Octavia."

"Child, why aren't you asleep in your bed instead of at the kitchen table? It's seven-twenty."

"I got up to fix Matt some coffee," Shannon explained, stretching her stiff arms over her head.

Octavia's gaze went to the automatic coffeepot. "Oh, Lord. I forgot to get things ready last night. That boy never could make good coffee."

Shannon smiled. "So I gathered from all the grumbling and banging I heard when I entered the kitchen. I'm surprised all the noise didn't wake you up."

"Once I'm out, I'm out. But my eyes open at seven each morning and there's no getting back to sleep. Matt comes in from working outside for breakfast a quarter to eight." Opening the refrigerator door, Octavia took out a box of sausage patties and a package of bacon.

"If I had known you were a deep sleeper I would have cooked breakfast." Shannon stood. "Is there anything I can do to help?"

"Hand me that big black skillet from the cabinet under the stove." Octavia placed the meats on the counter, opened another cabinet and took out a large crock bowl. "You never did tell me why you were asleep at the table."

Rinsing the skillet under tepid water from the faucet, Shannon smiled over her shoulder. "Showing Matt his partner is no slouch."

"Would you mind explaining that?" Octavia asked as she folded her arms across her wide girth.

Shannon smiled. Something she couldn't seem to stop doing. "Last night Matt asked me if I was willing to sweat and get dirty for my claim. He left before I could give him my answer. Getting up with him was my way of showing him that I can hang just as tough as he can."

Laughter burst from Shannon. "You should have seen his startled expression when I came into the kitchen. I've never seen a man so starved for coffee and too stubborn to ask for help."

"He's stubborn all right, but he's tricky, too," the housekeeper warned.

"I can handle Matt."

The housekeeper looked at her quizzically. "Seems you and *Matt* got along pretty well this morning."

Shannon ignored the comment and busied herself with opening the package of bacon. "How many slices should I put in the skillet?"

"Six for Matt and whatever you want for yourself. None for me, my cholesterol is up again. I sure do miss my bacon," Octavia lamented. "Some things are hard to give up, but you got to know what's best for you in the long run."

Shannon wondered if the housekeeper was talking about her cholesterol level or Shannon's situation with Matt. Not sure if she wanted to know, she didn't ask.

Matt had wolfed down four fluffy biscuits before he learned his unwanted junior partner had made them. The hungry side of him said it didn't matter, the suspicious side of him said this one knew all the tricks to get to a man. Dressed in an oversize bright-red-and-white striped shirt with the collar turned up and a pair of jeans, she shouldn't have looked elegant and chic in his kitchen, but she did. Well, he was adept at a few tricks himself.

Taking another sip of coffee from the stoneware cup, he pushed aside his plate and rocked back slightly in his chair. He was about to knock that confident smile right off Shannon's beautiful face. He didn't even mind Octavia's glare.

"Ready to work, Ms. Johnson?"

"Since we're in this together, why don't you call me Shannon and I'll call you Matt." Across the table, she folded both arms. "And to answer your question, I can't wait."

"Glad to hear it." Matt took a sip of coffee before continuing. "First, muck out the twenty-four stalls in the stable and lay in some fresh hay, then polish the tack in the work room. After that there's some brush down by the creek that needs clearing."

"And after that?"

Coffee was gliding over his tongue when Shannon asked the question. Matt, who knew the stables would probably keep an inexperienced person busy most of the day, choked on his coffee.

The flat of Octavia's hand slapped him hard between the shoulder blades. "What's the matter, Matt, something go down the wrong way?"

Matt scowled up into his housekeeper's cheerful face. Her grin widened.

"Are you all right?"

His head whipped around. Shannon was bending over him, her face filled with concern, her lips too close. Hastily, he pushed to his feet. "No need to make a fuss. Let's go outside and I'll introduce you to the hands."

"Shannon needs some work gloves and a hat before she goes to work." Octavia glanced at the younger woman's tennis-clad feet and shook her head. "Once you wear those shoes cleaning stables, you might as well throw them away."

Shannon bit her lower lip. "They're the sturdiest shoes I have. I don't have any money . . ." She didn't have to see Matt tense to know where his thoughts were leading. Melanie was going to wire Shannon her money and credit card in care of Arthur Ferguson. When she had called both of them this morning, each had been too glad to help. But in the meantime she only had thirty-six cents.

"I'm not asking you to buy me anything."

"Glad to hear it," Matt said.

"I know where you can find everything you need and

not worry about paying a cent," Octavia said. "You just come with me and I'll fix you up."

Grabbing Shannon's hand, Octavia left the kitchen and started across the den. Shannon looked back to see Matt wearing a scowl as black at his Stetson. Shrugging her shoulders, she allowed the housekeeper to lead her up the stairs.

Less than ten minutes later, Shannon came back downstairs wearing a faded blue shirt and jeans, scuffed boots, and a beat-up straw hat. Standing in the den in front of Matt in his younger sister's discarded clothes while his critical eyes skimmed over her was not easy.

"You look like a scarecrow."

"Perhaps you'd like to assign me to the alfalfa field instead of the barn?" Shannon asked politely. She'd eat worms before she'd show how much his remark hurt.

One dark brow lifted, but all he said was "Come on, you've wasted enough of my time."

Shannon followed his long strides out the front door and wished sticking your tongue out behind someone's back wasn't considered childish. Besides, with her luck, he'd catch her or, worse, think she was coming on to him again.

She saw the car as soon as she stepped off the porch. Moments later a smiling Arthur Ferguson emerged from the vehicle just as they reached the bottom steps.

"Good morning, Matt, Shannon. Wade would be proud of you, Matt. Shannon called me this morning to let me know she was all right thanks to your timely intervention."

"Hello, Ferguson," Matt said thinly. "Shannon prides herself on reassuring people."

Shannon spoke to the lawyer, then clamped her teeth together to keep her tongue from getting her into trouble.

The lawyer nodded. "Wade always said she was one of a kind." Ferguson reached into his breast pocket and pulled out two letters. "Since you two seem to have come to some sort of terms with the will, I have something for you from Wade."

Matt and Shannon looked questioningly at the lawyer before accepting the envelope, then lifting out the single sheet of paper.

Dear Shannon,
  Thank you.

                                        Wade

Dear Matt,
  Thank you.

                                        Wade

Matt's fingers curled around the letter as he lifted his head and asked, "You have any more of these?"

Ferguson's smile grew. "Might. You two have a good day." Getting back into his car, he drove off.

Shannon watched him leave, then shoved her letter into her hip pocket. She watched as Matt did the same. "I wonder if there was a letter for us if we didn't reach an agreement?"

"I can only hope," Matt said, and took off across the yard to the barn thirty yards away.

Unable to help herself, she made a face at his retreating back, than started after him. Trying her best to keep from looking as if she were running, which in fact she was, Shannon snatched her straw hat off her head so she wouldn't lose it. By the time they entered the dim interior of the barn, she was slightly winded.

"Jay, Elliott, Griff, Cleve. Get out here."

Four men emerged. One came from the hayloft, two from the interior of the barn, and one out of a stall. All came running. The three youngest men were first to reach Matt. Although they couldn't have been much younger than their boss, it wasn't difficult to see the adoration in their eyes. The last to arrive was a bearded elderly man who could have been Uncle Remus's twin.

"Men, I'd like you to meet the newest hand, Shannon Johnson." Four pairs of eyes bugged, then went from Matt to Shannon. "This is Jay Fisher, Griff Walker, Elliott Fox, and Cleve Redmon."

The elderly gentleman, Cleve Redmon, was the first to step forward. "Pleased to meet you, ma'am."

His gaze was as cautious as the hand he extended. Their hands barely touched before the light pressure of his hand was gone. Stepping back, he ducked his head.

If Cleve was reticent, the three other men were not. With their hats clutched to their chests with one hand, they pumped Shannon's arm with the other as if they were priming a pump. She hoped it meant they were going to accept her.

At least all of them were friendly except Cleve. For some reason her gaze strayed back to him. She was surprised to find him anxiously looking at her. "Is something the matter?"

"No, ma'am, I better get back to my chores."

"Shannon is going to muck out the barn for you," Matt told him.

Cleve straightened his slightly stooped shoulders. "You aren't pleased with my work no more?"

"You know if I hadn't been you would have heard it before now," Matt said.

"No offense, boss, but I'd rather do it by myself," the elderly cowhand argued.

"She cleans the stalls, Cleve." The flatness in Matt's voice brooked no argument. The other three hands found the pattern the toes of their boots were making in the dirt enticing.

The older man's shoulders slumped for a second, then

surged upward. "Yes, sir." There was no surliness in the tone, just hurt.

Wounded pride. Pride Shannon understood. She took the few steps that would bring her face-to-face with Cleve. "Cleve, I know it's an imposition, but I hope you can please put up with me for a little while. Since I now own a piece of the Circle T, Matt insists I learn what it takes to run the place."

Three dirt-staring heads popped up, their jaws unhinged. The scowl on Matt's face would have made most men run. Shannon smiled. He wasn't as fierce as he appeared. She had seen his face earlier and knew he hadn't wanted to hurt Cleve, either.

She turned to the elderly man. Lightly, her hand touched his stiff arm. "So, if you could please tolerate me and show me the ropes, I'd appreciate it."

"Well . . ."

She smiled. "I'd be so grateful." In a side whisper that everyone could hear, she said, "I might need to brush up on my riding, too, before Matt sends me out to scout the range."

Cleve looked horrified. "Ain't no such thing as scout the range. Where did you come from?"

"St. Louis. Where the West begins."

"The West begins in Fort Worth, Texas. You've got a lot to learn, girlie," Cleve told her.

"That's what I've been trying to tell her," Matt said. "You can give instructions, but I want her to do everything by herself."

"All right, boss. But don't be surprised if she don't last the day." Cleve turned and walked deeper into the barn's interior. "Ranching is man's work."

This time it was Shannon's jaw that came unhinged. After trying to help Cleve, he had turned on her. A bark of laughter swung her around.

Mesmerized, she watched Matt throw back his head

in laughter. He was framed in silhouette of the morning light. He looked like a dark angel, tempting and unbelievably handsome.

"I could have told you, Shannon. Some men are immune to your charm." Tipping his hat, he walked away.

Angel my foot! Devil was more like it. With determination in every step, she stomped off to find her reluctant teacher.

Seven

Matt crossed the yard in ground-eating strides. His foul mood was his own fault. All morning he had tried to forget the picture of injured pride on Cleve's face, but it wouldn't go away. In Matt's attempt to get rid of Shannon he had inadvertently hurt a man he loved and respected.

Cleve Redmon had been a fixture on the Taggart ranch for as long as Matt could remember. Like Wade, Cleve had never married. Unlike his uncle, Cleve tended to enjoy being by himself. Matt couldn't remember the elderly cowhand ever taking a vacation or a few days off. Working on the ranch seemed to be all he wanted. Even on his off day, he was never idle.

Yet, while Cleve's heart might be willing, his body was tired. His arthritis wasn't helping. More days than Matt wanted to remember, he had seen Cleve wrap his horse's reins around his wrist when his fingers were too stiff and pained him too much to hold the narrow leather strips. His pride was as big as the Texas sky. Pensioning him off would have slowly killed him. Easing him into taking care of things around the house and barn had required delicate maneuvering.

Wade had helped by constantly reminding Cleve they had worked in their youth for twenty-five cents a day and a rock-hard biscuit for lunch. Through rainstorm, broiling sun, and bad health they had stayed in the saddle and got the job done no matter how hard or how long it took. Without a word being said, Matt always knew Cleve was thinking Wade had been working for his father, then himself while Cleve had simply been one of the hands.

It surprised no one that Cleve had kicked against slowing down, but gradually he had settled into his new responsibilities off a horse. But he didn't like help from anyone. And in Matt's haste to get rid of Shannon, he had forgotten all that. Grudgingly, he had to admit she had been sensitive enough to Cleve's feelings to try to ease his mind.

Or was it another game she was running?

His mood darkened. Yanking open the back door, he entered the kitchen. From somewhere in the house he heard the vacuum cleaner shut off. The screen door banged shut behind him. Opening the refrigerator, he took out a pitcher of tea, then reached for a glass.

"Is that you, Shannon?" yelled the housekeeper.

"Nope, it's me."

Moments later Octavia entered the kitchen, her face wrinkled in a frown. "I thought you'd be out plowing most of the day."

"So did I," Matt said, then took a huge gulp of the ice-cold drink. "The clutch went bad on the tractor. I brought it back in to work on it."

"I don't suppose you got time for a bite to eat?" the housekeeper questioned.

"No, but thanks." Setting the glass down, he headed for the door again.

"If you see Shannon, send her in for lunch."

One hand on the knob, he glanced at his watch. "It's after one."

"I know, but I haven't seen her since the two of you left this morning," she answered. "You did tell her to come back for lunch, didn't you?"

"Any fool would know to stop for lunch."

Octavia crossed her arms in a familiar gesture. "That's the same thing I've been trying to tell *you* for years. Yet, you don't listen."

He scowled. "I'm working for what's mine."

"So is Shannon." The housekeeper nodded toward the kitchen clock on the wall. "Looks like she's willing to work just as long and as hard as you are."

"That remains to be seen." Opening the door, Matt headed for the barn. This was one time he was going to delight in proving Octavia wrong.

If there was one thing he had noticed about Shannon, it was her neatness. Despite the sassy red toenails her fingernails were short, rounded, and had a glossy shine. He'd bet his truck they were professionally cared for.

He hated to admit it, but she had the softest hair he'd ever touched. It smelled good, too. Whether ruffled by the wind or a man's hand, the lustrous, shoulder-length auburn hair somehow managed to look tempting. Automatically his mind conjured up the picture of the last time his hands had glided through her hair and pulled her body flush with his. Immediately, his body responded.

With ruthless determination, he brought his mind and desire under control. Shannon might be tempting as sin, but she was also manipulative, untrustworthy, and out for what she could get . . . the easiest way possible.

Nope, a woman like Shannon wouldn't like being sweaty and dirty. She'd probably spent most of the morning in the tackroom, not working, but washing her face and hands. Matt had no doubt she had already eaten with Cleve and the rest of the hands.

Cleve might not like women working on the ranch, but he wasn't mean-spirited. He'd offer her lunch. Shannon would accept; she wasn't the type of woman to pass up an opportunity to gain more allies or another conquest.

Matt entered the barn. A few feet inside he blinked, then blinked again.

A wheelbarrow was midway down the wide aisle. Dangling from one of the handles was the straw hat Shannon had been wearing that morning. His brows furrowed. She couldn't have gotten that far. Continuing, he didn't stop until he was at the open stall in front of the wheelbarrow.

Instead of using a pitchfork, Shannon was on her knees distributing hay and mumbling to herself. "I'm never going to think it's romantic to see a couple making love in the hay again. This stuff itches and it's dusty." She scooted over a bit. "You'd have to be in the depths of lust to forget where you were."

"Are you saying you've never forgotten where you were while making love?"

Her shoulders stiffened. Her eyes closed. Why couldn't it have been anyone but *him?* All too aware of how sweaty and dirty she was, she spoke without turning. "After I finish, I'll go to work on the tackroom."

One broad shoulder leaned against the stall door. "You didn't answer my question?"

His deep voice did strange things to her heart rate. "Don't you have work to do?"

He did, but at the moment he was oddly content to stay where he was. Shannon had a nice little backside. "You haven't chosen your lovers very well if not one of them could make you concentrate just on him."

The derision in his voice propelled her to her feet. "Oh, and I suppose your lovers wouldn't mind if they were on a roller coaster."

"High, hot, and wild. Why would they?"

Her body heated from one word to the next. She only had one defense. "And probably just as fast."

His darkly handsome face leaned within an inch of hers. "Keep pushing me and you're liable to find out the answer for yourself."

She staggered back. Her mouth felt bone dry. Her skin tight. "I . . . I. . . ." Her voice trailed off. She didn't know what she wanted to say. Worse, she didn't know if she wanted Matt to carry out his threat or leave her alone.

The sensual gaze left his eyes as quickly as it had come. "What did Cleve fix today for lunch?"

"B-beef stew."

Matt almost smiled. Better and better. If Cleve had fixed stew it meant he didn't plan to cook anything else for lunch until it was all gone. That could last a couple of days to a week.

"Octavia was concerned that you hadn't had lunch. I'll tell her you ate with the boys."

"But I didn't."

"You just said Cleve had beef stew."

"I did, but I didn't eat." Shannon stared down at her feet. "I wanted to get a bit more work done before I stopped for lunch."

Matt wanted to shake her. Why couldn't she act the way she was supposed to? She didn't appear a bit concerned that she had straw in her hair or that her jeans and shirt were dirt-smeared. He had too much to do to try to figure Shannon out. "Go in the house and eat."

Her head lifted. "I'd like to finish this first." She wiped a trickle of sweat from her brow. "I'm a little behind."

"That wasn't a request."

A glance at Matt's taut features told her arguing was useless and potentially dangerous. Not danger to her body, but danger to her emotions. Her feelings were too chaotic to risk another confrontation.

It was just her luck that Wade's nephew was the most sensually handsome man she had ever met. If that wasn't enough, something within her yearned to see him smile, to make him happy. She didn't know if it was her instincts as a nurse or as a woman.

He wouldn't appreciate either.

Stiff-backed, she walked past Matt. She had so wanted to impress him and she had failed. The thought had barely registered in her mind before her chin lifted. The day wasn't over. Her pace picked up as she hurried into the house.

"I saw you coming across the yard." Octavia set a plate on the table. "Chicken salad all right?"

Shannon grinned. "I'm hungry enough to eat a horse."

"Better not let Matt or the boys hear you say that." The older woman chuckled. "Go on and wash up."

Shannon glanced down at her soiled jeans and shirt. "I don't imagine I have time to change clothes."

"Just pretend you've been gardening."

Shaking her head at the housekeeper, Shannon quickly washed, returned to the table and said grace. The first bite of salad was delicious. "It's a wonder Matt doesn't weigh three hundred pounds."

"That boy barely eats sometimes," Octavia sniffed as she took a seat.

"Why? Is something wrong?" The words tumbled out of Shannon's mouth before she could stop them. "Forgive me, I have no right to pry into Matt's personal business."

"You didn't ask to be nosy. I know you care about him."

Sooty black lashes flew upward. Sherry-brown eyes widened.

Octavia patted Shannon's fluttering hand. "It's all right, child. Nurses are caring people."

She didn't answer. Instead, she concentrated on quickly eating lunch.

"Slow down or you're gonna choke," the housekeeper warned.

"I'm sorry, but I have to get back and finish." Draining her glass of iced tea, she stood and took her empty plate to the sink.

"I'll get that." Octavia took the plate out of Shannon's hand. "How far did you get?"

She made a face. "Only half through cleaning the stalls."

Black eyes rounded, Octavia grinned. "I knew you had it in you."

Shannon frowned. "Didn't you hear me? I still have to do the rest of the stalls, polish the tack, and clear the brush before I'm through for the day."

Leaving the dishes in the sink, Octavia faced the puzzled woman. "Did Matt give you a timetable or just tell you what he wanted you to do?"

"Just what he wanted me to do, but I assumed—" She stopped short as she said the taboo word in nursing. No one *assumed*. You went on facts. Period. If you didn't understand, you asked. A patient's life necessitated you to make the correct decision based on fact not assumption.

"Depending on the experience of the person, cleaning those stalls can take anywhere from six to seven hours. Matt knows that." She chuckled. "That's why he choked on his coffee when you asked him what else he wanted you to do after you finished."

"He didn't expect me to finish, did he?"

"I told you he could be tricky."

"The rat! I told him I had skipped lunch to try and finish," Shannon railed. "He could have said something."

"I don't think Matt exactly knows what to say to you."

Shannon's gaze narrowed in on the housekeeper. "What are you talking about?"

For a moment Shannon thought Octavia was going to sidestep the question as she had done before. "Matt's opinion of women, especially beautiful women, isn't the best. Can't say I blame him after what he went through with that woman. Never thought I'd see the day he'd meet one halfway, the way he has Victoria."

"Victoria?" The pang Shannon felt wasn't jealousy, she argued with herself. It wasn't.

"Victoria Taggart. Married to Matt's older brother." Octavia smiled. "Those two are so much in love they glow. Even a cynic like Matt had to admit Victoria's crazy about Kane. His size doesn't intimidate her a bit."

"Because I worked the eleven-to-seven shift I never met any of the family members. But I heard a lot. Matt might have set the women's hearts aflutter, but they were in awe of Kane and so were the doctors," Shannon recalled.

"That's Kane," Octavia said proudly.

"Even after Wade was discharged he talked mostly about the ranch and Matt. His uncle was worried about him."

"He wanted for Matt what Kane has with Victoria," Octavia said softly.

"That might take a miracle."

"Or the right woman."

Shannon bit her lower lip. "I guess I better get back to work. Thanks for lunch." Shannon escaped to the barn.

Her cheeks still burning, she finished scattering the rest of the hay in the stall. Plopping the hat on her head, she picked up the pitchfork and shovel leaning against the wall, placed them in the wheelbarrow, then went into the next stall.

She might feel a healthy dose of attraction toward Matt, but that was all. He was different, a challenge. What woman wouldn't be attracted to him? Just because she wanted to see him smile didn't mean she felt anything on a deeper level.

"Staring into space won't get the job done."

Letting the wheelbarrow drop, she turned to Cleve. "How was the beef stew?"

Bushy eyebrows lifted. "Filling."

"They're lucky to get it with all the work you do." Picking up the shovel, she began cleaning the stall.

"Forgot your gloves."

Propping the shovel against her leg, she put on the gloves and went back to work.

"You got good wrist action and swing."

Shannon smiled. "Didn't think I'd last the day, huh?"

"Day ain't over yet," he tossed back. "By the way, it's easier scattering the hay if you use the pitchfork."

Laughing, Shannon glanced over her shoulder and watched him walk away. This morning Cleve had pointed out the wheelbarrow, pitchfork, and shovel, then showed her where to dump the refuse. His battered straw hat jerked toward the loft where the baled hay was stored.

"How do I get it down?"

With a deadpan expression on his grizzled face he had said, "With your hands."

When the time came for her actually to get a bale of hay down from the loft, she saw Cleve standing nearby currying one of the horses she had brought back into the barn. He'd probably deny it to the last, but she had a feeling he had watched her take every cautious step upward.

Trying to move the hay was awkward; lifting it would have been impossible. So, she took a chapter from her nursing training. She rolled it off the loft.

The hay hit the barn floor with a solid thud. Cleve looked from the broken hay bale to her standing with her hands on her hips.

"I used my hands just like you told me," Shannon yelled.

"See that you don't waste any of that hay," Cleve admonished and left.

Shaking her head at the memory, Shannon went back to work. She liked the crusty old man. He didn't give her an inch, but she had the notion it wasn't because she was a woman. Clearly anyone who knew nothing about ranching was next to worthless. Before her three weeks of vacation was over, she was going to learn plenty.

"All finished. Ready to come see?"

Matt looked up from the belly of the tractor. Shannon was grinning from ear to ear. Her hair was pulled up on the top of her head by a rubber band, and she had managed to collect more straw and dirt all over her. Somehow she still managed to look beautiful.

He returned his attention to repairing the clutch. The sun had gone down an hour ago. He had spent too many hours repairing the thing. He wasn't in the mood to see Shannon gloating.

"Nope."

"Don't you want to see if the barn is up to your high standards?" she questioned, the cheery note in her voice scraping on his nerve endings like fingernails on a chalk board.

Callused hands closed more securely around the wrench. "Doesn't take a genius to muck out stalls."

"How about what you're doing?"

His head snapped up. Black eyes glittered. "Meaning?"

She had the grace to flush. "It's just that I've been seeing you working on this thing when I take the wheelbarrow out. How is it coming?"

"It's not." Giving her his back, he returned to tightening the bolt.

"Is there anything I could do to help? Like hold something?"

Matt gave the wrench one last yank, then turned his full attention on Shannon. "As a matter of fact there is."

"Yes?" she answered eagerly.

"Let me work in peace."

Shannon's expression faltered. "Oh."

Matt pushed away the twinge of guilt he felt at her shattered look. Shannon played the game better than most, but it was still that, a game where the woman walked away with everything, leaving a man nothing, not even the remnants of his pride.

He'd thought his ex-wife was the most beautiful, the most perfect woman he had ever met. He'd bragged to anyone who stood still long enough to listen how wonderful she was. He'd worked two jobs during the week and on weekends had followed the rodeo circuit to give her all the things she asked for.

She kept their apartment clean, meals on the table, and the sheets hot. She was a very inventive and tireless sexual partner. His grip on the wrench tightened. There was only one problem: she didn't mind whose bed she happened to find herself in . . . as long as the man in it had money. Once his popularity and his ranking started to decline, so had his wife's interest. The money problems that had ensued hadn't helped.

They had their disagreements when money had gotten tight, but he never suspected her infidelity. He had just worked harder to get his concentration level back up where he could finish ahead and stop his downward spiral in ranking as a calf roper.

He had been a fool going on blind faith and a stupid emotion called love. Never again. He chose honest lust and women who made no demands. Those who tried were left talking to thin air. He would never allow another woman to make a fool out of him. Never.

If he was a little hard on Shannon, she'd just have to learn that he couldn't be swayed and look for an easier mark.

* * *

"He's *so* rude!" Shannon said, the moment she entered the kitchen and saw Octavia. "All I did was ask him about that monstrosity he's been working on."

"That monstrosity is a top-of-the-line tractor that cost in the neighborhood of eighty thousand dollars. Without it working, Matt can't finish plowing the early crop of corn and he can't fertilize the alfalfa in the hay meadow for the cows' winter feed," Octavia explained patiently. "Matt's trying to fix it himself because if he can't . . . well, what kind of bill do you get when you take your fancy car in?"

"I thought he was . . ." She bit her lower lip. Once again she had assumed.

"Rich," Octavia accurately finished for her. "Depends on what you call rich. But even a rich person won't be that way for long if they don't watch how they spend their money. Especially on a ranch."

Shannon accepted the housekeeper's gentle reprimand. No one in the Johnson family had to work; they did so because they enjoyed the challenge. In the early thirties, forties, and fifties when many people were selling their land, her great-grandfather was buying it. The family still owned real estate in downtown St. Louis and on the riverfront.

From an early age she had been taught never to judge someone by the zeroes in their bank account but by their character. Her parents were always cognizant of how blessed they were and aware of the needs of those who were less fortunate.

"I owe you a hug after I'm cleaned up." Opening the door, Shannon went back outside.

At first she didn't see him, then she heard a clink from beneath the front of the tractor. Looking underneath, she saw him screwing on a bolt. Not wanting to interrupt him again, she dropped to her knees, took a deep breath and spoke to the top of his dark head, "I'm sorry for that crack earlier. Octavia just explained how important the tractor is to the ranch."

Not by one movement did he indicate that he had heard her. Or worse that he cared if he had.

Determined to apologize, she plunged on. "I worked very hard in the barn. It was childish of me to expect praise, but I did, and when you didn't give it, like a spoiled child, I struck back." Her shoulders squared. "Please accept my apology."

Matt moved, but it was to screw on another bolt. Her shoulders slumped in defeat. Her hand braced against the warm belly of the tractor to push to her feet.

"Come down here."

Without a moment's hesitation Shannon stuck her head underneath the tractor. It was as much of a concession as she was going to get from Matt. "Yes?"

He blew out an exasperated breath. "Down here, Shannon. With me. Go on the other side and scoot under beside me."

When she had ensconced herself under the tractor beside Matt on the well-worn blanket she asked, "What should I do?"

Unceremoniously, he dumped a handful of nuts and washers on her stomach. "Put those on all the bolts on both sides and I'll tighten them."

It sounded easy and it would have been if she hadn't kept brushing against Matt. Working in the small space together, it was impossible not to.

His hip bumped hers, her shoulders touched his, their thighs brushed together as one or the other turned. His touch inflamed her senses. With each contact, Shannon fought the temptation to conjure up what it would be like to leisurely explore the hard, muscled warmth of the man next to her, what it would feel like for him to explore her in return.

Hot. She was hot everywhere and it had nothing to do

with her sticky clothes or the temperature outside and everything to do with the man next to her.

"You're hot?"

"W-what?" Her gaze jerked to his.

"Is the heat getting to you? You haven't moved in the last minute," he explained. "Your cheeks look flushed."

If she could have sunk through the ground, she would have gladly done so. "I'm finished. I was waiting for you to tell me what to do next." Great. Now she could add lying to the list of uncharacteristic things she had started doing since she came to the Circle T.

"Right behind you," Matt said. He tightened the last nut. "Now to adjust it."

Matt stood before she did, then helped her up. His hand only touched her arm for a second, then it was gone. The warm imprint, however, lasted. "Start it up and hold down on the clutch." He dove back under the hood.

Shannon didn't move. She didn't know what the clutch was.

Matt's dark head popped up. "What's the matter?"

"My car is an automatic."

His eyes rolled heavenward. "Climb on and I'll show you. Pay attention because you may have to drive it before you leave."

"I . . . I don't think I could. I have problems with judging distances," she confessed, climbing onto the tractor

"Since you'll be in a field, that won't be a problem." He started the engine and pointed to the clutch. "Keep your foot on that and let me know how the tension feels."

She didn't know about the tension in the clutch, but hers was wound pretty tight. But slowly she relaxed as they worked.

"That should do it. Cut the engine," Matt told her.

Shannon climbed down. "It's fixed?"

"It's fixed." He began picking up tools and putting them away.

"I guess I better get cleaned up. Any suggestions about these?" She held up her grease-stained hands.

He started to lift his hand toward her face, then glanced at hands that were greasier than hers. "You also have it on your nose."

She rubbed the sleeve of her shirt across her nose and tried to ignore the stab of disappointment that he hadn't touched her. "There's probably not an inch of my body that doesn't crave a hot, soapy bath. So could yours," she suggested with an impish smile.

"You're offering to wash my back?"

Frantically Shannon tried to vanquish the images of her doing that and more to his body. "T-that's not in my job description."

Black eyes narrowed, and for a wild moment she thought he might tell her it was. "Ready to quit and head back to St. Louis?"

"And leave you short-handed? No way."

"The green bar of soap in the utility bathroom will cut through the grease. Under the sink in a pink jar is some cream for your hands."

Surprise and pleasure swept through her. "Thanks."

He shrugged. "No sense getting the grease all over the place for Octavia to clean up, and I don't want to hear you complaining because your soft hands are becoming as tough as mine."

She smiled and his jaw clenched. Imagine. *Matt had noticed her hands.*

"The ranch comes first," he said tightly.

"I quite agree. Never crossed my mind otherwise. Now, if you'll excuse me, I think that water is calling my name." Turning, she started for the house.

Halfway there she yelled, "Anytime you need an extra pair of hands, holler. That's what partners are for."

This time when she imagined Matt's scowl, she smiled instead of worrying. Every muscle in her body might ache, but she had showed him she wasn't a cream puff. She was going to make a believer out of him. Her smile faded as she recalled his irritation after he mentioned her soft hands. The mysterious woman must have really done a number on him if he had to rationalize being thoughtful to a woman. Deep in thought, Shannon entered the house.

"If I have to reheat this food again it won't be worth eating," Octavia warned from the stove.

"Sorry, but I had to help Matt fix the clutch." She held out her grease-smeared shirt. "Matt told me about the special soap. There's no way I can sit, let alone eat, until I get cleaned up all over."

"Hurry up then."

Upstairs in her room, Shannon resisted the urge to linger in the scented water. Instead, she quickly finished her bath, then washed and blew dry her hair. After liberally using the pink hand cream, she dressed in shorts and a blouse, then gingerly picked up her dirty clothes and went downstairs. Returning from putting them in the washing machine, she saw the place setting for one.

Her happy spirits faltered. "Did Matt already eat?"

"No. He went to the field," Octavia replied as she lifted boiled cabbage onto a plate.

"It's after eight. It'll be dark in less than an hour." Shannon looked out the window, frowning.

"The tractor has lights and he lost a lot of time today."

"He can't make it up by killing himself."

"I've been trying to tell him that for years. He won't listen."

"Did he at least come in for a sandwich or something to drink?" Concern laced Shannon's words.

"He wouldn't have eaten at all if I hadn't taken some

food to him." The stoneware plate hit the table with a soft thud.

"Why don't you go catch up on your reading?" Shannon suggested. "I'll clean up after I finish."

Octavia smiled in appreciation. "I think I'll take you up on your offer. Good night."

"Good night." Shannon took her seat, but she made no move to eat. Her mind was still on Matt.

Men and women pushed themselves past the limits for different reasons. Her parents and brothers for the sheer exuberance of winning, and the glory. The financial reward was icing on the cake.

None of them knew how to relax and enjoy themselves. Enjoyment for her family was zeroing in on a witness for the opposition and making them sweat. Relaxation was a breakneck-paced game of racquetball.

Her mother despised idleness as much as preachers despised sin. More than once, her grandfather had to rescue Shannon from some "project" her mother had assigned her. The two of them would escape and enjoy the time with each other. What they did didn't matter as long as they did it together. She'd miss him forever, but they had built some good memories. Her thoughts skidded to a halt.

How had she forgotten that?

Good memories lingered. She leaned back in the chair and remembered the happy times. The long talks, baking cookies, helping her study for a test, playing a game of chess. She smiled. He hated losing and hated it worse if she let him win. He was a special man.

It had been so very hard letting him go. Letting him know that it was okay to stop fighting, that it was okay to seek a place without pain. She had fought against it at first, begging him to fight although his body was racked with pain.

It wasn't until one night he had looked at her and said,

"I'm ready to go, Shan girl," that she realized he was trying to hold on for her. And her alone. She was the one selfishly keeping him in pain. So she had taken his hand and told him it was all right. She'd swallowed tears, railed against life and told him how much she loved him, and then she'd let him go.

He had taken part of her with him. But he had also left a part of himself with her. Tears rolled down her cheek and she made no move to stop them.

The healing process had finally begun.

A long time later she looked out the window. Darkness had descended. Maybe that's what Matt needed, to create some good memories to overshadow the bad ones.

But first she had to find out what drove him past the limits of other men. She had to admit she hadn't had much down time herself lately. When your mind was busy you didn't have time to think about yourself. That was the reason she pulled double shifts, to keep her mind occupied. And it hadn't done a bit of good. Her mind would drift: tears would fall.

She glanced out the window again and wondered at the reason behind Matt's long grueling hours of work. She knew somehow that she was going to find the answer.

Eight

It was after ten-thirty when Matt made his way toward the stairs. He was tired, but it was a good kind of tired. He had managed to plow a large section of the young corn, and the way he figured it, he was only a couple of days behind schedule. Everything would be going well if he didn't have to worry about Shannon.

He had to admit, she hadn't backed away from hard work or from getting herself dirty. After putting the tractor up he stopped by the barn to see the stalls. She had done a surprisingly good job.

Just as she had done a good job helping him with the tractor. He thought to push her a little further by getting her to help with the greasy, tedious clutch job and miscalculated badly. Instead of quitting, she stayed and put him through sheer torture squirming and rubbing against him.

Determined not to let her see how much she affected him, he had ordered her to stay and help him adjust the tension on the clutch. By the time she'd left, his body had ached for release.

He saw her as soon as he turned down the hallway. Dressed in a silky-looking pale-blue pants outfit, she leaned sideways against the wall facing him, her slim arms crossed beneath her generous breasts. If not for the pensive look on her face he would have thought she had seduction on her mind.

"Why do you do it?"

"What?" he asked, surprised at the slight edge to her voice.

She pushed away from the door and met him halfway. "Why do you work through meals and push yourself so hard? Is the ranch in some financial trouble?"

Now he understood the reason for her concern. "Worried about your profit margin?"

"Should I be?"

"This may come as a surprise, but I like what I do. I like pitting myself against all the capriciousness of Mother Nature and whatever else tries to take this place from me."

Her shoulders snapped back, her lips pressed together. Obviously she had caught his meaning. "If you keep on working these hours you won't be healthy enough to fight anything."

"Why should you care?"

"I asked myself the same thing."

"Care to share the answer you came up with?"

"Because Wade loved you."

The smug smile left his face.

"Good night and thanks for the hand cream."

She walked away leaving behind her a whiff of her exotic perfume and a burning ache in his body.

"I can make my own coffee," Matt announced without preamble as he entered the kitchen the next morning and saw Shannon standing by the counter.

"But can you make this?" she asked, and turned with a cherry-topped coffee cake in her hands.

So that was the mouth-watering smell he'd inhaled the moment his boot struck the bottom step of the stairs. She didn't give up easily, he'd admit that much. But to

get his land away from him she'd have to do more than
show him her skills in the kitchen.

Unbidden came the thought of other skills she knew
all too well, skills more suited to scented sheets and long
hot nights. Unbridled need rushed through him. With an
iron will, he brought his desire under control.

"Coffee will be fine until breakfast."

She shrugged slim shoulders beneath another oversize
shirt, this one yellow and white, and set the pastry next
to the coffeepot.

"Suit yourself, I'm a sucker for sweets." Leaning back
against the counter, she picked up a slice of coffee cake
and took a bite. Bread flakes clung to her lips. A pink
tongue flicked them away.

Matt watched in hungry fascination as her tongue disappeared inside her mouth and yanked hard on his slipping control. Lifting the cup, he took a drink. "Ohhh."

"What's the matter?"

"Nothing." He wasn't about to tell her he was paying
more attention to her mouth than the hot coffee.

Her elbow propped on her bent arm, she took another
bite. Crumbs fell. She lapped them up. "Are you sure
you won't have a slice?"

He picked up a wedge to stall for time until his coffee
cooled and to get his mind off her lush lips. The pastry
had barely settled on his tongue before he realized Shannon could be a rich man's dream or a poor man's nightmare.

So far hard work hadn't scared her and she cooked as
mouth-watering delicious as she looked. His ex-wife
hadn't cooked half this good or worked as hard, and she
had put his life into a tailspin. Shannon was in a class
by herself.

It would take a rich man to keep her happy. A poor
man would try and end up feeling less than a man because he couldn't.

"Do you like eggs rancheros?" She handed him a napkin.

He wiped his mouth and wished she'd stop looking at his lips. "Why?"

"Since I'm already up, I thought I'd give Octavia a break and cook breakfast."

Black eyes narrowed. He put the pastry down. "Why?"

She sighed. "Have you always been this suspicious?"

"Why?"

"Because I'm creating extra work for her by being here. It's the least I can do for her making me feel so welcome."

"You're still going to clean up the tackroom and polish the gear."

Her eyes rolled. "I can't believe you sometimes. Of course I'll do the tackroom. This isn't a trade-off, it's an act of kindness."

"Yeah." Sarcasm tinged the word. "What act of kindness did you perform for Wade to get him to give you the meadow? Or was it another kind of trade-off?"

Her eyes widened in shock, then darkened in pain. She started to flee the room.

Unyielding hands grasped her forearm. He was surprised to feel her body tremble, surprised even more to feel a twinge of guilt for hurting her.

"Turn me loose," she mumbled, her head downcast.

"Not until you understand I didn't mean it that way." He waited until his words sank in and she lifted her head.

"I've had some time to consider the situation and I admit I said some things without thinking them through. But the fact remains that you touched Wade enough for him to leave you the meadow," Matt stated, bewilderment in his voice. "He had a soft spot for women in trouble, but his connection to the land was unshakable. I want

to know what trouble you were in and why he thought
the meadow would help?"

"I'm glad you changed your mind about Wade," she
said softly. "That bothered me more than your anger and
mistrust."

"What did you expect me to do?" he asked coldly.
"Lay out the red carpet and throw a feast in your
honor?"

She sighed, her head lowered again as her body
seemed to shift closer to his. "I expected peace."

"Why, Shannon? Why did you need the peace?"

Her bangs brushed against his blue shirtfront. "Things
happened I had no control over and I had trouble accepting them. And before you ask, I don't want to talk about
it."

Secrets and pain he understood. There were things in
his past only Kane knew about. Some things, like his
talking through his ex-wife's deceit, he had never been
able to discuss with anyone. His pride had been hurt too
badly. Yet, there had been times he would have gladly
given a piece of his soul to make the ache in his gut go
away.

Shannon's head turned, her cheek pressed more solidly
against his chest. The warmth and softness cut through
the barrier of his clothes and his cynicism with lethal
effectiveness. His thumb absently stroked her arm beneath the cotton fabric.

With a trembling sigh, she leaned her upper body
closer to his. Blunt-tipped fingers flexed with every in-
dentation of bringing her even closer. Before his actions
became a reality he realized the risk. Abruptly, he set
her away.

Feeling sorry for Shannon was as dangerous as being
seduced by her body subtly shifting closer to his with
every heavy thud of his heart.

"As long as you want to take what's mine, you won't get the peace you're looking for here."

Heavy lids blinked. Sooty lashes lifted over slightly dazed amber eyes. Her gaze shifted. "There are different kinds of peace, Matt, I'm just beginning to figure that out." She turned away. "I need to fix breakfast and your coffee is getting cold."

Matt crossed the room, dumped the coffee without tasting it, then poured himself another cup. "You're hiding something and I'm going to find out what it is before you leave."

"Why?"

He didn't like his word turned on him. "I don't like surprises."

The doorbell rang. She started from the room.

"Leave it. We're not finished talking."

"It's not even seven. It must be important if someone is calling this early."

"It'll wait. This won't."

The chime came again. "There is never any excuse for rudeness."

This time he didn't try to stop her. Crossing his legs at the ankle, Matt leaned against the counter and sipped his coffee. *Run all you want, Shannon,* he thought with conviction. *But sooner or later, I'm going to run you to the ground and find out all your secrets.*

Taking a deep breath, Shannon raked an unsteady hand through her hair as she crossed the den. She had done it again, gone from boiling mad to hot and bothered in 0.9 seconds.

Try as she might to deny it, she could resist Matt no more than the increasing desire to get past his distrust and have him see her and not the woman he thought she was. And that was just the beginning of her problems.

Being around him was only going to make it more difficult for her to ignore her feelings.

Arthur Ferguson had delivered the money and credit card Melanie mailed to her so she could leave if she wanted to. She didn't want to. She wasn't running a step farther from whatever life tossed her way. And that included Matt Taggart.

What a time for her slumbering hormones to go on overdrive. She knew that's what it was. No woman in her right mind would fall in love with a suspicious, overbearing cowboy. A dependable, soft-spoken man like James Harper was more like it. With James fixed firmly in her mind as worthy of another look, she opened the front door.

The tall, rawboned man on the porch blinked in surprise on seeing her, then quickly jerked off his cream-colored Stetson to reveal a thinning patch of salt-and-pepper hair.

"Er, morning, miss. I'm Matt's neighbor. Is he home?"

Shannon smiled to put the older man at ease. "He's in the kitchen. Please come in." Closing the door behind the visitor, she led him back to the kitchen. "Matt, there's a gentleman here to see you."

The rancher stepped from behind Shannon. "Good morning, Matt."

The last person Matt expected was Adam Gordon. It was Wednesday. The Monday deadline had passed for them to agree on the sale of Sir Galahad. "Morning."

Shannon glanced between the two, her curiosity increasing. The elderly man's nervousness had increased, not decreased. Matt looked hard and uncompromising.

The rancher's gaze flicked back to Shannon, then swung to Matt. His grip on the brim of his hat tightened.

"Could I get you a cup of coffee or some coffee cake?" Shannon asked. She, of all people, knew how unnerving Matt could be.

"No, ma'am." He looked at Matt, then back at Shannon.

She offered a slight smile of encouragement.

Adam gulped.

Matt scowled. The speculative gleam in Adam's face when he entered the kitchen had gradually become one of male appreciation. He wasn't as interested in the relationship between Shannon and Matt as he was at looking at a beautiful woman.

"Something you wanted, Adam?"

The rancher jerked his attention back to Matt. "It . . . it's about the talk we had the other day."

"The deadline passed. I said all I had to say."

Gordon shifted from one polished ostrich-skin boot to the other. "Can we go someplace and talk in private?"

"Of course, I'll le—"

"You'll cook breakfast," Matt told her. "I don't intend to waste any more time today than I have to."

Head high, Shannon yanked open a cabinet door, then slammed it shut. Matt ignored her and the noise. "If you've changed your mind, it doesn't take privacy to tell me you're going to sell me the bull."

"Sir Galahad is worth a lot of money."

"Fifteen thousand dollars is a lot of money."

"Fifteen thousand dollars for a cow!" Shannon screeched, staring at both men as if they had lost their senses. Matt returned the look with one of censure, the older man with wry amusement. "Sorry," she mumbled and turned away.

"Pardon me for saying so, ma'am, but you must not know much about prize bulls."

"She doesn't know much about ranching period. But she will before she leaves," Matt promised.

"I'm not the only one who'll learn a lesson before I go," Shannon shot back, one hand on her slim hip, the other clutching a skillet handle.

Gordon's eyes skirted another glance between the two. Curiosity triumphed over good manners. "You're just visiting then, miss?"

Shannon gave up all pretense of cooking and extended her hand. "Yes. I'm Shannon Johnson."

"Adam Gordon." He pumped her hand up and down. "Welcome to Jackson Falls."

"If you two are finished . . ."

Gordon hastily withdrew his hand. Shannon faced Matt with a syrupy smile. "Drink your coffee. It might improve your disposition."

"Shannon," Matt gritted out.

"I know. Breakfast."

His jaw tight, Matt faced the rancher who looked stunned. Matt knew the women Adam usually saw around him went out of their way to please Matt. Shannon took pleasure in opposing him at every turn. "I'm waiting," he growled.

The man jumped, then blurted, "I brought someone for you to see."

Matt couldn't believe such audacity or callousness. His body became as rigid and cold as his voice, "Then you've wasted a trip and my time."

"I deserve that." The rancher looked at Shannon. "Miss Johnson, if Matt can spare you a moment from cooking breakfast, I'd like to show you the finest bull in the Southwest."

"Sir Galahad is here?" Matt thundered.

Gordon finally stopped gripping his Stetson. "I thought he could say it better than I could." He took a deep breath that strained the pearl snaps on his red-checkered shirt.

"At first I was angry with you and then I thought long and hard about things. It didn't take long to figure out you were right." Adam Gordon held out his hand. "You can't buy love or friendship. No one should try."

"I know." Matt clasped Adam's hand, but his steady black gaze was on Shannon. "But you'd be surprised at the people who haven't figured that out yet."

Matt's words stayed with Shannon all day as she worked in the tackroom. The reason for his distrust was clear. Money. She hung up a bridle she had just finished polishing and reached for another one.

Sitting down, she picked up the soft cloth and began rubbing cream into the leather. Telling him she had a trust fund that would see her very comfortably through two lifetimes wouldn't help. Maybe a certified letter from her father's law firm might, but she shied away from that idea.

Sighing, she leaned back in the wooden chair. As crazy as it seemed, she didn't want him to trust her because he knew she didn't need the meadow or his money. She wanted his trust because he was powerless to withhold it. It hardly seemed fair that she reacted so strongly to him and he barely noticed her unless it was to interrogate her or give her a command.

Her lips pursed. After breakfast he had ordered her to follow him to the small room in the back of the barn and told her that he wanted everything polished by the end of the day. It was almost two o'clock and she had barely made a dent in the numerous bridles, harnesses, and whatever else hung from the curved hooks scattered around the room.

Her stomach growled. There was no sense in skipping lunch. The gear would still be here. Maybe Matt wouldn't come back until late and she'd be finished by then. Even as her thoughts formed, she hoped he returned for dinner. She had gone into the house for a glass of water earlier and knew he hadn't returned for lunch.

Whatever else she could say about Matt, there was no doubt he worked hard.

Laying the bridle aside, she rolled her head to loosen stiff muscles, then stretched her hands over her head. She ached in places she had forgotten she had. Lunch, and then back to the grindstone.

Crossing the yard, she saw a late model Camaro coupe pull up in the circular drive in front of the ranch house. A young woman got out of the car and started for the front door. With each hip-swinging step the wind lifted the flared hem of her floral sundress to reveal a pair of long legs.

Shannon sighed. She had always envied women who could wear those flirty little numbers or body-hugging spandex. She had always been too conscious of the wind catching her at the wrong moment and too conscious of her upper proportions. She had only recently worked up to short skirts.

Sir Gallahad bellowed from the corral. The young woman's sandaled foot paused over the first wooden step on the porch. Shoulder-length, blunt-cut black hair swung around in an arc. Her gaze stopped on Shannon and for several seconds stayed there. Sir Gallahad bellowed again. The woman started toward Shannon.

"I'm Vivian Gordon," she said, her voice a slow, seductive drawl that was a captivating mix of the deep South and the West.

Shannon smiled at the pretty, cinnamon-hued woman and introduced herself. "I met your father this morning. I guess you came by to say good-bye to Sir Gallahad."

"I came to see Matt."

Shannon reassessed the unsmiling young woman. Obviously her father had mentioned Shannon and she was here to see what she thought might be the competition. "He's been out plowing since this morning. I don't expect him back until tonight."

Glistening red lips tightened. *"You* don't expect him back? What are you to him?"

If nothing else the woman was direct and Shannon had no intention of being caught between Matt and another woman. "Just what I look like. A hired hand."

The woman's calculating eyes traveled over Shannon who was in her work outfit of faded jeans, a sleeveless knit T, and an oversize shirt. "Is that Matt's shirt?"

Shannon laughed in the suspicious woman's face. She couldn't help it. Anyone who was that rude didn't deserve anything else.

Vivian bristled. "Daddy was wrong, there's nothing special about you. Matt wouldn't look at you twice when he can have me. I'm rich, prettier, and younger than you."

And spoiled rotten. Definitely not the type of woman Matt would choose. He wasn't a man to pamper a woman.

Shannon felt sorry for Vivian. The girl looked to be about twenty. Matt was probably the first thing in her life she wanted and she hadn't gotten. She wasn't dealing very well with the real world.

A girl's first love was often painful. Just because the person was older or entirely out of your reach or not an acceptable object of affection didn't stop you from wanting and hoping. Shannon's fixation had been on the captain of the high school football team who wanted her to be another notch on his jock strap. Her brothers had quickly wised her up.

"Mr. Gordon didn't mention he had children."

Her chin lifted. "I'm an only child and he gives me anything I want."

The conversation between the elderly rancher and Matt now made sense. Mr. Gordon might have come to his senses about Matt not being right for Vivian, but his daughter still needed convincing. And her father clearly wasn't up to telling her what you want isn't always best for you.

"I'm not a threat to any relationship you might have with Matt. He hardly knows I'm around." Vivian looked doubtful. "If there was anything going on here, do you think I'd be cleaning out stalls and polishing harnesses?"

The younger woman looked horrified. "Daddy said you were helping Octavia."

"Matt doesn't like for his workers to be idle," Shannon said sadly. If she was going to play the part of advice-giver she might as well do it right. Her brothers hadn't spared one rotten detail about the high school football captain.

"That's awful," Vivian said, looking at Shannon in a different way. "I don't have to do a thing around my house if I don't want to. Daddy would never ask me to do anything menial. I always thought Matt was just as considerate of women."

Shannon chortled. "Obviously you haven't disagreed with him on anything."

"We really haven't talked much." As if realizing what she had said, Vivian rushed on to add, "He's busy a lot on the ranch."

"If he's too busy to spend time with you, then he isn't worthy of you," Shannon said. "I bet there are plenty of young men around here who would jump at the chance to talk with you."

"Yes, but none of them are like Matt. They all seem so immature and insignificant compared to him. Matt has it all . . . money, success, a gorgeous body, and looks to make any woman's knees weak. He is one fine brother," the younger women said, her voice a breathy rush of adulation and yearning.

"I can't deny that, but I think I'd rather have a man who cared about me above everything else." Shannon's eyes twinkled. "Then again, I'm greedy at times. I bet you can find a man with it all."

Vivian laughed. Shannon joined in. The roar of the tractor drowned out the sound. Vivian's large brown eyes widened as she looked from a grim-faced Matt on the farm machinery to Shannon.

"Please don't tell him why I'm here." No longer did she sound like a self-assured woman trying to warn off another female from her man.

"He has a big enough ego as it is."

Matt stopped the tractor beside the women. As soon as he cut the engine, Shannon said, "I see the clutch I helped you fix is working fine on the tractor."

Vivian's eyes rounded in renewed horror. "He made you work on the tractor, too?"

With a long-suffering sigh, Shannon nodded.

The young woman glared up at Matt. "You shouldn't work her so hard. Daddy would never do that to a woman."

"What have you been telling her?" Matt growled and came off the tractor in a controlled rush.

Vivian stepped back from the harsh intensity of his glare. Shannon lifted her chin. "Only my work schedule."

"Apparently it's too light if you have time to lollygag," Matt told her.

"You're not the man I thought you were, Matt Taggart," Vivian said. She turned to Shannon. "My father's ranch is down the road about six miles on the left-hand side. Gordon's Angus Ranch. You'll always be welcome there."

"Thank you, Vivian," Shannon said. "And good luck."

Without a glance in Matt's direction, the young woman went to her car and drove off.

"What the hell was that all about?" Matt demanded. "That girl's been following me around with those big eyes of hers for the past three months. Now she acts like I'm the devil incarnate."

"Angry that you lost an admirer?" Shannon asked.

"Heck, no," he said, his face spreading into a wide grin. "I was just wondering if you could do it again."

His smile stole the air from her lungs. Her heart lurched in her chest. God. If he had smiled at Vivian that way, no wonder the young woman was so captivated.

"How did you do it?"

Shannon moistened her dry lips. There was no help for her throat. "I—I told her how hard you worked me."

He frowned and she smothered a small groan at the loss. "That's all?"

Shannon came out of her haze. "You aren't that irresistible."

The look he sent her obviously said he didn't care what she thought. "We're going to a party Saturday night."

"Why?"

"To meet your neighbors, of course."

"Try again?"

"Now who is being suspicious?"

Silence was her only answer.

"Adam and his wife are throwing a party in honor of Vivian's upcoming graduation from junior college," he explained. "Since you two hit it off I'm sure you'll want to go."

"And if I just happen to spread the word of what an arrogant, obnoxious tyrant you are, that wouldn't hurt," Shannon said tightly.

His lips thinned. "Hard taskmaster would be enough."

"Ohhhh! I can't believe you," Shannon railed. "That foolish young woman had some stupid notion of how fine and gallant you were. As much as I pity anyone else witless enough to believe such an idiotic idea, I am not,

I repeat *not* going to tell them what a jerk you are. You'll just have to be man enough and tell them yourself."

She turned to walk away, then abruptly swung back. "Or just open your mouth and they'll find out for themselves."

Black eyes blazed. His body became as taut as a plucked bow string.

Too late she realized she had let her temper run faster than her brain. One look at his hard face and she knew running would do little good.

Before she could draw another breath, unrelenting fingers closed around her forearms. "Let's just see how irresistible I am."

His dark head descended.

Nine

"I bite."

Barely leashed passion flared in his riveting black eyes. "So do I."

Shannon refused to give in to the sudden heat centered in her lower body. "I mean it, Matt. You don't want me, you only want to punish me."

"Maybe I just want to see what else that quick little tongue of yours can do."

The heat became a flame. "You deserved everything I said about you. I can't believe you'd be so unfeeling. I thought you were a better man than to lead a young woman on."

"You don't know what you're talking about."

"Yes, I do," she said. He had lifted his head, and she gave only minor thought that he continued to hold her upper arms. "I've known men like you who are thoughtless of women. Just because you're fairly good-looking doesn't mean you can treat women any way you want. You have no difficulty telling *me* what you think. I can't imagine you not setting Vivian or any other woman straight," she told him with certainty. "Failing that, all you need do is look at one of them the way you're glaring at me and they'd run for the hills."

"I have my reasons."

"Yes. I bet your giant ego is one." She shook her head

sadly. "One day you're going to find out what it is to love someone and not be loved in return."

"I already have," he said, his face bleak, his voice raw. "What?"

Releasing her arms, he started for the tractor. Shannon only hesitated a moment before she went after him. The pain in his face before he turned away had been devastating. And she had caused it in her anger, an anger she had used to keep her mind from the growing desire she felt for him. In trying to protect herself, she had hurt him.

Her fingertips touched his sleeve. He swung around, his expression remote. "You have work to do."

"The trouble with trying to judge people is that often it makes you take a good look at yourself. I don't like what I see," she told him. "I'm developing a bad habit of striking out at you when I'm angry. My problem, but you're the one who suffers. I'll try not to let it happen in the future."

"That's all?"

"Unless you want it in writing," she told him with frank calmness.

His Stetson-covered head tilted to one side. "What, no words of pity or polite inquiries?"

"You're too strong to need pity and too arrogant to accept any," Shannon told him quietly. "As for the inquiries, I won't deny I'd like to know the whole story, but you don't trust me enough to tell me. So why waste both of our time by asking?"

"You always have the answers, don't you?"

The way he said it wasn't a compliment. She smiled sadly and shoved her hands into the pockets of her jeans. "Once I thought I did, but life showed me how little I knew."

"Yeah, life is as fickle as any woman ever dared to be." He climbed on the tractor.

"Aren't you coming in for lunch?" she asked over the roar of the engine.

"No."

Shannon watched Matt drive the tractor over to the fuel tank and begin pumping gas. She started for the house. When she entered the kitchen, Octavia was nowhere in sight. Knowing she wouldn't mind, Shannon found the canvas bag and thermos the housekeeper had given her when she had gone fishing, fixed a ham sandwich, wrapped the last piece of coffee cake, and filled the thermos with iced tea. She took it all outside to Matt.

"Do you want to eat while I pump or do you want to take it with you?" she asked. If *she* was tired, he had to be near exhaustion. An empty stomach wouldn't help.

"Octavia send you?" he queried.

"Does it matter?" She dismissed the slight feeling of hurt.

"Leave it," he told her.

Hanging the canvas bag on the headlight, she started back. That woman had really done a number on Matt, cutting him more deeply than any surgeon's scalpel.

"Shannon."

Surprised to hear Matt call her name, she spun around. He stood with one hand on the wheel of the tractor, the other holding the canvas bag.

"Thanks."

"You're welcome," she called, knowing she was grinning foolishly and not caring one bit that he was scowling again. For a moment Matt had remembered what it was like to repay kindness with politeness not suspicion, and best of all he had shared it with her.

Shannon Johnson had to go and soon, Matt thought as he parked the tractor under the galvanized shed and cut the headlights. Darkness settled around him. It was almost nine, he had been up since six. His body should be ready to shut down. It wasn't. It hummed with a strange mixture of something. Whatever, Shannon Johnson was the reason.

It made no sense. Hell, who said life or women made sense?

One thing he knew, it was becoming more and more difficult to remain emotionally detached where she was concerned. This afternoon, she had been right. He had wanted to punish her, but he also wanted to taste her lips and go from there.

Climbing down from the tractor, he started for the barn. His mind knew she was out to take what she could, but his body wasn't listening.

Maybe it was time he went into Kerrville, have himself some fun. Just as quickly as the idea formed he discarded it. He wouldn't use anyone like that. And despite Shannon's accusations, he didn't lead women on. God knew he had ample opportunity.

Telling the women in the small town of Jackson Falls he wasn't interested was a lot trickier than telling the other women he met across the country. For starters, he respected the townswomen's families and didn't want to create hard feelings. The prodding of well-meaning family members like Adam Gordon was just what Matt wanted to avoid. Then, too, the women in town were too marriage-minded, and he was too easy to find.

He could just imagine the gossip if he flatly rejected one of them. Besides, he'd never forget the laughter and the scorn in his ex-wife's face when she told him she had never loved him, had only used him to get what she wanted. When he couldn't fill her needs, she used other men.

He could never do that to another person. He didn't understand why Shannon had sounded genuinely disappointed in him or why it continued to bother him. Like she said, she had no right to judge anyone. Strangely, at the time she had told him that, she really looked as if she wanted to comfort him, when moments earlier she had been chastising him.

He shook his head. Shannon was a chameleon. Somehow she had learned to adapt and change as the situation demanded, going from innocent to defiant to seductive before his eyes. And by doing so she interested him as no other woman ever had.

An interesting woman was a dangerous woman. A man tended to go on feelings, on what he saw instead of what he knew.

Wishing he'd never seen Shannon, he entered the barn and saw the one person he wanted to avoid.

"What are you doing?" he asked.

Startled, Shannon swung toward him and away from the stall she had been about to enter. "I think there's something wrong with your horse."

"What do you mean?" he asked, brushing past her and going to the horse who stood on three legs.

Shannon followed him inside. "This morning when Jay brought him out of the pasture, he was all over the stall. I could hear him stomping around while I was in the tackroom. As I passed just now, I realized I hadn't heard him in a long time," she explained.

Matt's hand slowly swept downward from Brazos's back to his rump to his leg, then finally to his hoof. His fetlock was hot to the touch and slightly swollen. Matt straightened "How long has he been this way?"

"I don't know." She looked at the horse's leg, then up into Matt's harsh expression. "He was standing in the same position he is in now when I went inside to get a drink of water at seven. I didn't think anything about it until I was passing just now."

"Very observant."

Shannon shrugged. "Will he be all right?"

"I think so. It's just tender. Nothing seemed broken or pulled. Cleve does wonders with his remedies," Matt said, sliding his hand over the horse's rump. "If he isn't better by morning, I'll call the vet."

"I'll go get Cleve."

"I'll stay here," he said, staring back down at the horse's leg.

"I thought you might," Shannon said with a smile and headed for the bunkhouse.

Shannon alerted Cleve to the problem.

The frown on Cleve's face quickly turned to one of concern. "I'll get my hat." With that, he was out the door of the bunkhouse and down the steps.

Inside the barn, he went straight to the sorrel stallion and inspected him just as Matt had. "He was kickin' up his usual fuss about being in the stall when I went to the bunkhouse a little after six."

"Shannon noticed he was quiet when she went inside around seven." Matt squatted by the older man. "What time did Jay bring him in?"

"Midday," Cleve answered. His gnarled fingers lightly ran over the stallion's leg, then he gently raised the hoof and just as gently, flexed and extended it. "Looks like he might have kicked the stall too hard and bruised himself. Don't look like it's botherin' him enough to worry about a fracture. I'll go fix up somethin'. He should be fine since we caught it early."

"Thanks to Shannon." Matt nodded in her direction. "She noticed the quiet."

"It was nothing," she said from the stall door. "Anyone would have done the same."

Cleve's free hand clenched, his battered gray hat tipped forward. Slowly he stood. "Meanin', I should have?"

Her eyes widened at the implication. "No. Of course not. I was here, you weren't."

"I guess we're lucky you were here then," he told her, then glanced down at Matt. "I'll fix the poultice."

Shannon stared after the elderly cowboy. "I didn't mean to offend him. I wouldn't intentionally do that to anyone."

"So you keep saying."

She faced Matt. "I know it might be hard to believe, but you're the only one who can make me forget reason."

Since she made him behave the same way, it wasn't difficult at all for him to believe her. "Yeah."

"We just rub each other the wrong way," she stated, folding her arms and catching her lower lip between her teeth.

"Rubbing each other the right way would create just as many sparks. Maybe more," he told her, his voice unnaturally gritty.

Her hand flew to the base of her throat where her pulse leaped wildly. "You . . . you shouldn't say things like that."

She was right, but hearing the breathless catch in her voice made the sudden tightness in his jeans worse, not better. Pivoting away from temptation, he stood facing the horse. "I wonder what's keeping Cleve."

"If you want, I'll go check."

"No, he likes fixing his remedies alone." Matt's hand ran over the horse's flank. "He takes his responsibilities seriously. This ranch is his life, the family he never had."

"Matt, I didn't mean to infer otherwise," she said earnestly, watching Matt's large hands glide reassuringly over the animal.

He glanced over his shoulder. Her face was filled with entreaty and a strange kind of hope. Shannon might be a lot of things, but so far he had yet to see her deliberately cruel. She was just as quick to soothe as she was to annoy him with her sharp tongue.

"I believe you," he finally answered.

Her face lit up. "Thank you."

"Cleve will probably come to the same conclusion once Brazos is all right." The horse neighed and Matt stroked him. "Although he knows it's not his fault the animal is hurt, Cleve feels guilty he wasn't the one to notice the problem."

"Just like family members feel guilty when a loved one becomes ill and they hadn't noticed sooner," Shannon said, remembering her own feeling of guilt about her grandfather.

Matt looked at her intently. "Sounds like you've been there."

Her breath came out shakily. "Yes, I have."

Matt watched her brown eyes darken, watched her struggle for composure and win. She had loved someone, and if he didn't miss his guess, she had lost them. Questions pounded in his brain, but he wasn't sure if he wanted to know the answers for himself or for the ranch's benefit . . . or why he felt the urge to pull her into his arms and console her.

"You better go on in. Cleve and I can finish things here."

"A men-only thing, huh?" she questioned with a laugh.

He struggled to keep from being affected by the twinkle in her eyes and the laughter. "I won't have you sleeping on the job tomorrow because you stayed up needlessly tonight."

"I've pulled double shifts before. I can take it," she told him. "I'll go see if Cleve needs any help."

"Shannon, go to the house." She kept walking. Matt shook his head. "And she called *me* stubborn," he muttered.

* * *

She opened the door to the tackroom and saw Cleve sniffing the contents of a quart-size brown bottle clutched in his right hand. She tensed. "What are you doing?"

He whirled around. Shannon was confused. Instead of the glazed look she had often seen in the eyes of people who had inhaled substances, Cleve's were sharp and accusing. "You ruined everything."

He was still upset with her. "You've got to believe me when I say I didn't mean anything earlier."

"I mean this," he said angrily, the wide arc of his arm encompassing the top two shelves where various bottles and metal containers sat.

Shannon looked at the shelves she had worked on most of the early morning rearranging and cleaning. From over-the-counter liniment to grooming needs, all the various bottles, jars, and cans were now neatly in groups instead of the chaotic mess she found this morning. She could find anything she wanted without . . . Her mind came to a halt.

This was Cleve's domain, not hers.

"I'm sorry. Before I moved anything I should have asked first. I needed some extra saddle soap. While I searched for another can, I started cleaning and rearranging." She studied his unhappy face. "If you'll tell me where, I'll put everything back tomorrow. Right now Matt is waiting."

"Tell him I'm comin'," he said sharply, and set the bottle on the table with several other similar-looking ones and turned away.

She started to go, then frowned when she read the label on the bottle. Iodine. "I'll straighten things out tomorrow. Matt is waiting."

"I know what I'm doin'," he told her flatly. "You just tell the boss I'm comin'."

"I'm glad to know it," said Matt.

On hearing Matt's voice, the cowhand tensed and slowly turned. Lines bracketed his mouth and raced across his dark forehead. He glanced at Matt, then away.

"It's my fault," Shannon blurted. "I rearranged the shelves and now he can't find anything."

"You what?" Matt shouted. His gaze swept the neat shelves, then Cleve's tense body before coming to rest on an anxious Shannon. "I told you to polish the harnesses and other gear, that's all."

She explained what had led up to her cleaning session.

Matt's stony expression didn't soften. "Go to the house, Shannon, and this time I mean it."

She started across the room. "Cleve—"

Matt blocked her path. "I'm not going to tell you again."

Shoulders back, chin lifted, she accepted his angry glare unflinchingly. "I messed up. The least you can do is let me apologize."

"You've already done that." Matt took her by the elbow and led her to the door. "I don't have time to waste arguing with you."

"But I could help. I know where I put things."

"We'll find them."

Digging her heels in did little good. His callused hands were gentle and powerful and determined. "The old bottles like the ones on the table are in the back of the second shelf."

Matt stopped. "You didn't throw them away?"

"What kind of an idiot would do that without asking?" She wrinkled her nose at his raised eyebrow and answered her own question. "The same kind that would rearrange someone's work space without asking."

She twisted to look at Cleve. His shoulders sagged. She had done that. "I really am sorry. The only reason Octavia hasn't thrown me out of her kitchen is that she feels the same way about keeping things in order. I forgot men aren't the same way."

Once again she was on her way to the door. "Good night, Shannon."

Looking up into Matt's unrelenting face, she bowed to the inevitable. "If you're not too tired, please let me know how they both are when you come up to bed."

His hand clenched on her arm.

She swallowed. The tip of her tongue ran across her lower lip. Matt's narrowed eyes followed. "I . . . I mean when you come upstairs."

"Good night." Spinning on his heels, he went inside the tackroom and closed the door, shutting her out.

"Need any help?" Matt asked on reentering the tackroom.

Cleve lifted his head. His eyes were old, tired. "You think she suspected anything?"

Matt gritted his teeth to hold back a curse word. He had learned a colorful array of words on the rodeo circuit and as a rancher. But respect for his elders was bone deep. "No."

Nodding his head, the elderly man began pulling bottles from the second shelf. "I know what you told me, but I can't help how I feel."

"I shouldn't have sent her in here," Matt replied, turning on the faucet and filling a bucket with water. "I never thought she'd do more than what I asked her to do."

"She looks like fluff, but she's as scrappy as I've ever seen."

Matt shut the gushing water off with a snap of his wrist. "Sounds like you like her."

Taking three quart-size brown bottles from the shelf, Cleve hugged them to his chest. "Just speakin' the truth."

The bucket of water plumped on the table. "She won't be here much longer. In the meantime, I'll set her to riding fence or something."

A battered straw hat came upward sharply. "Meanin' I can't handle one female."

Matt had seen that stubborn look before. "Meaning I had already planned on seeing how well she liked being in the saddle for eight hours." As soon as the words were out of his mouth, his body reacted with predictable swiftness.

Cleve's laughter sounded more like a rusty cough. "Might have known you wouldn't let that those big brown eyes get to you."

"You noticed her eyes?"

Cleve shot Matt a long, level look. "Might be old, but I ain't six feet under." Opening the bottle in his hand, he sniffed the contents, nodded his satisfaction, then poured about a cup into the water. A medicinal smell wafted upward. "She's got grit to go along with all them other things a man my age can only admire."

"You about ready?" Matt asked, his words sharper than intended.

The cowhand didn't appear to notice. "Yep, a man regrets a lot of things when he gets old," Cleve reminisced.

A younger man also had regrets.

Matt wanted Shannon with an increasing fervor that kept him awake at night, then invaded his dreams when he finally fell asleep. The taste, the feel, the scent of her was never far from his mind. Somehow he knew with a gut certainty that if he took her to bed, his need for her would only increase.

Once before he had been suckered in by wanting a woman so badly he wouldn't listen to his family, only the wild clamoring of his body. He had paid the price.

This time he was staying in control. "Come on, Brazos is waiting."

Cleve quickly poured from the other two bottles he had taken from the second shelf. "Grab some clean towels from the drawer over there. This might be a long night."

"In more ways than one," Matt mumbled and followed the older man out the door.

Shannon was waiting for him at the top of the stairs. She had on another of those silky pants outfits, this one the color of peaches. Her knees were propped up, her folded arms across them. A faint exotic scent drifted to him as his booted foot touched the bottom step. "It's after midnight."

"I couldn't sleep."

"The meadow losing its magic already?"

She rocked. "Cleve's remedy must have worked faster than you thought."

Matt peered at her closer. If he didn't know better he'd think there were dried tears on her cheeks. "Morning is going to be here before you know it."

She nodded and slowly stood. For some reason, she hadn't wanted to be alone. She had never minded solitude before. Her grandfather wasn't the reason. She just felt incredibly sad.

Before she knew it, she was on the steps waiting for Matt. But his aloofness made her feel worse, not better. Without another word she started down the hall.

Knowing he shouldn't, but somehow unable to help himself, he followed. "What's the matter? Are you sick?"

Head down, hands jammed in the pants pockets, she continued down the hallway. "I'm not sick."

"Then what's wrong with you?"

"Good night, Matt." She reached for the doorknob.

His hand shot out and closed around her delicate wrist. "All right? I'll bite." Her head lowered even more at his choice of words. "You were waiting for me so the least you can do is tell me what's wrong."

She shook her head. It was too late.

Two fingers lifted her chin. Her skin was velvet smooth, but what caught his attention were the tears shimmering in her sad brown eyes. They affected him more than he wanted to admit.

"Shannon, what is it?" he asked, unaware of the husky note of entreaty in his voice.

She swallowed around the lump in her throat and the desire to ask him to hold her. "I just wanted to say good night."

Sadness stared back up at him. He should leave her and go to his room. Yet something tore through him. "Ah, hell. Come here." Strong arms closed around her. Instantly her hands came up to push him away. Using his greater strength, he pulled her closer. Again and again in one continuous motion his hand brushed from the base of her spine to her shoulder.

She shuddered, then relaxed against him. "I'm sorry," she gulped.

She fit perfectly beneath his chin. It seemed natural for his cheek to rest against the top of her head. "You smell like some exotic flower."

"You don't."

Matt tensed, then laughed, a deep rumbling sound. Once again she had caught him off guard. "I don't suppose I do."

Shannon leaned back and looked up at him. A smile started at the corner of her mouth and blossomed into a laugh. "That wasn't very nice of me."

"You certainly don't pull any punches."

"Neither do you."

"You offering to wash my back again?"

"No, and you know it."

They stood smiling at each other. Then the smiles were gone, replaced by an intensity neither wanted and neither could deny.

Air became harder for Shannon to draw into her lungs. Every place their bodies touched, her skin tingled. She suddenly knew why she had waited for Matt. The realization made her take a hasty step backward.

She didn't need this. Dear Lord. She didn't need this. "Thanks for helping me to laugh. I—I think I can sleep now."

"Don't bet on it."

Shannon escaped into her room, away from the blazing fire of Matt's eyes. She glanced at her bed, then away. Matt was right.

Sleep would not come easy.

Ten

She couldn't go down to breakfast, face Matt across the table and act as if he hadn't touched her last night as no man ever had.

He scared her. He excited her.

Sitting on the bed, Shannon tucked her lower lip between her teeth. Matt disturbed her in ways she didn't want and didn't understand. She finally had to admit those feelings he drew from her had nothing to do with her instincts as a nurse, and everything as a woman.

Sixteen days remained of her vacation. Sixteen long days of pretending that Matt didn't set her body afire with a look, make her want with a simple touch.

And he didn't trust her as far as he could throw his horse.

Her stomach rumbled. A not-so-subtle reminder that she hadn't eaten since her late lunch yesterday. After leaving Cleve and Matt last night, she hadn't been hungry.

She glanced at her watch. Seven fifty-five. She stood. Matt should be finishing breakfast. She'd go down and get her assignment. Whatever detail around the ranch he put her on today she'd find time to grab a bite once he left. She knew she was being a coward, but at the moment being a coward was safer than being vulnerable.

Grabbing her straw hat, she went downstairs and into

the kitchen. Matt's unreadable gaze touched her the instant she opened the swinging doors.

She smiled and spoke despite the familiar lurch in her stomach, the catch in her breath. "Good morning, Octavia, Matt."

"Good morning, child. I was just going up to wake you for breakfast," said the housekeeper, smiling.

"She doesn't have time." Matt sat his coffee cup down and stood. "Let's go."

She accepted the brisk command with relief. If she was having difficulties resisting a suspicious Matt, a tender, caring Matt would melt her like snow on a hot stove.

"She hasn't eaten," Octavia protested.

"Shannon knows what time work starts." Setting his Stetson on his head, Matt headed for the door.

With a reassuring smile at the housekeeper, Shannon followed. Let him stay annoyed with her. That way, she'd keep out of trouble.

Halfway to the barn they were met by the three range hands, Jay, Elliott, and Griff. Five horses trailed behind them. Matt grabbed the reins of a huge black satin-skinned animal and swung up in the saddle in one graceful motion. Gazing down at her, he looked at once intimidating and compelling.

"You'll be riding the fence line today with Griff," he informed Shannon.

"Boss, you gave *me* that assignment," said Jay, the youngest and best-looking of the two single ranch hands. His appreciative gaze on Shannon, he smiled. "I never thought I'd ever see the day I'd be looking forward to riding the fence line."

"You'll enjoy moving the cattle to the north pasture just as much." Matt's tone was curt, final. "Trade horses with Griff."

His confusion obvious, the young cowboy's brows bunched together in his rich mahogany face as he glanced over his shoulder at his boss. The implacable face wasn't reassuring. Jay hastened to do as he was told. Griff and Elliott wisely said nothing.

"The roan's yours, Shannon," Matt indicated with a curt jerk of his Stetson. "Mount up. We're wasting time."

Her eyes rounded. "I haven't ridden for years."

"Riding is something you never forget." When his spirited horse sidestepped, Matt controlled the blaze-faced animal with effortless ease. "Give her the reins, Griff."

"Morning, miss." Griff, tall, homely, and happily married, tipped his hat and extended the reins.

Gripping the leather strips, she stared at Matt. He stared back, his face resolute, inflexible. Another challenge. Being on the Circle T made her remember something she had forgotten in the past months. Once you commit to something never give up until either the job is done or the last breath is gone from your body.

Looping the reins over the horse's docile head, she put her left foot into the stirrup, grabbed the horn cap and swung into the saddle. She was certain she heard a sigh of relief from Griff.

Matt's expression didn't change as his encompassing gaze swept from her booted foot resting comfortably in the stirrup to her face. "What if I didn't know how to ride?"

"The fence in the south pasture needs checking. You're assigned to do it. One way or another, you would have gotten the job done." The heel of his dusty brown boot touched the horse's flank. Instantly, the black animal sprang forward. The ranch hands took off after them.

After one longing look toward the back door of the kitchen, Shannon urged her horse to follow. This wasn't exactly the way she had planned her morning. Matt had outwitted her.

She just wished she knew if it was because of the

incident with Cleve or he had decided to turn up the pressure and make her quit. Either way she hoped her gluteus maximus didn't give out before Matt gave in.

In ICCU when she had been too busy to take a break let alone eat lunch, she had worked through hunger and thirst. There was no reason for her not to do so today. It was after ten and Griff said they'd head back for lunch around twelve. She could make it until then. As when she was on the hospital floor, she just needed to focus on getting the job done.

After giving herself the pep talk, Shannon gazed dispassionately at the meandering line of fence stretched out before her. She sighed. Getting excited about barbless wire was simply beyond her capability.

Now she understood Jay's earlier comment. This had to be the most boring and monotonous job on the ranch. If it wasn't for the beautiful countryside and the lanky cowboy beside her, she would have had a hard time continuing.

Griff Walker was forty something, balding, and as thin as the proverbial rail. He was also soft-spoken, kind, and loved his family. She knew all about his three sons ranging in age from four to nine, his wife who worked at the hardware store, his hope of buying a place of their own one day. He was a talker and good company.

"You wanna get down and rest a minute under one of those oak trees, ma'am?" Griff asked, looking sideways at the stooped shoulders of the slender woman riding beside him.

Shannon wiped her shirtsleeve across her perspiration-damp forehead before answering. "If I get off this horse, I may not get back on."

"You're doing fine, ma'am. The boss will be real proud of you."

"Somehow that doesn't inspire me at the moment." She shifted from one hip to the other. Thank goodness she was in pretty good shape.

"The boss might work you hard sometimes, but *he* works just as hard," the tall cowboy said with conviction. "Ain't nothing he asked you to do, he won't do himself."

She wasn't surprised Matt had the loyalty of his men. He certainly had jumped to defend Cleve and reassure the elderly hand. It was *women* Matt didn't trust. "I'm sure he treats his *men* fairly."

Leather creaked as Griff shifted in his saddle. "That he does. Never looks down on us or treats us different because he's the boss. If we're running a little short until payday and need money and have a good reason, he'll advance us the cash without interest. Ain't many a worker who can say the same thing."

From personal knowledge, she knew he was right. Although the hospital frowned upon loan transactions between employees during working hours, it was common practice. Sometimes the borrower just signed over their paycheck to the lender.

Wade also had been right. Matt wasn't as hard as he pretended. "He doesn't sound like Hardcase to me."

"The boss don't deserve that name," Griff said with heat. "Without him my youngest wouldn't be alive."

Slender hands clenched on the reins. "What happened?"

The cowhand looked embarrassed he had blurted out the information. "He don't want me telling folks, but I don't like hearing things 'bout a man who helped Clint when no one else could or would."

"I understand, it's just that I'm having difficulty understanding Matt," Shannon told him.

"No wonder since you two are partners and all. Must be hard for him to get used to." Griff shook his head.

"I've lived in Jackson Falls all my life. Never thought anyone but a Taggart would own Taggart land."

"I'm only a temporary owner," Shannon confessed, holding her hat against the sudden gust of wind that tried to blow it off. "I'm leaving in a couple of weeks, but before I go, I'm signing the land back over to Matt."

"I'll be." Griff grinned and guided his horse around a clump of stunt cedar. "The boss will be happy to hear that."

"If you don't mind, I'd rather you not mention it to him or anyone else." Matt wouldn't believe Griff any more than he believed her.

The cowhand nodded. "You're good people, ma'am."

"Thank you."

"The boss is the same way." Griff looked away for a long moment. "Clint was stung by a bee. I didn't think much 'bout it. I been stung lots of times and so had my other two boys. Told him he'd be all right." The cowboy swallowed. "I left him in the truck while I went in the hardware store to pick up my Millie from work. By the time we came out, Clint was having trouble breathing. The boss had walked outside with me.

"He took one look at Clint, grabbed him from me and ran back in the store giving instructions for the other clerk to call 911 and Dr. Carter. Then my boy stopped breathing. My wife started screaming. I was shaking so bad I didn't know what to do. Everyone stood back, not knowing what to do. The boss bent over Clint and breathed for him."

The cowhand looked at her with eyes that unashamedly shone with tears. "He saved my Clint's life. Every day I thank him and thank God for giving me another chance."

"Not many people know what to do with a second chance."

"I know. Come on, we better get to checking this

fence." He urged his horse from a walk to a canter. "The boss don't give second chances."

She grunted. "Tell me something I don't know."

He had been right to send Shannon off without breakfast. She hadn't overslept as Octavia suspected, she had stayed in her room to avoid him. When he didn't see her in the kitchen when he first went down, he had gone upstairs to check on her. Outside her door, he had heard her pacing the floor, yet when he knocked, there had been no answer.

Maybe she regretted last night's encounter in the hall as much as he did. He had spent a miserable night, and when he did fall asleep, it had been to dream of Shannon a living flame in his bed.

His gritted his teeth at the memory. No breakfast was her choice. Yet he couldn't get out of his mind the sound of her stomach rumbling as they crossed the yard. It was too much of a reminder of when they first met and how exhausted she was and how stubborn.

His horse jumped a small ditch, and the canvas bag on his saddle horn bumped against his knee. He wasn't taking her food because he cared. Shannon had to learn that she didn't have the stamina it took to help run a ranch, but at the same time he didn't want her fainting from lack of nourishment and falling off her horse. He had enough on his mind without dealing with an injured woman.

Matt came over the slight rise and saw Griff and Shannon standing by the fence. Shannon was gesturing toward the fence with something in her hand. Griff was shaking his head. Matt urged his horse toward them.

They turned to him when Matt was several yards away. Stopping in front of them, he saw a break in the barbless wire fence. Shannon had a wire stretcher in her hands. A hammer lay on the ground.

"Is there a problem?"

Shannon shot a look at Griff. Her chin lifted. "No."

Matt leaned over and crossed one arm over the horn, then propped the other arm on top. Griff looked uncomfortable. He wasn't going to get his range-riding partner in trouble. Score another conquest for Shannon. Matt had known the impressionable and unmarried Jay would be easy prey for a captivating woman like Shannon, but Matt figured a happily married man like Griff would be a little stronger.

Hell. He had a hard time not being suckered in by her beauty and her spirit, and he knew she was after his land. He couldn't expect a good-hearted man like Griff to resist falling under her spell. But as boss, Matt expected the hands' first loyalty to be to him.

"Griff, if there's a problem I want to know about it. Now."

The cowhand ignored the plea in Shannon's eyes. Matt wasn't known for his patience. "Miss Shannon wants to help."

Matt straightened. "Then let her help. That's what she's here for."

"She don't have any gloves."

Matt looked at Shannon's delicate hands. In spite of himself he recalled their softness. Without gloves, the firm grip needed to use the wire stretcher would blister her hands in no time.

"Why didn't you say something before we left the ranch?"

The impertinent chin went higher. "How would I know I needed gloves? You said check the fence, you didn't say anything about repairing it. Besides, if you'll remember, you were in a hurry."

Matt barely bit back an expletive. "Let her nail in the staples."

Griff appeared even more uncomfortable. "We, er . . . already tried that."

When Matt's probing gaze went to Shannon, she stuck her hand behind her back. He swung out of the saddle. In the two strides it took to reach her, he removed his gloves.

Superior strength easily pulled her hand from behind her back. The knuckle of her thumb was bruised, slightly swollen. Tenderly, his thumb stroked hers.

Air hissed through her teeth. Huge brown eyes stared up at him.

"I didn't mean to hurt you." He was surprised his voice came out so husky, surprised more that he didn't want to release her hand.

"You . . . you didn't." Her lips were slightly parted as if she was having difficulty drawing in air. The pulse in her throat leaped wildly.

He recognized desire not pain, but if he didn't stop this craziness, one could quickly lead to the other. Releasing her hand, he stepped back. "Go back to the ranch house and put some ice on your thumb."

"I haven't fin—"

"Yes you have," he interrupted her. "Afterward, help Octavia. Today is her half day."

"Gladly. When I finish here."

"I don't give an order twice."

"Neither do you send a hired hand home and give them light duty simply because their thumb got in the way of a hammer." She went to the fence and, using the wire stretcher, tightened the wire. "Ready, Griff."

The cowhand didn't move.

She sighed. "Matt, I'm not being argumentative or stubborn. I've done worse and survived. When I bang my knee against a bedrail at work I can't take time to pamper myself any more than you or one of your men can." He didn't move. "I don't like walking away from something until it's done. You assigned me a job, now let me do it."

He studied the determined features of his unwanted junior partner for a long time. Short of throwing her on her horse, he didn't have a choice. Touching her was the last thing he wanted to do at the moment. Even with her battered straw hat punched down on her head, reddish-brown hair whipping around her face damp with perspiration, she was too tempting for his peace of mind.

He handed her his gloves.

Surprise widened her eyes, then she smiled. "Thanks, boss." Sticking the wire stretcher under her arm, she put on the too-large gloves, then resumed holding the wire.

Matt watched her eager expression and tried not to read too much into her calling him boss. She sure as hell wasn't going to take his orders without letting him know her opinion. He decided to stop trying to figure out this woman for now, and bent to pick up the hammer. Without asking, Griff handed him the staples.

With one glance to make sure Shannon held the wire securely, he drove in staple after staple, then moved to the next wire and the next. Each time Shannon had to adjust the oversize gloves, and each time Matt waited. At last the break in the fence was repaired.

"We did it." She grinned, testing the wire. "My best friend Melanie will never believe this."

"Perhaps you should send her a picture," Matt suggested dryly.

Shannon tilted her head to one side. "Maybe I will. Do you have a camera I could borrow?"

His mustache flattened. "Go home, Shannon."

Her heart lurched. As much as she didn't understand

her feelings about Matt, the thought of leaving him sent her into a panic. "You can't make me go back to St. Louis. I've done everything you asked me."

"I meant the ranch house," Matt explained curtly.

"Oh, my mistake," Shannon mumbled in embarrassment. Pulling off his gloves, she handed them back. "I'm going. Sorry, Griff, to leave you without help."

"That's all right, Miss Shannon, I done this before by myself," the cowhand placated.

"But I bet the time goes faster when you're not by yourself," she told him with a mischievous grin.

"That it does, ma'am," he agreed.

"Griff, you still have work to do," Matt said.

Gathering the tools from Matt and Shannon, the hand put them in his saddlebag and mounted. "Nice ridin' with you."

"You're a gallant man, Griff." Shannon wiped her shirtsleeve across her brow as she watched him ride away.

"Is there a man you can't wrap around your finger?"

Since there was no accusation in his voice or in the midnight-black eyes watching her so intently, she answered him. "Men *and* women seem to find it easy to talk with me. My nursing instructor called it my special gift."

"You thirsty?"

The question was so far afield, Shannon blinked. "What did you say?"

"Are you thirsty?"

"What do you think?"

"What I think doesn't bear saying." Matt walked over to his horse, took off the canvas bag and handed it to her.

Shannon's avid gaze went from the bag to Matt. A tongue moistened her dry lips. "I'll wait. That has to last you until tonight."

Guilt struck him like a physical blow. Yet, he could no more admit the bag was for her than he could admit wanting her was slowly driving him crazy. Reaching inside, he handed her the thermos. "It's enough."

She didn't need any further urging. Unscrewing the lid, she poured the cap half full and drank. Finished, she recapped the thermos and handed it back to him with thanks.

Blunt-tipped fingers closed around the container. "Can you find your way back?"

A disarming smile lit her face. "I thought I'd give my horse his head and he'd lead me home like in the movies."

"More likely to the spot with the sweetest clover," Matt told her. "Follow the fence until it juts sharply to the left, then head due west for about two miles. The ranch is over the next rise."

"Okay."

"Remember, due west."

She nodded. Still unmoving. Two hours ago she hadn't wanted to face him and now she didn't want to leave him. The hot sun didn't seem to matter. "How is Brazos today?"

"Fine."

"Cleve."

"Fine."

"Is he still upset with me?"

"He thinks you have grit."

"He does?"

"He does."

"What do you think?" The question was out before she had time to stop herself.

"I think you should get on your horse and leave while we're both thinking at all."

Shannon recognized the dark, smoldering passion in

Matt's eyes and quickly went to her horse, mounted and rode away. She rode fast because she so wanted to stay.

God help her. How was she going to last until her vacation was over?

Eleven

"I'll do that."

Shannon glanced around to see Cleve behind her. She stepped away from the horse she had been trying to unsaddle. "Thanks."

Gnarled hands finished uncinching the horse, then removed the saddle and blanket. "Saw you ride out this morning."

"He put me to riding the fence line." It was easier to think of Matt impersonally.

Cleve straightened the blanket on the rail to dry. "And?"

"I seem to have a knack for doing the wrong thing." She held up her thumb. "I'm on light duty."

"Better go inside and put some ice on it."

"You sound like him," she said, pleased that Cleve didn't appear upset with her any longer.

"Well, if us men don't take care of those with less sense, who will?" Untying the horse's reins, he walked off.

"You sure you two aren't related?" she called after the bow-legged cowhand. She didn't expect an answer and she didn't get one. Shaking her head, she headed for the kitchen. Octavia glanced up from the kitchen table. The frown on her face curved into a smile.

"Oh, Shannon, I'm glad you're back."

"It's nice knowing I'm wanted somewhere."

The frown returned. "Matt giving you a hard time? I thought he was coming around. I know he fixed you some food."

"That was for him."

"No, it wasn't. He might fill a canteen with water, but that's about it no matter how long he plans to stay out." Octavia's smile returned. "He certainly would never put a napkin and a wash cloth inside."

"He only offered me a drink. He didn't say anything about food," she said.

"He didn't have to since he was sending you back to the house. That way he didn't have to admit he was wrong this morning or that he was worried about you. Told you he was sneaky."

Shannon suppressed a warm rush of happiness. "He's only worried that I won't sign over the meadow and leave."

"Wouldn't be so sure about that." The housekeeper's level gaze studied Shannon for a long moment. "Matt pays about as much attention to women around here as a horse does to a fly. Less. For him they simply don't exist. I'm sure it's a different story with women away from here, but for whatever his reason, the women in the area are off limits. Since you're living here, logic says he should ignore you, too. But he doesn't. You have his attention and I don't think the land has anything to do with it."

Shannon didn't like the way the conversation was going. "Was there a particular reason you're glad I'm back?"

"I can take a hint," the housekeeper said. "The ladies auxiliary is having a call meeting and I need to go. I had already switched my half day off from yesterday to today because of my hair appointment. I just called the beautician and, thank goodness, she can work me in tomorrow. Lord only knows how long I'll be there. Matt won't care if I take off, but I had planned on going grocery shopping."

"Say no more. I'll do the grocery shopping."

"Oh, Shannon, that would help me out so much. I truly hate going to the grocery store, so we're almost out of everything," she confessed and handed Shannon a three-column list on a sheet of paper.

"You weren't kidding."

"If it's too much—"

Shannon shook her head. "I was just wondering how I'm going to get all this in my car."

Octavia brightened. "Cleve always drives me in his truck, so he can help with the groceries."

"Oh, wonderful," she said drolly.

"Like Matt, he just takes a bit of getting used to."

"Define a bit."

The corner of Octavia's mouth twitched. Shannon's lips curved upward. Simultaneously both women broke into laughter.

"Cleve, this would go a lot faster if you'd just read over the list and help me find the right aisles." Shannon remembered why she stayed with her old grocery store back home after a new superstore opened. Even with the signs overhead, she still had to find the exact spot the item was located.

"I just push the cart," he said, moving his chewing tobacco from one side of his jaw to the other.

She sighed. "You cook for the other hands. You must know something."

"I just tell Mrs. Ralston what I need and she adds it to her list. She understands how a man feels about grocery shopping."

"I wonder how that same macho man would feel if there was no food on the table when he came home."

"Mighty upset" came the reply.

"Then I suggest you find your memory or your boss is going to know why there's no food prepared when he comes home for dinner tonight." She tore off the third column, handed it to a startled Cleve. "I'll do the rest of the list."

Halfway down the next aisle, Shannon stopped. She shouldn't have done that. She had promised Octavia she'd do the grocery shopping, it wasn't Cleve's responsibility. Perhaps if he didn't act as if she didn't have sense enough to come out of the rain, he wouldn't upset her so.

He thinks you have grit. Matt's words came back to her.

Wheeling the basket sharply, she went in search of Cleve. She turned the aisle to see him unmoved from the spot she had left him, the list clutched in his fist, his eyes shut tight. Misery radiated from him like a physical thing.

His eyes opened. He turned away, but not before she saw the pain and confusion in them. Suddenly, she remembered Cleve sniffing the bottles, not reading the labels.

He couldn't read.

Her chest tightened. He couldn't read and she had embarrassed and hurt him. She started toward him, praying somehow she'd find the right words not to injure his pride further.

"I was thinking, Matt isn't going to be too pleased with me if I don't get this done and I sure don't want to let Octavia down, so how about we do this systematically and compromise?"

Gently, she pulled the rumpled list from his hand and put it with the other one. If he knew what she wanted, she didn't doubt he could take her to every item. People who couldn't read were visual learners.

Get **3 FREE** Arabesque
Contemporary Romances
Delivered to Your
Doorstep and Join the
Only New Book Club
That Delivers These
Bestselling African American
Romances Directly to You
Each Month!

No Obligation!

WE INVITE YOU TO JOIN THE ONLY BOOK CLUB THAT DELIVERS HEARTFELT ROMANCE FEATURING AFRICAN AMERICAN HEROES AND HEROINES IN STORIES THAT ARE RICH IN PASSION AND CULTURAL SPICE...

And Your First 3 Books Are FREE!

Arabesque is the newest contemporary romance line offered by Pinnacle Books. Arabesque has been so successful that our readers have asked us about direct home delivery. We responded to your requests. You can start receiving three bestselling Arabesque novels a month delivered right to your door. Subscribe now and you'll get:

⬦ 3 FREE Arabesque romances as our introductory gift—a value of almost $15! (pay only $1 to help cover postage & handling)

⬦ 3 BRAND-NEW Arabesque romances delivered to your doorstep each month thereafter (usually arriving before they're available in bookstores!)

⬦ 20% off each title—a savings of almost $3.00 each month

⬦ FREE home delivery

⬦ A FREE monthly newsletter, Zebra/Pinnacle Romance News that features author profiles, contests, special member benefits, book previews and more

⬦ No risks or obligations...in other words, you can cancel whenever you wish with no questions asked

So subscribe to Arabesque today and see why these books are winning awards and readers' hearts.

After you've enjoyed our FREE gift of 3 Arabesques, you'll begin to receive monthly shipments of the newest Arabesque titles. Each shipment will be yours to examine for 10 days. If you decide to keep the books, you'll pay the preferred subscriber's price of just $4.00 per title. That's $12 for all 3 books with FREE home delivery! And if you want us to stop sending books, just say the word...it's that simple.

*See why reviewers are raving about ARABESQUE
and order your FREE books today!*

"Let's see, baking products are next. You can get the flour, cornmeal, sugar, and I'll get the rest."

Dark-brown eyes shifted away from her. "Pardon me, but I don't feel like grocery shopping no more."

The elderly cowboy slowly walked away from her as if every step was an effort. She had never felt so helpless in her life. He had seen through her subterfuge as easily as seeing through spring water. Without giving the groceries another thought she walked after him.

As soon as she opened the door of his truck, the engine roared to life. Her door closed and the vehicle took off. She stole one furtive peek at Cleve's rigid profile and slumped against the leather seat. He wasn't up to listening to her. Besides, she had had her chance and blown it. There was only one person who could help him now.

Matt.

This time when he yelled at her, she knew she would deserve every second of his condemnation.

"Octavia, I need Matt to come back to the ranch at once," Shannon said as soon as the housekeeper came to the phone. She didn't know what she would have done if Octavia hadn't left a number where she could be reached.

"Child, what's the matter? You all right?"

Shannon spoke around the lump in her throat. "I can't explain things now, but it's very important that I talk to Matt immediately." She took a deep breath. "Do you have an emergency code or something? I tried to catch that stupid horse, but he wouldn't come."

"Shan—"

"Please, Octavia. I don't have time for questions." Twisting the phone cord around her finger, she stared at the entrance of the barn. Cleve had gone inside about fifteen minutes ago and she hadn't seen him since.

"Just tell me you're all right."

"I'm fine. I'm not the one . . . I'm fine."

The housekeeper gave her Matt's number, then instructed, "Put in 911 and your name. He'll know it's you calling and come running."

Shannon sniffed. "Thank you for not demanding an explanation."

A none too delicate snort came through the receiver. "I'm not sure you would have given me one. I guess I'll have to wait until you're ready to explain things."

"That's not my decision to make," she said softly. Pressing the disconnect button, she put in Matt's beeper number, the emergency information, then went outside on the porch to wait.

Matt came thundering over the rise looking down on the ranch in less than five minutes. Low in the saddle, he leaned over the horse's long neck as if they were connected in some way. Shannon's breath caught in her throat when she saw he was headed straight for the white wooden fence of the outer corral instead of taking the time to go to the gate.

Horse and rider cleared the fence with room to spare and Shannon let out a grateful breath that he was an excellent rider. Her gaze glued to him, she watched him take the next fence with the same reckless ease. He was aiming straight for her.

Her eyes widened in apprehension as he swung from the still-moving horse with an agility and skill that left her breathless again. In seconds he was on the porch. His gloved hands closed around her forearms, his black eyes drilled into her.

"What's the matter? Are you hurt?"

Despite his voice, the gentleness of the hands holding her finally got through to her. "He's hurting."

"Who?" he barked, clearly at his limits.

"Cleve. He and I went to the grocery store together." She took in a huge gulp of air. "I thought he was acting macho and I gave him part of the grocery list."

Matt's fingers tightened on her arms.

"He's hurting, Matt. He's a proud man. I didn't know what else to do but call you."

"Where is he?"

"The barn."

Matt turned and started back down the stairs. Grabbing the reins of his horse, he tried to slow his drumming heartbeat and get the bitter taste of fear out of his mouth.

He had never been so frightened in his life. Seeing the concern in Shannon's teary eyes had been like someone twisting his insides. The fear hadn't been for herself, but for a man she had only known a few days.

Nearing the barn, he wondered if he'd ever know the real Shannon, or if he dared. He saw Cleve sitting a few feet inside on a small stool, three strands of hemp in his dark, calloused hands.

Making handmade rope was time-consuming. To Matt's knowledge, Cleve had never made over a few dollars' profit from a single one of the highly prized ropes he "sold" to friends. The elderly cowhand considered it a dying art, and since he had no children, he was leaving a part of himself behind. He blessed the good days when his arthritis allowed him the strength and dexterity to work without pain. He'd always said it proved he wasn't useless.

Cleve certainly had a need to feel useful today.

Matt leaned against the stall door beside Cleve and glanced out the door. Shannon still stood on the porch, her slim arms wrapped around her, her gaze fixed on the barn door.

He looked at the top of Cleve's battered, sweat-rimmed

hat. Matt would rather be locked in a chute with an angry bull than see the old man hurt.

"You all right?"

"She call you?" Hemp twisted around hemp.

"Yeah."

"Haven't seen you ride that crazy in a long time."

Matt propped his elbows on top of the stall door. "She put in the emergency code."

The battered hat lifted, then swung in the direction of Shannon. "You should have seen her tryin' to catch Flapjack again. Had a carrot in her hand."

"She watched a lot of westerns."

Cleve's head lowered. A long time passed before he said, "I never wanted anyone else to know."

"She won't tell anyone."

"She knows." The words came out tightly, embarrassment mixed with resentment.

"She knows and she's so worried about you that she has tears in her eyes."

The arch of the old cowhand's neck brought Matt into his line of vision. "You must be wrong. Why would she cry for an old nobody like me?"

It was all Matt could do not to yell he wasn't a nobody, that the person, not the education, not the money made the man. But he had yelled before and Cleve hadn't listened. "A nobody wouldn't drop out of school and stay at home to help with his four younger brothers and sisters after his father was killed when a mule kicked him. A nobody wouldn't work from sunup to sundown for the price of a soft drink in today's money. You gave up your education for your sisters and brothers. Without you, they wouldn't have made it."

"They're gone now, but all of 'em got an education," he said proudly.

"They had you to thank," Matt said, his hand clamping

on the older man's shoulder. "A nobody couldn't have done that."

Cleve's hand gripped the rope. "A grown man should know how to read."

"I told you I'd teach you anytime you're ready."

The elderly man's sigh was long. "What if I don't have it in me to learn?" His shoulder moved helplessly beneath Matt's strong hand. "That's a failure I don't want to face in this lifetime. I don't even know if I can face her again."

"She regrets what happened," Matt said.

"She's sassy, but she's got a good heart."

Matt's gaze followed the direction of Cleve's. Shannon hadn't moved from the porch. She might be concerned, but he wasn't ready to concede her goodness. A good woman would be more disruptive to his peace of mind than a selfish one. "She's stubborn and opinionated."

A dry bark of laughter erupted from the old man. "Just like you."

"Now who's calling the kettle black?" Matt asked.

"She don't know spit about ranchin'," Cleve snorted.

"I don't know what Wade was thinking to leave her the meadow."

Cleve came to his feet, his eyes wide. "She wasn't kiddin'? She really owns a part of the Circle T?"

Matt lips tightened. "Yeah."

"Why?"

Matt gave the only truth he knew. "She was Wade's nurse."

"I'll be," the older man said. He looked back at Shannon with new interest. "So she's the 'angel' in the hospital Wade talked about. He thought highly of her. Can't say he said the same thing for her beau."

Matt had been about to ask why everyone seemed to know something about Wade and Shannon when he didn't, until Cleve said "beau." Every nerve in his body snapped to attention. He came away from the stall and faced the cowhand. "Beau?"

"Yep. Wade spoke of some citified fellow up in St. Louis. Should have made the connection sooner." Rope in one hand, Cleve took his hat off and scratched his balding pate with the other. "Wade thought she might marry the fellow. Guess he was wrong. Didn't see no ring."

Something inside Matt tightened. His ex-wife had kept hers in the coin holder of her billfold. After he filed for divorce she had pawned her rings and sent him a useless part of the ticket to show him just how little she thought of him. Enclosed with the torn receipt was a note telling him how angry he had made her by not fulfilling her dreams of fame and riches as the wife of a top rodeo star.

The laughing, caring woman he had met in line at the grocery store and married a month later didn't exist. He had been suckered all the way by her beautiful face and lying lips. He wasn't going to be that gullible or that stupid again no matter how tempted.

"I better get back."

"You shouldn't have come," Cleve told him. "I ain't made out of fluff."

"Never thought you were." Untying the horse, Matt went to the waiting Shannon.

"Is he all right?"

He wanted to ask Shannon questions of his own, such as who was this man Wade had mentioned. Matt shut the words away because he shouldn't care about the woman whose gaze kept darting from him to the barn. Or care that the perspiration dampening her face indicated she was uncomfortable in the heat. Most of all, he shouldn't have the strangest urge to run his tongue across the moisture beaded on her brow, the curve of her upper lip.

His jaw hardened. Hell, he'd like to taste her all over and then start again.

"Matt?" Concern etched her face, echoed in that one word.

Somehow he drew his rampaging mind from his fantasy of her body to the need in her face. She cared and she was worried.

Unbidden came the memory of being in the emergency room with a broken collarbone. With his shoulder feeling like someone had taken a branding iron to it, he kept asking why his wife wasn't there. She'd been in the stands when the bronc threw him four seconds into his ride; she should have been there.

Kane had told him she probably didn't like to see Matt in pain. He had wholeheartedly believed his big brother, because he hadn't wanted to face the alternative. Two months later, he had no choice.

A tornado wouldn't have kept Shannon away. She was capable of caring, possibly even loving. Somehow he knew, if she had been in the stands, nothing would have kept her away.

"Matt, please say something."

He shook off the memories with practiced ease. "He'll be all right."

"I knew you could help him." She reached out her hand to touch him, then as if realizing what she had been about to do, jerked it back. "He respects you so much."

"Hard to believe, huh?"

Her smile was tremulous. "No. You can be nice when you put your mind to it."

The smile; the rosy lips, were too much. She smelled good and looked better. He turned and swung up on his horse.

"Wait!" she cried, and stepped off the porch. "At least come in and eat something."

"I haven't time." He gathered the reins tighter in his hands.

She grabbed the canvas bag and stepped back. "Then I'll fix you something fresh. I won't be but a minute." She whirled and ran up the steps.

He should go. He didn't.

Shannon's big brown eyes staring at him one moment as though she'd like to lay his head on her soft breast and comfort him and the next as though she'd like to eat him with a spoon was too much of a temptation to see again.

He waited and, of course, it took longer than a minute. A smile on her face, she came rushing out of the house and handed him the bag.

"You eat every bit of it."

"You're beginning to sound like Octavia." He hooked the bag over the saddle horn. She was in her comfort mode. His gaze flickered to her breasts.

Her smile widened. "Maybe you'll listen to one of us."

"I'm hardheaded, remember."

"You're a lot of things, I'm just beginning to learn," she said softly and went into the house.

Matt had one leg over the saddle before he realized his intention of going after Shannon and asking what she meant. Calling himself crazy, he regained his saddle and took off. He didn't care what she thought of him. Even as the words formed in his thoughts, he knew he lied.

Good or bad, he wanted Shannon Johnson with a soul-burning urgency. It was stupid, it was dangerous. His mind knew, his body just wasn't listening.

Her grocery basket was exactly where she had left it earlier. Thank goodness there had been nothing perishable inside. Hands clamped on the handle, she headed to aisle 4. Baking products. Rounding the corner, she came to a halt.

Cleve. A smile started at the curve of her lips and spread.

He put a ten-pound bag of flour inside his cart next to the cornmeal and the sugar. "What else is on that list?" he asked.

Grinning, Shannon started toward him. "Cleve."

He backed up a step when she lifted her arms. "Ain't no call for all that."

Her arms lowered. "I'm glad you came."

He shrugged. "Ain't much gonna fit in that little toy car of yours, so I followed in my truck. I got a taste for a German sweet chocolate cake."

"I'll fix you one tonight."

"Hmph. Hope you cook better than you can catch a horse."

She laughed. "Cleve, you're priceless. You and Matt must have given Wade a run for his money."

His smile was warm with memories. "Wade was one of a kind. Left me that truck of his." He fixed her with a stare. "Left you the meadow, I hear."

She hadn't told Griff the exact location of the property or why she owned Taggart land. "Matt told you."

"He did."

"You needn't worry. I'll be gone soon and, when I go, the ranch will be his alone." She said the words calmly, as if something inside her wasn't protesting at the thought of leaving the ranch, leaving Matt.

Cleve picked up a box of pancake mix. "This on the list?"

Glad to have the matter dropped, she scanned the list. "Yes," she answered, then named several other items.

Without pausing, Cleve plucked them from the shelves. For the first time, she really looked at the various items and realized how difficult it must be for someone to memorize labels, especially when some products by the same manufacturer were packaged in so similar a manner.

She was just beginning to fully understand something Matt already knew. A man's character was measured by many things. Strength and courage and intelligence were shown in many different ways.

Matt cared about the person inside, not what they were, not who they were. A hardcase wouldn't care or know the difference. Wade had been right. But was it possible to find the gentleness inside Matt and bring it to the surface?

"You gonna daydream or what?"

Cleve's terse voice snapped her back to the present. "Sorry."

"You thinking about that feller of yours?"

Shannon blinked. "What!"

"Wade said you had a feller you might marry."

Shannon's mind flashed not to James but to Matt. Strong, compelling, and so handsome he made her knees weak. She looked away from Cleve's sharp gaze. "We're just dating."

He nodded tersely. "Glad to hear it. Wade wanted better for you."

So did her grandfather, but she felt it disloyal not to speak up in James's defense. "James is a very successful lawyer and well respected by everyone."

Cleve's gaze sharpened. "Is that the only way you take the measure of a man?"

"No," she answered without thought.

He nodded. "You'll do. You're not like the other one."

"What other one?" she questioned, afraid she already knew.

"If you don't know, ain't my place to say." Wheeling his basket around her, he started down the aisle.

Abandoning her cart, she caught him in two steps. "You can't make a statement like that and leave me hanging."

Cleve's lips clamped tighter than a two-year-old's mouth with a spoonful of spinach in front of him.

"Everyone alludes to a woman in Matt's past. What did she do to him?" she asked, unaware that her voice trembled.

"You got your feller back East," Cleve finally said. "Why so interested in the boss's life?"

"I-I'm just concerned."

Bushy eyebrows rose. "You're sure that's all?"

"Yes." Matt wasn't for her.

"Probably just as well. A city lady like you wouldn't be much good to a hard-working rancher like the boss," Cleve said. "He needs a sturdier woman."

"Is that how you measure a woman, by her sturdiness?" she asked sarcastically.

His crackling laughter boomed. "You give as good as you get, girlie. Does that mean you're interested in the job?"

She jerked back. Her mouth worked several seconds before any words came out, and when they did they were filled with indignation. "Matt means nothing to me."

"You don't have to hurt my ears. A simple no would have gotten the job done."

"You shouldn't ask such personal questions."

"I figure if you don't ask, you won't learn." Cleve started down the aisle again. "Anyway, it would take a mighty special woman to get the boss to the altar, mighty special indeed."

Twelve

"Melanie, I think I'm in trouble," Shannon said softly into the receiver.

Her best friend laughed. "That's usually my line."

Shannon leaned against the wooden chair in the kitchen and almost smiled. She could picture this woman who had been her best friend since college with one foot draped over the side of her hammock in her living room, her tortoiseshell glasses perched on her nose, a mischievous smile on her coffee-colored face.

But that smile could turn intimidating in seconds if she was thwarted. The staff and patients in the rehabilitation center where she headed the physical therapy department quickly learned to respect both.

"I'm serious. There's a man——"

A loud screech came through the line. "Way to go, girl. I always knew James was too stiff for you. Now, tell me every delicious and dirty detail, and don't leave anything juicy out."

Shannon cast a glance at the oven where Cleve's German sweet chocolate cake was baking, as if to make sure the loud noise hadn't made the cake fall. He was the cause of all these doubts resurfacing. Matt wasn't for her. She couldn't heal his heart. But Lord, how did she stop herself from wanting to do that very thing?

"Shannon?" Melanie prompted.

"Well, there's nothing much to tell ex——"

"What! After I've waited all these years for some guy to knock your socks off, you're telling me you're still at the looking stages?"

"If you'd stop cutting me off, I'd tell you."

"So talk."

Impatient. Melanie had always been impatient. She rushed headlong into everything. She wasn't afraid to take chances. Shannon marveled at her best friend as much as she envied her free-wheeling spirit. Nothing intimidated Melanie, especially not a man.

Yet, she never thought less of Shannon because she weighed everything carefully before making a decision. Melanie had always said it was because of Shannon's single-minded determination once she made up her mind. Melanie's friendship and loyalty were unwavering.

"Thanks for sending me the money."

"You're welcome. Now, tell me everything before I start thinking your parents might be right about you being in trouble. Has this brother got it going on or what?"

Shannon had no difficulty answering that question. "He's the most compelling and the most irritating man I've ever met."

"Oh, girl. I wish I could see the man who finally melted your butter."

"You've seen him."

"When?"

Shannon sighed. "Four years ago. He's Matt Taggart, the Walking Hunk, the nephew of Wade Taggart."

"You come home right now or, better yet, I'll fly down and we can drive back together," Melanie told her, all playfulness gone. "That man disrupted the entire department every time he came to therapy with his uncle. Work virtually came to a standstill. There were so many tongues hanging on the floor you had to be careful where you stepped."

"I heard it was the same way on the unit," Shannon admitted.

"Exactly. No woman was immune to him, and although he took several of the staff women out, once his uncle was discharged they never heard from Matt Taggart again. You worked the night shift so you didn't get to see all the pitiful weeping and moaning when he moved on to the next woman or if he chose one woman over another." Melanie snorted delicately.

"I thought," she continued, "they were all being foolish until his uncle introduced us. If his good looks didn't get you, that molasses voice or those devilish eyes would. Let's not even get into his body. Oh, Lord! That's one man who looks as good going as he does coming."

"I know."

"You're too vulnerable to tangle with a heartbreaker like that. Lord only knows if any woman could," Melanie said flatly. "He's the kind of man who'll give you heaven for a few days, then drop you straight into hell for a lifetime. Come home."

"I can't. I can't explain it, I just can't leave." Shannon might be unsure of her feelings, unsure of her control, but one thing she was sure of was that if she ran this time it would be the worst mistake of her life.

"No, you didn't, Shannon Elaine Johnson," Melanie riled. "Tell me you didn't go and fall in love with this guy."

She had never lied to Melanie and she wasn't about to start. "I don't know."

"Then don't. Get your soft-hearted behind out while you still can," her friend advised. "Marry Mr. Conservative and be happy."

"Melanie, you know how I feel about marriage. It's forever. I couldn't do that to James."

"So you're gonna stay and let Taggart leave his boot

marks on your back as well as on your heart," her friend said tightly.

"Matt hardly pays me any attention unless I do something wrong," she confessed.

"What's wrong with that man? Men fall all over themselves trying to get your attention. We had to have an unlisted phone number in college because of all the guys trying to hit on you."

"The way I remember it, half of those calls were for you."

"From men trying to get to you through me. And they're still doing it," Melanie said. "It's a good thing my ego can take it or I might end up in therapy."

"Men don't ignore you, but Matt does ignore me."

"He must have fallen off his horse one time too many. You're the best thing that could happen to a hard man like Taggart."

Shannon smiled at her friend's quick defense. "He doesn't think so."

"His loss. Come home."

"I can't. I just needed to talk to someone." It went unsaid that it had always been her grandfather whose counsel she sought.

Silence. "How's it going?"

"Better," she answered, and for the first time since she lost her grandfather, she actually meant the words. "I'm going to be all right. I know that now. I'll miss him forever, but I can make it."

"I never doubted."

The oven timer dinged. "I better get off the phone. Thanks for listening."

"Anytime. Just guard that heart of yours."

"Good-bye, Melanie." Slowly she hung up the phone and realized her best friend's warning had come too late.

* * *

"Is Brazos's fetlock worse?" Matt asked as soon as he entered the barn that evening and saw Cleve standing by the horse's stall.

"Nope," the cowhand answered. "Just walkin' off two big slices of German sweet chocolate cake."

Matt dismounted with a smile. Cleve's sweet tooth was well known. "How did you talk Octavia into baking on her off day?"

"I don't recall sayin' Mrs. Ralston baked the cake."

Strong fingers paused in the middle of tying the reins. "Who else could . . . Shannon?"

The dusty brim of a battered hat dipped. "Yes, siree. She may not know squat about ranchin', but she shore can bake. Best tastin' cake that ever passed these lips. The man who puts a ring on her finger is gonna be mighty lucky."

"Or mighty miserable," Matt said, throwing back the stirrup to unbuckle the cinch.

"I bet that successful lawyer feller in St. Louis doesn't think so."

Matt stilled, then turned, his eyes intent. "How do you know so much about him?" he asked, unaware of the sharpness of his voice.

"I asked while we were grocery shoppin'," Cleve answered with satisfaction.

"You two all right now?"

"I reckon. Figured anyone who'd shed a tear for me deserved a second chance. Besides, that fancy car of hers couldn't have brought back all the groceries Mrs. Ralston usually buys." A crafty smile brightened his lined face. "Got me a cake out of it, too."

Matt grunted and turned back to his horse. Looks like he was the only man in Jackson Falls who wasn't tripping over himself trying to sing Shannon's praises. "She seems to have a knack for making some men happy."

"That feller in St. Louis must have a lot of competition," Cleve said thoughtfully. "When it came time to check out, we had more sackers than a dog has fleas."

"That must have made *her* happy." The saddle landed with a solid thunk on the wooden rail.

Cleve shook his head. "Miss Shannon didn't seem to notice. She was laughing at some silly front-page story in one of them tabloids. She sure has a pretty laugh."

Matt had had enough. He faced the elderly cowhand. "You sound as if she's your best friend."

"I'm just tellin' it like it tis. She's a mighty interesting lady even if she had the misfortune not to be born a Texan."

"Somehow I think she would take exception to hearing that."

"Reckon you're right." Cleve grasped the horse's reins. "I'll take care of Sundance for you. You better get inside and see if any of that cake is left. Jay and the boys were just ridin' in when she came out to tell me to come and get mine."

"I'll pass."

Cleve lifted a heavy eyebrow. "Since when didn't you like anything chocolate?"

"I don't want any cake. I'm not going to eat some just to please Shannon. I'm sure the rest of you have praised her cooking skills enough. She doesn't need mine."

"Well, I'm sure Miss Shannon won't force any down your throat." With that remark, the cowhand turned and led the horse away.

Matt started for the house at a ground-eating pace. He had overreacted. Cleve knew it and he knew it. He just hoped the elderly cowhand didn't know the reason.

Shannon.

He wasn't able to get her out of his mind. No matter how hard he tried, he couldn't dismiss her as easily as he had other women. It was more than the softness of her skin, the tenderness of her touch, more than her beautiful face, her shapely body.

He kept remembering her stubbornness in repairing the fence, her tears for a man she barely knew, her admonishment for him to eat his lunch. She was like no other woman he had ever met. She fascinated and confused the hell out of him. He may not have succumbed to Shannon, but he was sure teetering on the brink.

Somehow he had to keep from going over. His life wasn't what he wanted, that was for sure, but he wasn't about to go through the hell his ex-wife put him through trying to get it. Having his niece and nephew, Chandler and Kane Jr., was almost as good as having his own children. Against a gut full of pain, almost wasn't so bad.

Snatching open the door, he entered the kitchen and came to a dead halt. Shannon stood by the stove, a shy smile on her toffee-colored face, a plate of steaming, delicious-smelling food in her hand. Without asking, he knew it was for him. She was not going to get to him as she had all the other men.

"Where's Octavia?"

The smile on her beautiful face slipped a notch. "Eating dinner at Mama Sophia's with her church auxiliary group."

Matt's gaze swept the stove noting the skillet and the two pots. "You cooked."

"Octavia wanted to stay. She didn't have time this morning to cook something for you." Shannon tucked her lower lip between startling white teeth. "She said you liked stuffed pork chops."

"Sometimes." They were one of his favorites. "You can go. I can handle things from here."

She turned back to the stove. "That's all right. I have to get mine."

He glanced at the clock. Seven-thirty. "You haven't eaten?"

"No. I got kind of busy. While you wash up, I'll set the table," she told him, her voice oddly breathless.

Placing his hat on the back of his chair, he went to the kitchen sink. Water gushed out of the faucet, and he stuck his hands underneath.

"You know Octavia doesn't like for you to do that."

Matt glanced over his shoulder to see Shannon setting two plates on the table. "So we won't tell her."

She smiled and brought him a towel. "Do you always get your way?"

His gaze roamed over her face. "Am I going to get my way with you?"

Her eyes rounded. Her sharp intake of breath cut across the small space separating them. She took an unsteady step back.

He had meant the ranch. At least that's what he *thought* he had meant. But watching the tip of her tongue glide across the sensual fullness of her glistening red lower lip, the rise and fall of her full breasts beneath her sleeveless beige blouse, he wasn't sure.

It was suddenly very important that he made sure. "Are you going to sign over the meadow?"

Disappointment. Surely that wasn't disappointment in her brown eyes. "I—I told you I would when I leave."

He studied her closely as she went to the refrigerator, returned to the table with a pitcher of tea and filled their glasses with a hand that trembled. Tonight, instead of her usual long pants, she wore wheat-colored shorts that clearly showed her long, shapely legs. Legs that could easily wrap around a man's waist.

"I just thought you might have a special reason to sign now so you can leave here sooner."

"No. No reason," she answered, her gaze as direct as his.

Her answer shouldn't have mattered. It did.

He shouldn't have asked the question. He had.

There shouldn't be a need to sit down before she noticed his jeans had gotten considerably tighter. There definitely was.

"We better eat before it gets cold," he said, his voice rough with suppressed need.

Shannon took her seat and said grace for them. Without glancing across the table at Matt, she picked up her fork. So much for waiting to share dinner with him. He didn't notice her any more than he usually did. Nor did he notice the wildflowers she had picked for the table. He would be glad to see her leave.

Perhaps that would be for the best.

"Aren't you hungry or are you one of those people who eats while they cook?"

Her hand paused on cutting another floret from the broccoli stalk. Gathering her fraying courage, she finally glanced up. "I guess I'm just tired."

"From doing what?" he asked, cutting into the second pork chop on his plate.

She blinked. "I beg your pardon?"

"All you did was go grocery shopping and cook." He forked the pork chop into his mouth and reached for a biscuit. There had been seven on the plate. Only four remained.

Shannon snatched the plate away from his questing fingers. "Let me have another one before you put more on."

"I have no intention of putting any more on." She stood and reached for his plate. "In fact, the kitchen is closed."

"That's not funny."

"It wasn't meant to be," Shannon said, incensed he thought so little of all her time and effort. Learning how to cook had been as much of a requirement as etiquette in her house. A meal to her practical-minded mother was more than nourishment, it was a necessary business asset.

At a well-appointed table set with sparkling crystal, polished silver and fresh flowers, careers were advanced, deals made, lifelong friendships cemented, tempers and hurt feelings soothed. Apparently, her mother had yet to meet a man like Matt Taggart.

"If you hurry you can get to the grocery store before it closes, then come back and peel onions, chop celery, bake cornbread for your stuffing, make biscuits, wash broccoli. Shall I continue?"

Matt noticed the glint in her eyes and knew he had better be careful how he answered her question if he wanted his dinner back. With one wrong word, she'd have his hide and his supper. Cleve was right, the woman could burn.

Cleve.

"This is how Cleve got into trouble at the grocery store, isn't it?"

The glint in her eyes brightened.

Matt looked from Shannon's rigid stance to his plate. He probably could put together a meal, but he wanted his pork chops. "Octavia expected you to feed me."

"She suggested leftovers."

Matt wondered if he could get to her plate before her, then dismissed the idea. No self-respecting man would fight over food . . . unless he hadn't eaten more than a couple of mouthfuls in the last twenty-four hours.

He scowled. Shannon's fault again. He hadn't been able to eat breakfast because he had been worried about her. Now, she wanted to deprive him of his dinner.

Just like you deprived her of breakfast.

"Is this your way of getting back at me for this morning?"

"No. This is for your chauvinistic attitude toward

women doing housework," Shannon told him. "Your mother would probably brain you with a frying pan if she were here."

Matt flushed. There was no *probably* to it. From his earliest memories, everyone in the Taggart family had shared the household duties. He still remembered hiding the mop when one of the guys had dropped by unexpectedly.

"Then you'd have to administer first aid," Matt said, the corner of his mouth curved upward.

"Oh, you're incorrigible." Plopping the platter and the plate back on the table, she turned to leave.

Matt stood. Gentle fingers closed around her arms and brought her to him before she took one step. "Wait."

"You can make me so angry sometimes."

"You seem to have the same effect on me."

"I—I don't want to fight with you."

"Something tells me the alternative would only create more problems." His thumb stroked the smoothness of her forearm and he felt her shiver.

Breathless. She felt breathless and lightheaded. She also felt the blunt hardness of his body against her and, God help her, she wanted to press closer. Heat zipped through her like lightning, oversensitizing her skin.

Matt wasn't ignoring her now and neither was his body. *If* she wanted him, all she had to do was step closer, lift her lips to his and . . . step off a precipice.

He offered no guarantees, no happily-ever-after. He offered nothing but an overpowering passion that would probably sear her very soul. Although she had no sexual experience to speak of, she didn't doubt he would be a magnificent lover, but, God help her, she wanted more, much more.

Fighting herself, fighting need, she glanced away from compelling black eyes that made her ache. "I forgot the salad."

Callused hands released her before she completed the sentence. "Sit down. I'll get it."

Shannon sat. He had a better chance of finding the salad in the well-stocked refrigerator than she did of walking on her shaking legs.

"Which dressing?"

"T-the vinaigrette. It's the clear bottle with the green top next to the salad." Her voice sounded almost normal.

Matt placed both items on the table, then refilled his plate before taking his seat. "Can I get you anything?"

She was as surprised by the question as she was by the total indifference in his eyes, eyes that had earlier seared her soul. Then, she experienced the loss. Her fault. She hadn't been willing to take a chance.

"No, I'm fine." Since he continued to watch her, she picked up her fork and began to eat. The food had grown cold. It didn't matter. She wasn't tasting it anyway.

The phone rang. She pushed her chair back to answer it. Matt was already up.

"Hello."

He straightened. Black eyes drilled into her. "Who's calling?" he asked, his voice harsh.

Dread tripped down her spine as he continued to stare at her.

He held out the phone. "It's for you."

She didn't like the way Matt was looking at her. "Who is it?"

"Lover boy."

Her brows bunched, then she drew back. "The man from the motel?"

"I forgot, you probably have trouble keeping all of them straight," he said sarcastically. "I'll give you a hint. He says you're engaged."

"James."

"Bingo."

Thirteen

"What?" Shannon cried in disbelief as she ran to the phone and snatched the receiver from Matt.

Heavy black brows arched. "I don't think I've ever seen you move so fast."

She sent Matt a quelling glare, then spoke into the phone, "James?"

"Oh, Shannon, it's so good hearing your voice" came James Harper's cultured voice. Then it took on a cutting edge he usually reserved for the courtroom. "Who answered the phone? I had to tell the man who I was before he'd put you on."

"Never mind that. Why did you tell him we're engaged?" she asked, turning her back on Matt. He could have the decency to leave.

"Now, sweetheart," James said and laughed cajolingly. "Although it's not official, everyone knows it's only a matter of time."

He was patting her on the head again and making her decisions. Only this time she didn't like it. She had told James and her family she wanted this time alone with no interference from either of them. Both had a tendency to try and pressure her into doing what they thought best for her. Because she didn't like arguments, more times than she liked to remember, she had given in to them. No more. "Then everyone knows more than I do."

Worry finally sounded in his voice. "I'm sorry if my

call upset you, but you know how much I love you. You've changed since your grandfather died, become pre-occupied. You've spent more time at work than with me and now you're gone again," he said, accusation creeping into his tone. "If there is a problem, I'm the one you should be with. I want to marry you."

"James, please, I've told you before, I can't think about marriage now."

"Darling, I'm sorry. I didn't mean to distress you any further. I know how devastated you've been and I didn't want you to do anything rash."

"Taking a vacation is hardly rash," she said. "I told you when I left that I needed some time by myself."

"I know, but it isn't like you to be so secretive," James explained. "I want you to come home."

Shannon stiffened at his commanding tone. "I'm staying until the end of my vacation."

"Then I'm coming to you," he stated flatly.

"Melanie told you where I was?" Shannon asked, astonishment in her voice.

"Not yet," James said. "But she's just as worried about you as I am. As is your entire family."

"Put her on the phone."

"We haven't finished talking."

"Please, James. Now is not the time to try and win an argument."

A defeated sigh echoed through the line. "All right, but I want to speak with you before you hang up."

"Shan—" Melanie began.

"I trusted you," Shannon said, cutting off her best friend.

"He was worried," Melanie defended. "I had him turn his back while I dialed. He doesn't know any more than he did five minutes ago."

"We both know that's not true." He knew there was a man with her.

"I told him a married couple ran the lodge where you were staying and the place had only one phone," Melanie placated. "I just thought you needed to hear from him."

And remember he was safer than Matt Taggart.

"Melanie, I know you meant well, but you've only made matters worse for everyone."

"Sorry."

"I am, too."

"You mad?"

"Because you worried about me? No. Annoyed that you, like everyone else thinks I can't handle my own life? A little. But you're my best friend and I love you."

"I won't interfere again."

"Thank you. Now please put James back on." Shannon cast a glance at Matt who had finally moved a few feet away. Arms folded, legs crossed at the ankle, he leaned against the counter watching her like a hawk watching a mousehole.

"Shannon darling, if I have upset you, please forgive me," James coaxed. "We'll talk when you're up to it."

So nice, so forgiving . . . so very wrong for her.

Shannon closed her eyes at the thought of what she had to do. She should have been stronger and never let things get this far. For months she had known what she felt for James wasn't enough. Instead of putting an end to it, she had succumbed to the coercion from both him and her family. She'd had the foolish idea her affection for him would increase with time.

It had taken midnight-black eyes and a voice like subdued thunder to let her know she had deluded both of them.

"It's all right, James," she told him softly. Her forehead rested against the wall by the phone. She couldn't end things between them over the phone. But was it kinder to let him hope or set him free?

Melanie, why couldn't you have had more faith in me?

"Shannon, are you still there?"

"Yes, James, I was just thinking."

"Take your time. I'll be here when you get home," he told her as if sensing her doubts.

But you'll never be the man for me, she wanted to say and knew she couldn't. How do you explain to a man that when he held you you felt no more than a faint warmth, not the white-hot heat of a raging inferno? How do you explain to him that it had taken another man to make you realize the difference.

"Yes, James, we'll talk when I get back."

"I'll be waiting for your call." Relief sounded clearly through the line.

"Just promise me there'll be no more talk about an engagement. Please."

"Whatever you want, Shannon," he assured her.

She heard the swinging door close and glanced around. Matt was gone. "Take care of yourself, James. Please put Melanie back on."

Her friend came back on the line. "Next time I'm minding my own business."

"Take care of James. Good-bye." Gently, Shannon replaced the receiver. As if on cue, Matt reentered the kitchen. If he said one nasty remark, she wasn't going to be responsible.

"Sit down and eat. Afterward I'll take you to your meadow. You look like you could use your sleep aid." When she didn't move, he crossed the room, took her by the elbow and gently urged her to sit. "I'll even do the dishes."

They drove to the meadow in silence.

Every once in a while Matt glanced at his passenger. If she was any stiffer, the next rut they'd hit, she'd break. She had looked so lost in the kitchen that for some inexplicable reason, he had wanted to take her in his arms and offer solace.

He had no idea where that crazy idea had come from, so he decided to do the only other thing he could think of . . . which was almost as crazy as the first. Despite what she and his uncle thought, the meadow didn't have any special powers.

He couldn't see her face clearly in the dark cab, but he didn't think she was crying. The woman shed more water than a leaky faucet! But after she hung up the phone she looked more melancholy than teary. He pulled out a clean handkerchief and handed it to her just in case he was wrong.

"Thank you."

Polite. Just the way her conversation had been with Harper. Matt had heard enough of the one-ended conversation to figure out she wasn't going to marry the guy. Matt didn't know why the thought pleased him so much or why it had angered him just as much when he thought she was.

He pulled to a stop in front of the cabin, pressed a button to roll down the automatic windows, then turned off the lights and cut the engine.

The scent of wildflowers drifted inside the truck. Through the cypress trees moonlight glinted on the surface of the stream two hundred feet away.

Now that he was here, he felt like an idiot. Women sure had a way of messing with a man's mind, especially this particular woman sitting next to him. He couldn't even enjoy his stuffed pork chops for trying to make sure she ate her dinner.

He stilled. Was that a sniff or her shifting on the leather seat? Out of nowhere came the urge again to pull her close.

"How do you do it?"

He frowned and tried to see her face more clearly. "Do what?"

"End a relationship and remain friends?" she asked so quietly he had to lean closer to hear her.

"I'm not sure that you can," Matt answered honestly. "That's why I never mix the two. But the longer you stay in one the more difficult it is to break off."

"I see," she said, not knowing if the sadness in her voice was because of her conversation with James or knowing Matt's involvements with women were brief and sexually motivated. She was very afraid it was the latter. She wasn't as worried about breaking off with James as she was at the frightening possibility of never having a relationship with Matt or, worse, having one and watching him walk away.

"You cool enough with the air-conditioning off?"

"Yes." She clamped her hands in her lap, because she wanted so very much to wrap them around Matt and ask him to hold her. Friendship was better than nothing. Her head lowered.

The impulse was stronger this time to offer her the comfort and strength of his arms. He needed some air. "You want to get out?"

"I haven't gotten used to the total darkness in the country," she admitted softly. "It makes me feel small and rather insignificant. Except for the few stars there's no other light in the sky except the moon."

Propping his arm on the back of the seat to keep himself out of trouble, Matt stretched out his legs. "I like the isolation, the quiet."

"That's because you have never probably known a moment of fear in your life," Shannon said.

"Anyone who says he's never been afraid of something is a liar."

"You don't impress me as a man afraid of anything."

"A man without fear is a fool waiting to get his comeuppance," Matt said with feeling. "There's not a man or woman who has ridden the rodeo circuit or ranched who hasn't been a tiny bit afraid of the animal they drew, afraid they won't make the slack, or worried about the weather, or fluctuating beef prices. I went from one profession to another, where each new day brought new problems."

"And you wouldn't change it for anything."

The certainty in her voice somehow pleased him. "No. There's not another place I'd rather be."

Shannon leaned her head against the seat. "It must be nice knowing where you belong, where you're going."

Something about the wistfulness in her voice pricked at him. His fingers touched something soft and silky. Her hair. Instead of moving away as he planned, he wrapped a curl around his finger. "You don't?"

"I thought I did, but now I'm not so sure." She glanced out the window. "I'm ready to go back if you are."

She'd shut him out. She'd done it politely, but she had done it just the same. Just as she had the jerk who wanted to marry her. Somehow that angered him. He didn't want her to treat him like every other man in her life.

He knew one way to get her attention. Warm fingers settled more firmly in her hair, then turned her head toward his descending one. He felt the warmth of her breath, inhaled the exotic scent that seemed so much a part of her, savored the gentle touch of her lips against his.

He stopped thinking.

His arms gathered her closer, his mouth slanted across hers. Her lips opened without hesitation. He needed no further invitation. His tongue swept inside the dark interior. Forbidden and delicious and hot.

At the first taste of him Shannon forgot everything but the need to get closer. He kissed her relentlessly, taking from her, giving to her until her mind was filled only with incredible sensations that began and ended with Matt. She felt as if she were being enveloped in a thick, sensual haze of passion.

Under his nimble fingers, her blouse eagerly parted. The touch of his hand on her stomach wrenched a low moan of pleasure from her. Her breasts tingled and tightened in anticipation as his searching hand slowly moved upward. Then, he was there, cupping her.

She arched against his hand, her entire body quivered in mindless pleasure. He caught her lower lip between his and suckled. She felt restless, needy, hungry. She needed to touch him the way he was touching her.

Hands that trembled somehow unbuttoned his shirt, then touched almost reverently the hard, hot muscled flesh beneath. His mouth found her again. She whimpered and strained against him.

She was burning him alive and he was enjoying every consuming flame.

His thumb raked across the tight bud of her nipple, then caught her low groan of pleasure. He never knew a woman to be so responsive or her skin to be so soft. He didn't seem to be able to get enough of touching her, of tasting her.

He wanted to taste her everywhere and then start again. The agony was exquisite torture. He had never wanted anything as badly as he wanted to bury himself in Shannon's sleek body.

The last thought rocketed through his brain. With wild desperation he tore his lips from hers and fought for control. Somehow he had forgotten she wasn't for him.

Her breathing as labored as his, her eyes dazed, she stared up at him. Her hands remained on his skin, her soft curves pressed to him. With more power than grace he set her across the seat from him. And prayed she stayed there.

She did, but it wasn't far enough. His senses were too

attuned to her. He still smelled her, still remembered the satiny texture of her skin, still tasted the honeyed sweetness of her lips, still wanted her so much he ached.

Every button she slowly did in the lengthening silence he wanted to undo. All he had to do was . . .

He gripped the steering wheel instead of reaching for Shannon. His head spun, his body was in torment.

Shannon kissed like she did everything else, with power and passion. She put her entire body into it. More than his next ragged breath, he wanted to pull her down on the seat and make love to her until nothing else mattered.

He started the engine, backed up and took off to the ranch. He left the windows down. Maybe the wind whipping across his face would cool him off. As delectable as Shannon's body was, she wasn't worth his ranch.

The truck tires screeched as he came to a halt in front of the ranch house. He stared straight ahead. The passenger door opened, material glided over the leather seat. When he didn't hear the door close, he glanced around. And wished he hadn't.

The porch light behind Shannon threw her into sharp relief. He saw her tousled hair, her kiss-swollen lips, the mismatched button on her blouse. She looked rumpled and needy.

"Somehow I don't think going to the meadow will help either of us sleep tonight." The door closed.

Matt stomped the accelerator and took off for the garage. That was the last time he'd try to be nice. From now on, Shannon was on her own. He didn't care if she flooded the entire state with tears.

Matt was avoiding her.

Sighing, Shannon lifted the curtain in the kitchen and looked out. Lightning streaked across the night sky followed by an ominous rumble of thunder. The weatherman had predicted a rainstorm. And Matt was out there somewhere. She shivered and let the curtain fall.

Today he had assigned her to Octavia and Cleve. This morning over the strained atmosphere of the breakfast table she had tried to talk to him about her duties, but he had brushed her aside saying he had more important things to do than listen to her complain.

The unfairness of his remark hurt. He was the one who said she needed to learn about the ranch. Somehow she didn't think he meant tending the vegetable garden or taking over Cleve's job as cook. She wanted to be out working on the ranch. She had enjoyed being outdoors, enjoyed knowing she was helping Matt in some small way.

But the kiss last night had changed things.

Now there was an awareness between them. Almost like an electric charge. All it would take was a tiny spark to set it off.

Matt was going to make sure that didn't happen.

In principle she agreed with his decision. When he touched her, her brain turned to mush. She wished this awareness didn't keep them from being friends.

She wanted to get to know him better. There was a tenderness beneath Matt's tough exterior just as Wade had said, just as she was slowly discovering.

For all his gruffness and arrogance, he had cared that James's call had upset her. In Matt's own way he had been trying to help her.

Then they had kissed and everything had changed.

A loud clap of thunder shook the house. Startled, Shannon lifted the curtain again, praying Matt wasn't still out there moving the herd as Cleve had told her earlier, praying he was safe in the barn.

In her mind came the memory of a horse spooked by lightning, an unseated rider injured and alone as the rain unmercifully plummeted his body. It had been in a movie, but it was still a real possibility.

Shivering, she strained her eyes to see past the slight drizzle of rain that had begun to fall. He was probably all right. She had seen for herself how well Matt rode. Octavia wasn't worried. The housekeeper had retired to her bed an hour ago. Shannon had gone to her room, but she hadn't been able to stay put. So she had come to the kitchen, the first room Matt always entered when he came home.

A flash of lightning illuminated the yard. Shannon gasped. A cloaked figure in a duster-style rain slicker and Stetson strode toward the house. Head bent against the rain, he came toward her.

Matt.

She wanted to run to the door and berate him for scaring her, hold him to make sure he was safe. She could do neither. It was after nine. He'd know she had waited for him. She started from the room.

The back door opened. Light flooded the kitchen. It was too late. Slowly she faced Matt. Hat in hand, his black rain slicker glistening with water, he looked dangerous. A dark angel.

"What are you doing here in the dark?"

"I'm thirsty." It wasn't exactly a lie, her mouth was dry. Deciding to brave it out, she crossed to the refrigerator. She had taken two steps before she remembered she was wearing pajamas. Her steps faltered. The oversize boxy top and above-the-knee leggings in a rose print covered everything, yet knowing she didn't have on any underwear caused her to wish she had been a coward and gone to her room.

Out of the corner of her eye, she glanced at Matt. He hadn't moved. His stillness unnerved her. He was watching her, his black eyes stripping away her clothes, touching her, wanting her, making her body tingle and burn and want his.

"Y-you're making a puddle."

His head jerked up, then down. Water ran from his duster and pooled on the floor around him. His gaze arched upward. His mouth tightened beneath his mustache. Shrugging off his slicker, he headed for the utility room.

Trembling so badly she could hardly walk, Shannon somehow managed to get a towel and clean up the floor. The door to the utility room reopened. Her skin felt hot, prickly, too tight for her body.

"Get your water and leave. I'll take care of the floor."

Gripping the towel, she stood. This was one time she was glad to take orders from Matt. She needed to leave while she was still thinking clearly. Placing the towel on the far end of the counter, she washed her hands, then got a glass of water.

The glass clinked against her teeth. Hoping Matt hadn't heard the sound, she clutched the shaking glass tighter and lowered it from her lips. Preparing to make her escape, she took a steadying breath and faced Matt. "I . . . er, think I'll take this upstairs."

"Night." The word was low, husky, as if forced through clenched teeth.

"Good night," she said, and began inching her way across the room, her eyes unable to keep from roaming over his powerful body one last time to reassure herself he was all right.

He needed a haircut. There were dark smudges beneath his eyes. His shoulders, encased in a faded green shirt, were as wide as she remembered. The wide silver belt buckle emphasized his trim waist. His hands—

"You're hurt," she cried. Crossing the room, she reached for his bandaged hand.

Matt moved it out of reach. "It's nothing."

Shannon glanced from the blood-specked white handkerchief tied around the palm of his left hand to Matt's tight features. *This* she felt fully confident to handle. "Then you won't mind me taking a look."

Setting the glass down, she retrieved the first-aid kit from beneath the sink. After putting away the groceries and cooking, she knew where everything was located in the kitchen. Without giving him a chance to protest further, she caught him by the arm of the injured hand and led him to the sink.

"I can do this myself."

"I didn't say you couldn't." Her back to him, she pulled his arm under hers and began untying the bandage. She breathed a sign of relief as the bandage easily slid off. "How did it happen?"

"Barbed wire" came the succinct reply.

She glanced at him over her shoulder. "Why weren't you wearing your gloves?"

Black eyes drilled into hers. "Are you gonna fix my hand or ask foolish questions?"

She glared right back. "Is your tetanus shot—"

"Yes," he snapped.

"At least you remembered something important." With that parting shot, she opened the first-aid kit with one hand, held Matt's hand with the other, then turned the water faucet on low. "This cleaning solution might sting a little."

Matt remained silent.

Slanting his hand downward beneath the stream of water, she cleaned the two-inch wound at the base of his palm, then gently probed the area. It wasn't very deep; the sides easily met. But it must have hurt, must still be hurting. The thought of him in pain caused her stomach to knot.

She shut off the water. The pads of her fingertips brushed across his upper palm, the callused ridges of his hand, trying to soothe away the pain. Once, twice.

Matt shifted from one foot to the other. The front of

his thighs brushed against her hips. Awareness shot through her like lightning. The hand that had been so steady moments earlier trembled.

His uninjured hand came to rest on the sink by her waist, effectively trapping her. Her throat dried. Trying to regain her professionalism, she took a deep breath. And felt his muscled hardness from her shoulder blades to the bend of her knees.

Air wobbled out of her lungs.

Fingers that refused to remain steady and cooperate finally dried his injured hand, applied too much antibiotic ointment, and put on the adhesive bandage about as well as a four-year-old could.

"T-that should do it." Not wanting to step back against him, she glanced over her shoulder with what she hoped was a professional smile.

Hypnotic black eyes smoldered. "Not quite." His head slowly lowered, giving her enough time to stop him if she wanted.

His lips brushed against hers. Once. Twice.

With a sound between a moan and a groan, she turned fully toward him. Parting her lips, she welcomed him inside. Her arms circled his neck, her hands clasped his head bringing him closer.

His large hands found their way beneath her top, stroking her warm skin. His thumb grazed across her pebble-hard nipple and she shivered with pleasure.

He smelled of wind and rain and his unique male scent. She was surrounded by him, by sensations she had only imagined until last night. His hand cupped her hips, pressing her closer to his hardness, then lifted . . . and hurt his injured hand.

"Ouch!"

Shannon's eyelids blinked upward. Her body stiffened an instant before she pushed away. She hadn't meant for this to happen.

Matt reached for her.

"N-no. Please." She staggered backward, her palm thrust out in supplication.

"You want this as much as I do."

"I don—" She couldn't finish the lie. She wanted him more than she ever thought it possible to want a man. With the realization came fear. If there was one thing she had learned about Matt, it was his distrust of her and his cavalier ways. She wasn't going to be any man's castoff.

"I'm sorry." She turned and ran from the kitchen.

Matt started after her, then stopped at the swinging doors. His growing need was a danger to his self-control. Needs made a man weak. Another lesson his ex-wife had taught him.

But with Shannon he had difficulty remembering. Shannon tempted him as much as her mixed signals puzzled him. One second she was getting away from him as fast as she could, the next she was insisting on taking care of his hand.

He hadn't meant to brush against her; somehow he just had. He had tried not to be affected by the exotic scent of the woman so tenderly taking care of him, to disregard her soft curves brushing against him, to dismiss the warm brown eyes filled with concern.

He hadn't lasted two minutes.

"I thought I heard you," the housekeeper greeted as she entered the kitchen.

"Hello, Octavia," Matt said, glad she hadn't entered a minute earlier. He walked over to the first-aid kit.

"Hurt yourself?"

"Barbed wire."

Picking up his hand, she inspected the bandage. "You never could get one on straight. You want me to put another one on?"

His hand fisted. "No."

"Sit down and I'll get your plate."

After putting away the first-aid kit and the towel Shannon had used to wipe up the water, Matt took a seat. A steaming bowl of beef vegetable stew was waiting.

Instead of leaving, Octavia took the chair across from him. "Why don't you take Shannon to the dance at the community center tomorrow night so she can meet her neighbors?"

"They aren't her neighbors. Besides, she'd probably be bored stiff." He reached for a piece of cornbread.

"As long as she owns the meadow, they're her neighbors," the housekeeper pointed out. "And I don't think she'd be any more bored than she was today stuck here with me and Cleve."

"Octavia, not tonight."

"Shannon is a beautiful, caring woman. What's the harm in taking her out?"

The harm was, if he came within two feet of her, his brain went South. The harm was, he had been thinking about her instead of paying attention when he had injured his hand.

"You know I don't date women this close to home."

"Make an exception. Any other man would jump at the chance."

"Octavia."

She studied his set features for a long time, then heaved her bulk from the chair. "I'm going. I can see you're tired. Just think about it. Good night."

Matt returned to his meal. If he didn't know better, he'd think Octavia was matchmaking. She should realize by now, he never planned to remarry. There could never be anything between him and his unwanted partner except mind-blowing lust.

A lust that he had to deny or risk losing more than the meadow.

Fourteen

The last thing Matt expected to see as he came over the ridge was Shannon's car parked in front of the rustic cabin in the meadow. He frowned as he pulled his horse to a halt.

He hadn't seen Shannon at breakfast, but since it was Saturday he thought she was either sleeping late or avoiding him. He had secretly hoped it was the latter.

The morning after their first kiss she was in the kitchen acting as if nothing had happened. When she hadn't shown up this morning, he had been strangely pleased. He thought he had finally gotten to her. Now he wasn't sure.

But what was so important to Shannon that would bring her out so early? The only reason he was out was to see how the livestock and the crops had fared following the storm. It hadn't rained hard at the house, but years of experience as a rancher told him that didn't mean it hadn't caused some damage elsewhere on his ranch.

Suddenly the answer to Shannon's presence hit him. Despite everything, she still planned to take the meadow. White-hot anger swept through him. He urged the horse down the incline.

The cabin door stood open. He didn't knock, just walked inside. Immediately he smelled the strong scent of cleaning agents and saw that the cabin had reaped the benefits of them. Shannon stood by the open window.

Wide-eyed, she stared at him, paper towels in one hand, a bottle of spray window cleaner in the other. "W-what are you doing here?"

"I might ask you the same thing."

She faced the only window in the cabin and began rubbing the dingy pane. "I think I should stay here."

"So your claim on the meadow will be stronger?" he clipped out.

Her hand paused, then resumed rubbing the glass. "So last night won't happen again."

Her answer drowned his anger and left him speechless. It had been his experience that women didn't like to admit their vulnerability to a man, yet Shannon had just admitted hers. She was up to something again. "It was just a kiss."

"I—I know, but it has happened twice. There mustn't be a third time."

A scowl swept across his face. She knew damn well it was more than just a kiss. It had left them hot, breathless, hungry. He knew he couldn't trust her. "Don't worry, it won't."

She sprayed the pane again and rubbed. Sweat trickled down his back. Dressed in a sleeveless knit shirt and shorts, Shannon probably was only a little cooler.

"There's no electricity for even a fan." he pointed out.

"I'm sure it will be cooler at night."

"I thought you didn't like the darkness."

"I'll manage."

She was being calm and polite again and Matt wanted to shake her. Then, he noticed something else: she had not stopped spraying and scrubbing that same plate of glass.

He rocked back on his heels and crossed his arms. "Are you running from me or yourself?"

Her shoulders tensed, then she faced him with the spray bottle clutched to her chest. "All right, Matt. We'll have it your way."

She had the lost look again. He pressed his arms tighter to his chest. He was not falling for that again. "I'm waiting."

"You asked questions about my past that I wasn't up to talking about before. Now I'm going to tell you because I hope you'll understand and know why I can't have any more complications in my life."

Her eyes closed briefly, then opened. When she spoke her words thickened. "The—the reason Wade left me the meadow was as I told you. He believed it would heal me."

Brown eyes glittered with unshed tears. "I desperately needed to be healed."

Matt's arms came to his side. His chest hurt. He barely pushed the words past his lips. "You're sick."

"In a way. My grandfather, the man who believed in me when I didn't believe in myself, the man who was never too busy to listen to my dreams, the man who was always there for me, was dying." A tear slipped down her cheek. "There was nothing I could do to help him. After all the times he had helped me, I couldn't help him."

Matt crossed the room and closed his arms around her. He was sure he was hearing the entire truth this time. Somehow he wished he wasn't. "Don't."

"All I could do was hold his hand and tell him it was all right to let go." Tears soaked into his shirt. "He was worried about me more than he was about dying. I couldn't leave him to come to Wade's funeral. I was afraid he wouldn't last until I got back. I wanted every precious second."

His hand swept up and down Shannon's rigid back. "Don't, Shannon. Everything is going to be fine."

She pushed frantically out of his arms. "No, it isn't. That's the problem. I was a damn good ICCU nurse, but the thought of going back to the unit or anywhere with direct patient care is too much of a reminder of losing my grandfather. I know in my head that I did all I could, but in my heart . . . My heart just aches." She drew a deep, steadying breath. "Yet, if I don't return to nursing, I'll let my grandfather down, let myself down, let Wade down."

"Only if you give up."

"What is that supposed to mean?"

"If you don't like how your life is going, change it," Matt told her. "No one is going to do it for you. Feeling sorry for yourself is a waste of time. Believe me, I know."

"Who was she, Matt?"

His face became shuttered. In trying to help Shannon he had revealed too much. "I'm sorry about your grandfather. You obviously loved him very much, so maybe you'll understand where I'm coming from." His gaze piercing, he kicked his Stetson back with his thumb. "I love the land, the ranch, the same way. It's a part of me. It's in my blood. Just like you fought to save your grandfather, I'll fight to save what's mine."

"There's no need for us to be enemies. I told you I plan to sign over the meadow when I leave. You'll just have to trust me,"

"Women can't be trusted."

"Wade didn't believe that."

"Yeah, and look where that got me." Spinning on his heels, he left the cabin and mounted his horse.

Shannon walked to the door and watched him ride off. In a way, Matt was right about one thing. Feeling sorry for herself wasn't going to change her life. She had to do that for herself. That meant taking charge. Deciding to end her relationship with James had been a start. She just didn't know what to do next.

One thing she knew, she wasn't ready to admit defeat and leave. She had accepted Matt's challenge and she was staying to see it through no matter how much of a dangerous temptation he was.

Sighing, she returned to the window. Matt wasn't for her. He excited her, left her breathless with wanting, but she would only be another notch on his bedpost. He might want her body, but he wanted the meadow more. She was certain if she signed it over to him, he'd put her off the ranch before the day was out.

Spraying the window cleaner on another pane, she scrubbed the glass. Her life was in St. Louis. She just wished her heart agreed with her.

Several hours later, Matt sat at the Horseshoe Bar nourishing his anger with a beer. How could Wade have saddled him with a stubborn, irritating woman like Shannon Johnson?

"Hello, handsome. You finally ready to see what you've been missing out on?" a sultry voice cooed.

Matt slowly turned to see Irene Nobles, a Saturday-night regular, in gold spandex and lace. Bosomy and nicely curved, Irene had been known to jump-start more than one man's heart, but not his, and not for want of trying on Irene's part.

"Sorry."

Irene pouted passion-red lips, then ran two-inch gold-lacquered and glittering nails up his muscled thigh. "Give me three minutes."

His hand caught hers before it reached its objective. "I'm not in the mood."

She leaned over, her breast rubbing against his arm, her heavy perfume cloying. "Two minutes."

"I don't think so." He moved her hand away.

"Your loss," she said, and glided across the room to another male customer. This time the man was all smiles. Irene settled in the man's lap instead of the chair.

Matt knew she had probably forgotten about him before she took two steps across the room. She didn't care who paid for the things she wanted, just as long as she got them. Just like his ex-wife.

Although he wanted to think the same of Shannon, it wouldn't fit any longer. Which made matters worse for him. It wasn't money she was looking for, but peace of mind. While she sought hers, she tampered with his.

Finishing off his beer, he left the honky-tonk and headed outside. It was completely dark and the parking lot was beginning to fill up. Getting into his truck, he pulled out of the graveled parking lot onto the main highway and headed back to the ranch.

Shannon and Octavia should be gone by now. He could go home to some quiet.

His housekeeper had been like a broken record once he came back to the house. "Take Shannon to the dance." "Take Shannon to the dance." To escape he had to leave his own house. He'd put in a perfunctory appearance at Vivian Gordon's party, then headed for the door. She might have given up on him, but the other single women had not.

He glanced at the clock in the dashboard. Nine fourteen. The monthly community social should be in as much of a high gear as it was going to get.

Matt knew that the pot-luck gathering with a fifteen-year-old record player wasn't what Shannon was used to. Perhaps her going to the social would be to his advantage. She'd see another reason why living in a ranching community wasn't for her.

Parking the truck in the garage, he entered the house. As usual, Octavia had left the lights on downstairs. She

said seeing the lights gave her the sense of being welcomed home. He hoped that wasn't for at least another
hour and a half. The ranch accounts needed to be updated, and he had a feeling Octavia wasn't through with
him. Once she learned Shannon planned to live in the
cabin at night, he was going to be in for the chastising
of his life.

Opening the door to his study, he was halfway across
the room when he realized he wasn't alone. He spun
around.

A shy smile on her face, Shannon uncurled her sock-
covered feet from beneath her. "I didn't mean to startle
you."

"What are you doing here?"

The smile slipped as she held out a thick black leather-
bound book. "Reading."

"Why aren't you at the dance?"

Slim shoulders shrugged beneath an off-the-shoulder
oversize top. The knit material dropped another inch, bar-
ing smooth brown skin. "I didn't feel up to meeting a
lot of new people. Octavia said she understood."

Matt gritted his teeth. Irene had practically crawled
into his lap and it hadn't bothered him at all. Now he
sees a couple of inches of Shannon's bare shoulder and
his jeans get tight. He was going to get Octavia for this.
"I'll bet."

"I hope you don't mind me borrowing some of your
books," Shannon said hesitantly. "You have quite a collection."

"Most of the books belonged to Wade." Continuing
across the room, he took a seat behind his desk, opened
a drawer and took out a large red-and-gold book. Pen in
hand, he began writing. No woman was going to make
him lose control.

If Melanie could see Matt now she'd know she didn't

have anything to worry about, Shannon thought. She barely kept from sighing aloud.

Deciding if he could act as if she didn't exist, she could do the same thing, she sat back down with her book. However, she couldn't concentrate with him in the room. Standing, she began to roam around the oak-paneled room filled with plaques, trophies, and pictures.

"All these trophies and things belong to you?"

"Yeah."

"Wade said you were a champion calf roper a few years back."

"I was."

"I've never been to a rodeo."

That remark earned her a long, level look.

"It's a shame I won't get to see one while I'm in Texas."

"I can tell you where several are being held."

Shannon gritted a smile. "I'm sure you could."

Matt grunted and went back to his books.

Her fingers trailed over a pair of binoculars, a collection of silver belt buckles, a lariat. She moved to a picture on the wall. Matt sat on a magnificent black stallion holding two toddlers, a boy and a girl. All three were grinning from ear to ear. "What beautiful children."

He glanced up, saw the photograph and smiled. "Kane Jr. and Chandler. My nephew and niece."

Her heart knocked against her chest at the beautiful smile on Matt's face. "You sound as proud as their parents must be."

"I don't think that's possible," he said, a wistful note in his voice.

She moved to the next picture on the wall. Matt stood beside a man as tall and broad-shouldered as he. Both stared directly into the camera as if they barely tolerated the imposition. Both were strikingly handsome. "Who is he?"

"Daniel Falcon."

"Is he a rodeo performer?"

"Hardly. He owns several firms across the country. You probably heard of Falcon Industries. His logo is a falcon, legs outstretched, talons poised to capture its prey."

"Not a very nice picture."

"That's exactly what Daniel intended. If he comes after you, he's coming for blood."

"I'm glad I won't be meeting him."

"Then you better leave before next Monday."

"What?" She whirled to face Matt and noted the strangely pleased expression on his face. Probably the happy thought of her leaving.

Matt reared back in his chair. "Daniel and a film crew he's hired are coming to the ranch to get footage of the African-American cowboy of today. Too much of our heritage has been lost and Daniel intends to set some records straight."

"For instance?"

"Black men and women contributed to the settling of the West as much as anybody. Nearly one-third of all the cowboys in the West were black. The word cowboys comes from ranchers telling the black man to 'go into the brush and get the cow, boy.' Many black cowboys were hired to do the hardest work, busting broncs. The typical trail crew of eight usually included a couple of black cowboys. Many came West after emancipation, hoping they would be judged by their skills and not by their skin color."

"It must have been extremely difficult for them."

"It was, and most people don't even know the true history of the black men and women in the West. Their trials and tribulations might be in the history books, but not their triumphs."

Shannon glanced back at the picture. "It seems I was

wrong about Mr. Falcon. I'm looking forward to meeting him after all."

"When you do, don't forget his logo."

"Is that a warning?"

Matt went back to his book. "Take it any way you want."

"I will." Going to the built-in bookcase, she replaced the book in her hand. "Good night."

"Shannon."

"Yes?" She glanced over her shoulder.

"When do you think the cabin will be ready?"

She looked stricken. "Soon." The door closed softly behind her.

Matt's hands clenched atop his desk. His desire for Shannon was testing his control with every breath he took. Finding her on the couch reminded him too much of the first time he saw her in the meadow, looking both beautiful and innocent.

All the ranch hands certainly liked her. The men watched their language around her and were as polite as choir boys. The bunkhouse no longer looked like a tornado just blew through, and all of the hands had taken to cleaning up and wearing cologne.

She certainly had made an impression on everyone, including him. He didn't understand why. He steered clear of women he couldn't walk away from. Becoming involved with one under his roof was crazy. He had his share of lady friends and past lovers, but to date no woman had ever managed to be both. He and Shannon weren't friends, but neither could they be lovers.

Picking up his pen, he went back to the account books. Maybe if he kept telling himself that enough, he might actually begin to believe it.

* * *

"You look stunning in that navy suit. And how about that white blouse. I love the draped collar!" Octavia said.

Shannon's brown eyes sparkled. "Thank you, and you look good, too. I love that hat."

The housekeeper beamed with pleasure as she turned her head from side to side for Shannon to get a better look at the pale-pink wide-brimmed straw hat with two large, deep pink roses in full bloom on the crown. "Besides my romance books, hats are my weakness."

"I hope it's all right that I'm not wearing a hat to church."

"Sure it is. Lots of the young folk these days go bareheaded," Octavia said as she picked up her gloves, purse, and Bible. "Matt, better hurry or we'll be late."

The smile slid from Shannon's face. "He's going with us?"

"Of course. My grandson has my car again."

Breakfast had been difficult enough, she didn't want to have to sit by a silent Matt for the next couple of hours. "Octavia, why don't we go in my car?"

"Waste of gas to take both cars. Here's Matt now. We better hurry or we'll be late for prayer service." Without waiting for an answer, Octavia went out the back door of the kitchen.

Sensing Matt's eyes on her, Shannon followed. Outside, Olivia waited by the truck with the passenger door open. "I'll sit by the door," Shannon said.

"I have to ride by the window or I'll get sick," the housekeeper told her.

Shannon's steps faltered. This definitely wasn't a good idea.

"Will you two stop dragging your feet?" Octavia ordered.

All of a sudden Shannon realized Matt was as reluctant as she. He didn't want to be near her, either. She had more pride than to let him know how much that hurt. Head high, she continued to the truck. Her courage faltered as she put one foot on the running board and realized how high her skirt would rise and how difficult it would be for her to get inside gracefully.

She turned back to suggest they take her car and looked straight into Matt's piercing black eyes. The fluttering feeling returned to her stomach. Dressed in an almond-colored suit that fit his powerful body flawlessly, he was magnificent. And totally out of reach. She didn't want them to be enemies anymore.

"Matt?"

His sensual mouth compressed into a thin line beneath his mustache. Strong hands circled her waist and lifted her into the truck. As soon as her bottom touched the seat, he stepped back.

"Move over, child."

Afraid to look at Matt again, Shannon did as requested. Octavia settled in beside her. Matt closed the door and went around and got inside.

Matt's muscled warmth touched her from shoulder to knee. She swallowed and tried to pull her skirt down from midthigh. It wouldn't budge. Placing her small box purse in her lap over her sheer navy hose didn't help hide her exposed flesh.

Matt leaned forward to start the engine and brushed the outside of her breast. Shannon froze from trying to inch down her skirt. Her heart rate doubled. Swallowing again, she stared straight ahead.

Something soft touched her hands. A large lilac handkerchief bordered with lace covered her lap.

"I have four teenage granddaughters," Octavia said and grinned.

Shannon smiled and some of the tension drained away. Now, if Octavia had a two-inch steel divider that Shannon could place between herself and Matt, she might stay sane.

* * *

Pastor Billows never had a chance. He paced in front
of the pulpit, shouted in his fine bass voice, called sin-
ners to repent, Christians to rejoice. He had never been
in finer form. He rose to the occasion, but it wasn't
enough.

He was no competition against Shannon.

Matt had never been so annoyed in his life. You'd think
the citizens of Jackson Falls had never seen a woman.
So much rubbernecking was going on, it was a wonder
some of the participants didn't get whiplash.

More children had to be taken outside by a parent than
in the past year. The second a baby whimpered, out it
went. Each time with a different person.

Not even Leola Price and her glare could quiet the
murmurs. Leola liked the audience to pay attention. They
usually did. No one wanted to make the unofficial ma-
triarch of Jackson Falls upset with them. Today she might
as well have been calling hogs. In an effort to gain control, she decided to direct her attention to the person who
was causing the problem. Shannon.

Shannon smiled encouragingly at the singer and nodded as if every word went straight to her soul. Soon
Leola stopped glaring and sang her heart out. Leola finished on a note that shook the wooden beams.

Nobody seemed to notice but Shannon, the pastor and
Octavia, who certainly hadn't helped by forcing Matt and
Shannon to sit together. He hoped he didn't sink to such
low levels when he got older. He and Shannon could sit
hip to hip, flesh to flesh until hell froze over and . . .

"Let us pray."

Matt bowed his head, his eyes going instinctively to
the lilac handkerchief. Since hell hadn't frozen over as
far as he knew, he asked for God's forgiveness and turned

his head slightly and saw three other men looking exactly where he wasn't supposed to be looking.

He plopped his hat in her lap. Shannon glanced at him from beneath her lashes. He flexed his leg.

Leaning over, she whispered to Matt, "Would you like to go outside and stretch your legs?"

There was nothing he'd like better, but he was sure if they left, the entire congregation would follow them outside. "We'll stay."

She looked so disappointed, he smiled. She blinked, then smiled back.

"Brother Taggart, please introduce your guest."

They jumped and their heads jerked up and around. Every adult and some of the children watched them with undisguised interest. Matt wanted to howl. He didn't need to see Octavia's pleased expression to know he and Shannon had been caught grinning at each other like two idiots.

And how in the hel— *heaven* was he supposed to introduce her? People knew Wade helped people, but they also knew how he loved the ranch. Talk was going to run through the community like a brush fire. He didn't want that for either of them.

While he was trying to think of something, Shannon stood. "If you don't mind, Pastor Billows, since I was more a friend of Wade's than Matt's I'd like to introduce myself."

Fifteen

You could hear a pin drop.

Shannon had often heard that expression and, until this moment, had laughed at the fallacy. She wasn't laughing now. She didn't have to see Matt's face to know he probably wanted to pull her down in her seat. She wasn't so sure about this herself.

Octavia gave her an encouraging smile. Shannon's hand clenched the stiff brim of Matt's hat. He'd never stop shouting if she ruined his Sunday Stetson.

Her fingers relaxed and she met the expectant gaze of the pastor. "My name is Shannon Johnson and I was fortunate enough to be assigned as Wade Taggart's nurse while he recovered in St. Louis. He was a fine, caring man. I wanted to come and see the place Wade loved."

She glanced around the congregation. "I've met so many wonderful people since I've been here and now being in church today, I see why Wade loved Jackson Falls. Thank you."

The church exploded in applause as she sat down. The person on her right stuck out her hand, and so did the next person.

"Please stand for the benediction."

Shannon came to her feet still clutching Matt's hat, her purse strap slung over her shoulder. As soon as Pastor Billows said, "Amen" she was surrounded by parishioners.

"Welcome to Jackson Falls."

"Wade and I go way back."

"Nice having you at church."

"Hope you enjoy your stay."

Out of the corner of her eye, she noticed Matt had drawn his own crowd. Three attractive women and two matronly ladies hemmed him in. She couldn't make out what the females were saying, but she had no difficulty hearing Matt repeatedly tell them how tied up he was with the ranch.

"Shannon can tell you how busy I am; she's even riding fence."

Everyone stopped talking. Once again she became the center of attention. She had told Matt she wasn't going to help him discourage women, but she could see his problem since Octavia said he didn't date the local women. Those five weren't taking no for an answer. If he wanted to be painted in a bad light, who was she to say no.

"One morning he was so anxious to get started, I didn't have time to eat breakfast or get my work gloves." Every eye whipped to Matt. Shannon smiled into his scowling face. "But he did put me on light duty after my thumb was a bigger target than the staple."

"He hit you with a hammer?" the woman next to her asked in horror.

"No, I did that myself." Maybe she was laying it on a bit thick. "Matt took one look at my bruised thumb and sent me back to the ranch. He cares for his people very well. Wade was justifiably proud of him."

All around people murmured their agreement. The women resumed gazing adoringly at Matt. He pulled his hat from her hand. His face was smiling, but his eyes promised retribution.

"If you'll excuse us, we have to be going." Catching Shannon's arm, Matt started out of the church. Sneaky.

Nobody seemed to notice that flaw in her character except him.

"Matt, Pastor Billows and Sister Price want to meet Shannon," Octavia called.

Matt clenched his jaw and halted. People clustered around and waited. He cast a sideways glance at Shannon and saw her smiling. Sneaky as they come.

Octavia quickly made the introductions, beaming at Shannon as if she were her own child. "Shannon's the head nurse now in the ICCU unit where Wade was a patient. You can tell just by looking at her what a warm, gentle lady our Shannon is."

There were several loud amens. All from men.

"You only see the goodness in people because you're so nice," Shannon said. "Pastor Billows, I really enjoyed your sermon, and Mrs. Price, you touched my heart."

Pastor Billows stuck his chest way out. His round, dark face glowed with pleasure. "I'm but the instrument of God."

"I give all praise and glory to Him," added Leola Price, glancing around the audience as if to let them know she was taking account as to who agreed and giving them a second chance.

Women took the hint and sent out another chorus of amens and praises for Leola's voice.

Matt had had enough. "Octavia, we need to be going." Thanks to Shannon he still hadn't updated the ranch accounts.

"Any chance of you staying with us permanently, Miss Johnson?" Pastor Billows asked.

Matt wasn't the only one who stared at the pastor. Tall, midforties, widowed, and handsome, he had the respect of the entire congregation. Matt always admired him for his ability to keep so many women in the church happy and willing to work.

Shannon moistened her lips before answering firmly. "No."

"That's a pity. We need someone of your obvious experience in our community. Our only doctor retired last month and referred all the patients to a colleague forty-five miles away. It's tough on our senior citizens getting there."

"I'm sorry, but I'm only here for a short time," Shannon told him.

"How long?" Leola asked. "Maybe you could help out while you're here."

"I don't have the authority to practice nursing in Texas," Shannon explained with more calm than she felt.

"Is taking a blood pressure practicing nursing?" asked a frail woman holding the hand of a equally frail man. "My name is Rose Badget and this is my husband, Henry."

Shannon said how pleased she was to meet them.

"I bought that pressure thing, but I can't hear the sound. Now I have to drive my Henry every week to the doctor because he has glaucoma and they have to watch the medicine he takes for his pressure. The traffic and the drive are a bit much for me, Henry, and our car."

Shannon saw the desperation in the woman's face, felt her need. Dressed in a print cotton dress and small straw hat, she appeared to be in her early seventies. Henry wore a crisp khaki shirt and pants. Her grandfather had been seventy-two when he died.

"Couldn't someone in the church or in your family take his blood pressure for you?" Shannon asked hopefully.

"The doctor has to regulate the medicine sometimes and he says he won't take the responsibility unless it's taken by someone he trusts or a professional person," the woman said. "Our daughter lives in Atlanta."

"I'm sorry." Shannon crossed to the older woman.

"Then that means I would be acting as a RN because I would report directly to your husband's doctor. For that I'd need reciprocity."

"Reci—what's that?"

"Validation of my nursing license to work as a RN in Texas, since I took my nursing exams in Missouri. I'm not even sure how long that takes." She rushed on at the woman's crestfallen expression. "I'd be happy to come over and I'll try to help you learn to take your husband's blood pressure."

The woman looked away, then back at Shannon. "I spent two hours trying already with those double things where the nurse and I both could hear the sounds." She blinked. "We'll make it. Have a nice stay, Miss Johnson."

Helpless to stop them, Shannon watched them leave. Callused fingers curled around her arm. She didn't have to glance up to know it was Matt.

"We're leaving."

This time no one tried to stop them. Once in the truck, Octavia spread her handkerchief in Shannon's lap.

"I'm sorry."

Octavia patted Shannon's knee. "Ain't your fault, child. Nobody's blaming you. We know you'd help if you could."

But she could help . . . if she wasn't afraid of falling apart again.

"You think I'm a coward, don't you?"

"What I think doesn't matter," Matt said and braced his shoulder against the trunk of an oak tree. "Dinner is ready."

"I'm not hungry." Arms clasped around updrawn legs, Shannon laid her cheek against her knee.

She was hurting and he didn't know how to help her. Shannon might be a lot of things he hadn't figured out, but mean wasn't one of them. As soon as they had reached the ranch house, she had gone upstairs.

She had passed him going back downstairs as he was going up. Wearing the same yellow T-shirt and shorts as when they met and carrying her quilt, it wasn't difficult for him to figure out where she was headed.

After changing, he told Octavia to eat without them. Now that he was here, he didn't know what to say. After his divorce, his family telling him to get himself together hadn't helped him a bit. He had to work through his anger.

The land had been his salvation. He wasn't sure if it was Shannon's. He looked around the flower-strewn meadow, saw a jackrabbit scurry for safety, heard a blue jay in the trees.

It was a peaceful place, but sooner or later you had to leave. And when you did, your peace had to come from within. He knew that better than anyone.

"Did you really enjoy Leola's singing?" Matt asked.

"Yes."

He picked up a rock and threw it in the direction of the stream. "Those high notes of hers always remind me of a whooping crane."

She lifted her head. The wind playfully tossed her thick auburn hair. "That's not a very nice thing for you to say."

"I'm not a nice guy."

"Yes, you are. You just don't like anyone to know."

"How did you come up with an idea like that?"

"Wade. You helped. I didn't mean for that lady to think you hit me with a hammer."

"Forget it." She was trying to comfort him again when she was the one in need of consolation. Lowering her chin to her knee, she stared out across the meadow. "You better go back and eat. You know how Octavia hates to rewarm food and there's no one there to eat."

"She knows we might be late." Matt sent another rock toward the stream.

Her lush, plum-colored lips curved into an alluring smile. "I said you were a nice guy."

Another rock went sailing. "Your grandmother give you that quilt?"

"My grandmother died before I was born. My grandfather gave it to me when I spent the night with him for the first time." She looked wistful. "I was four years old. I had the chicken pox and couldn't go on the family vacation to Disneyland."

"He kept you by himself?"

"Yes."

"Brave man."

Shannon looked at him as if unsure if he was serious or joking. "Granddaddy Rhodes was the best. He wouldn't like knowing his only granddaughter turned her back on people in need."

"He'd probably understand better than you think." Matt squatted down beside her. "People who love you are less judgmental than you are of yourself."

Shannon wrinkled her small nose. "You haven't met my parents or brothers. They all think they know what's best for me better than I do."

Matt tossed the one remaining rock in his hand. He wanted to ask if her ex-boyfriend was one of the things her family thought best for her, then discarded the idea. He didn't want to become entangled in Shannon's life any more than necessary. Trying to help her through this bad time was the same as he'd do for any of his other ranch hands who faced a problem.

He pushed to his feet. "Are you going to show them they're wrong or sit here and feel sorry for yourself?"

Amber eyes glinted. "I take back what I said about you being nice."

"You only have to decide one thing: can you live with

yourself knowing you could have helped and didn't? I
don't think you can. You had no control over what happened to your grandfather. You do over this. I'll see you
back at the ranch."

He had gone only a short distance before he heard her
say, "I don't think I could, either."

He turned to see her folding up her quilt. He waited
until she caught up with him.

"Granddaddy Rhodes would have liked you." On tip-
toe, she kissed his cheek. "Thanks." Getting into her car,
she drove off.

It took Matt a full thirty seconds to realize he was
smiling. The smile vanished in the next heartbeat.

She wasn't adding him to her list of admirers. He had
only done what was best for the ranch. She would be
unable to do her job effectively if she was upset all the
time.

Walking to his truck he ignored the voice that whispered, she might have left sooner if she was unhappy.

"Come in," Matt called from behind his desk.

The door slowly opened and Shannon hesitantly stuck
her head inside the room. "I know you're busy, but could
I talk to you for a minute?"

"What is it?"

"Stop frowning, I'm not going to ask for a raise."

"Very funny."

Shannon had thought this was going to be so simple,
but the stern-faced man staring at her wasn't the same
compassionate man who had helped her in the meadow
this afternoon. Matt looked at her now as if he didn't
care if she dropped off the face of the earth.

"Shannon, if you have something to say, please get on
with it. I'm busy."

"I wanted to thank you again for this afternoon. Octavia and I just got back from visiting with Henry and Rose Badget. They're a wonderful couple."

He tossed his pen down. "I've known them most of my life. You interrupted me to tell me that?"

No, I interrupted you because I just wanted to see you smile at me again. Maybe say I knew you could do it, Shannon.

"Octavia took me to meet two other elderly people. I'd forgotten how frightened of the unknown and doctors the elderly can be," she confessed. "We're going to see a Mrs. Snyder tomorrow. She's recovering from a stroke, but she's depressed and her daughter can't get her out of bed."

Heavy brows arched. "You seem to be jumping with both feet into something you were scared witless of a few hours ago."

"I still am, but whenever it gets too much, I think of Granddaddy and thank God someone was there to help him." *Just as I thank God you were there to talk me through a difficult time just as Granddaddy did.*

She stuck her hands into the back pockets of her shorts. "Like you said, I couldn't live with myself if I didn't help."

"What about reciprocity?"

"I talked with the director of nursing where I work in St. Louis and she doesn't see a problem. Once I made a promise I wasn't thinking of leaving, she was a lot of help," she told him, becoming more animated. "She even thinks I'll be able to take Mr. Badget's blood pressure as a lay person, but because of my background, the doctor will probably accept the reading."

He rocked back in his chair. "You seem to have it all worked out except when you're going to have time for all this."

Her smile faltered as she drug her hands out of her pockets. "I'm sure I'll manage."

"That's your little spiel for everything, 'I'll manage.' Now I see why you came in here." He pushed to his feet and rounded the desk. "If you think I'm going to cut back on your duties so you can run around the countryside playing Shannon Nightingale, think again. Tomorrow you ride fence with Griff and you better remember to wear your gloves."

Her chin came up. "I've never shirked my duties. You're the one who assigned me to work around the house."

"Consider yourself unassigned."

"I don't know why I'd thought you'd understand." She left the room, slamming the door.

"What's the matter, child?" Octavia asked as she stormed into the kitchen.

"He can make me so mad."

The older woman chuckled and went back to readying the automatic coffee maker for Matt to use in the morning. "I get the feeling you do the same thing to him. Better to strike sparks than complacency, I always say. At least you know the person knows you're around."

Shannon grunted and picked up the plate of chicken and dressing with a huge wedge of lemon cake on the side. "I guess I'll go take this to Cleve."

"You're gonna spoil that old rascal."

"What about you?" Shannon asked with a smile. "I saw you add more food to this plate when you thought I wasn't looking."

"I'd just throw it out," the housekeeper defended. "Now take that on over and be back before it gets full dark."

"Yes, ma'am." Still smiling, Shannon left the kitchen. Everyone was so nice to her. Why did Matt have to be such an obstinate . . .

Her shoulders sagged. It wasn't Matt's fault that she wanted more from him than he was willing to give—or could give for that matter. She wanted his trust, his laughter, his love.

She stumbled as the full impact of her words struck her. To want Matt's love she'd have to care deeply for him. She'd have to be . . . in love with him.

She wasn't. She wasn't. Each way she tried to escape the truth, no matter how she ran, it was always there waiting for her.

She loved Matt. Wildly. Passionately. Endlessly. And he would never love her in return. Despair as deep as a bottomless pit swept over her. She had found the love her heart always knew was out there and it would only bring her heartache.

Matt didn't trust her and showed no signs of changing his opinion. But then came those rare moments like this afternoon. She could see the tenderness in him, feel him reaching out to her, but then it would disappear behind a shuttered mask of indifference. It was almost as if he were *afraid* to reach out to her.

Which was crazy. Although he had told her otherwise, she didn't think anything on earth could scare Matt. Least of all Shannon Johnson.

Loosening her grip on the plate, she continued to Cleve's house. There was nothing she could do about loving Matt, except hope he never learned her secret. That would be the ultimate humiliation.

Why did she have to fall in love with someone who couldn't love her back?

"Daydreaming again?"

Shannon jerked out of her musing to see Cleve sitting on his porch. She grasped at the chance to get her mind off Matt. "Hi, Cleve. I guess I was."

His booted feet on the step below, he reached for his plate. "If you're bringin' that to me, I better take it 'fore somethin' happens to it."

Giving him the plate, she sat down beside him and handed him a fork. "In case you didn't want to wait."

After removing the plastic wrap, Cleve reached for the utensil. "For that I might put you to muckin' out the stalls again."

"Matt has me riding the fence line with Griff." Bringing up her knees, she circled them with her arms, then held up her face to the gentle evening breeze.

The hand that had been bringing a cake-laden fork to his mouth paused. "You're a good worker."

His boss didn't think so. "For a woman from the city, you mean."

"For anybody." He laid down the fork.

"You don't like my cake?"

"Just thinkin'." Carefully, he replaced the wrapper.

"About me teaching you to read?" She had taken a chance and brought up the subject the day they were weeding the vegetable garden.

She had glanced up to see him with a package of seeds in his hand, his thumb grazing over and over the letters for cabbage. "I could teach you."

His head had lifted, hope glittered in his eyes, then died. Replacing the package on the stick at the head of the row, he began hoeing again.

His not saying a flat out no encouraged her. "If you ever change your mind, the offer remains. It'll just be between the two of us."

Returning to the present, she gently touched his arm. "Cleve?"

Gnarled fingers smoothed the plastic wrap over and over. "I've been thinkin' about it a little, I guess."

She strove to keep her enthusiasm down. "First we start with what you know and go from there."

"I know a few letters, but not any words."

"It's a beginning. Once you learn the alphabet sounds

you're going to learn to sound the words out. All we'll need to start is pencil and paper."

"I already have that stuff and some books, too. I told the saleslady I was buyin' 'em for my grandchildren," he admitted softly.

Her heart went out to him. "You can learn, Cleve, I know you can."

"We won't have time if you're out on the range all day."

"We'll manage," she said, then grimaced as she thought of Matt's reaction to her words and the reason why. She looked at Cleve's wishful expression and brushed aside any doubts. She couldn't turn her back on him. If he had enough courage to ask for help, she could get up an hour earlier each morning.

"I promised Octavia to look in on a couple of people in the afternoons, but I could come around seven each morning."

"The boss would suspect somethin'." Cleve shook his head. "I couldn't stand him knowin' I tried this and failed. I don't know why, but he's always thought highly of me, I kinda like him to keep thinkin' that way. That's why I never let him teach me."

"He offered to teach you?"

Cleve looked offended by her startled reaction. "Course he did. Offered again just the other day. Don't many come finer than the boss."

Matt cared for his people on the ranch, she just wished he cared for her as well. "Then we'll just put things in reverse."

Bushy salt-and-pepper eyebrows lifted. "What are you talkin' 'bout?"

"Instead of me teaching you how to read, you'll be teaching me how to make rope," she told him with growing enthusiasm.

Cleve looked at her as if she had said he'd teach her

to belly dance. "I don't know why I thought you were smart." He pushed to his feet and stomped into the bunk-house.

Shannon was right behind him. He reminded her of Matt so much, sometimes she wanted to shake him. "What's so unbelievable about that? You told me it's a dying art. Doesn't it stand to reason you'd want to pass it on to someone?"

"An easterner?"

Momentarily, she lifted her eyes heavenward. "If I didn't care about you so much, I'd walk out that door after an unfair crack like that. You just said I was a good worker."

"Don't get your feathers all ruffled," Cleve said, putting the plate on the table. "The boss is too smart to believe you'd want to learn how to make rope."

"Matt doesn't pay attention to me except to give orders or ask if I'm ready to leave the Circle T," she said, unaware of how wistful her voice sounded.

"There you go talkin' foolishness again."

Shannon braced her hands on her hips. "As long as I'm there by eight to take orders in the morning he'll never miss me."

Dark-brown eyes sparkled as leathery fingers rubbed a stubbled jaw. "A peach cobbler says he will."

"What do I get?"

"The satisfaction of bestin' me."

She extended her hand. "Done."

"Done."

"Where're you going?"

The whiplash in Matt's voice stopped Shannon in mid-step going down the stairs. "It's not eight yet."

Booted feet pounded on the hall runner. Firm fingers curled around her forearm and turned her to him. "I didn't ask you for the time, I asked you where you were going."

Her explanation fled as she gazed at the heavy matting of chest hair visible through his unbuttoned red shirt. He must have been dressing when he heard her leaving. The curly black hair looked soft and crinkly at the same time. Her hand lifted toward beckoning temptation.

"Shannon."

Her gaze flew up to his face, dark and uncompromising. Guilty, she stuck her hand behind her back. "Out."

A muscle leaped in his jaw. "My patience is wearing thin."

"You have my time from eight in the morning until my job is done. The rest of the time belongs to me or did you forget?"

Charcoal-black eyes searched her face, noted the way her glance kept sliding away. His sensual mouth hardened. "Who is he?"

"You always think the worst of me. I'll tell you one thing, if there was a man, he'd treat me much better than you treat me," she snapped without thinking.

He struck without warning. Both hands lifted her to him so they were eye-to-eye. "Is that a challenge, Shannon?"

The lazy sensuality in his voice curled around her body and held her tighter than his hands. She wanted and couldn't have. "Matt."

He shuddered, then briefly closed his eyes. When they opened, his eyes were as devoid of emotions as his voice. "Did I hurt you?"

"No. You could never do that," she told him softly.

He set her on her feet. "You think the best of people too easily."

"Only when it's deserved."

"Be careful you don't trust the wrong person. See you

at eight." He left her on the stairwell and started for his room.

Shannon bit her lower lip. He wouldn't bother her again if he saw her leaving, but she couldn't stand the thought of him thinking she was sneaking out to meet someone. "Cleve's teaching me how to make rope."

He faced her with an expression on his dark face much like's Cleve when she had suggested the ruse. "Rope?"

"Now you see why I didn't want to tell you? I knew what your reaction would be." It wasn't difficult to look irritated. Cleve would never let her forget this.

"You're getting up before seven to learn how to make rope?"

"It's a dying art form," she unnecessarily reminded him. "I thought I'd make one for a friend back home."

"So you've added something else to do." His scowl returned. "When did you plan to rest?"

"I'll man—"

"Manage," he finished sharply for her. "You get hurt while you're working because you're tired and you'll answer to me, is that clear?"

"I don't pl—"

"Is that clear?"

"Yes."

Spinning on his heels, he went back to his room. The door closed with a crisp thump.

Sighing, Shannon continued down the stairs and out the back door. That's what she got for trying to reassure him, someone else to treat her as if she didn't have two brain cells. Next time he could think what he wanted.

Going up the last step to Cleve's house, she crossed the porch. The door opened before she lifted her hand to knock.

Cleve opened the door, took one look at her mutinous expression and laughed. "I like lots of peaches."

Sixteen

He had acted like a jealous maniac. He had never touched a woman in anger in his life. Not even when he caught his ex-wife in the bar with her body and her lips plastered against her boss's.

The bastard hadn't been so lucky.

"Gritting your teeth is bad for them."

Matt snapped his head up. Shannon sat across the breakfast table from him, her comforting smile firmly in place. He didn't want to be comforted. "They're my teeth."

"The dentist's drill will remind you of that quite nicely."

"Now, children," Octavia chuckled from her chair between them.

Being chastised in his own home was the last straw. His chair scraped against the floor as he rose. "Let's go."

Shannon picked up her hat, gloves, and the canvas tote bag and was at the door before he was. "If we're going, let's go." Then, she was gone.

Octavia's chuckles grew louder. "I prayed for this day."

"For Wade to saddle me with a stubborn woman who doesn't have the sense God gave a chicken?" Matt railed, trying to calm down before he followed Shannon.

"For you to meet a woman you couldn't ignore. A

woman who could stand toe-to-toe with you and make you like it."

Matt scowled. "Lay off the house-cleaning today. You've been inhaling too many fumes." Laughter followed him out the door.

All the hands including Shannon were mounted and waiting for him. He didn't waste time giving orders. They rode off as soon as he finished. Over the noise of the hoofbeats, he heard Shannon's laughter.

He caught himself turning his head trying to catch the captivating sound. His hands tightened on the reins. She had to go before he completely lost it.

"Somethin' wrong with Brazos again?"

Startled, Matt glanced around to see Cleve making his way toward him from the barn. "No. Just thinking."

Cleve cocked a brow. "Miss Shannon does the same thing sometimes."

Matt held on to his temper with both hands. "Shannon and I have nothing in common."

"Try tellin' that to my ears." He tugged one earlobe, then the other. "It's a wonder I ain't deaf."

"Don't you have work to do?"

"We both do," Cleve said, and started back to the barn. "Ain't no shame in likin' a pretty woman," he called over his shoulder.

"Cleve."

"Have a nice day, boss."

Booted heels touched the horse's flank and he took off. Was everyone around him crazy? He did not like Shannon. He might feel a little sorry for her at times, but he certainly didn't like her.

He could, however, understand why her parents thought she needed guidance. She took too much on herself. She had let this comforting business get out of hand. If helping the senior citizens wasn't enough, she had added Cleve to the list.

He had thought she had lied to him at first about learning to make rope, but the more he thought about it, the more he reasoned she might be telling the truth. It was just like her to help Cleve preserve the craft he loved so much.

Matt would have to remind Cleve to teach her with cured leather instead of sisal or hemp. The amount of strength and tension it took to keep the twisted strands together might be too much for Shannon's delicate skin if they used anything else. Matt didn't want to see it marred—

Shannon's skin was of no concern to him!

He gritted his teeth, remembered what Shannon said about the dentist's drill and pulled his horse to a halt. No woman had ever gotten to him the way she did. He didn't know whether he wanted to berate her for being so stubborn or pull her down and bury himself deep inside her.

A trickle of sweat glided down the side of his face. He was worse than a kid. He glanced around, saw the cabin and bit back a groan. He was nowhere near where he had planned to be today.

Beseeching eyes lifted heavenward. "Wade, I never would have thought you'd do this to me." Whirling Brazos, he headed for the south pasture two miles away.

Sometimes she didn't understand Matt. And now was one of those times. Honking her horn, Shannon turned into the road leading to the ranch house. The sound was answered by the truck behind her. In her rearview mirror, she watched the vehicle back up, then go back the way it had come.

Her escort had gotten her safely back on Taggart land. Matt's orders. No one had wanted to admit it at first, until she insisted she didn't need anyone following her home. No one had listened. Matt had said she needed an escort and that was what she was going to get.

The respect his neighbors had for him gave her a warm glow. There was talk of his financial help in putting a roof on the church, sponsoring a summer camp for teens. He wasn't a hardcase. She wanted to see him happy and loved. With all her heart she wished she could be the one to help him discover both. Parking the car, she went inside and knocked on Octavia's door and told her she was home.

"Good night, child."

Shannon smiled. No one had waited up for her since high school. Shoving open the swinging doors, she wasn't surprised to see light spilling from beneath the door of Matt's study. He worked too hard.

She started in that direction, then changed her mind and continued toward the stairs. He didn't like to be interrupted. She'd tell him an escort wasn't necessary in the morning. Absently rubbing her neck, she started up the stairs.

"Kind of late, isn't it?"

The rich timbre of Matt's voice sent a shiver down her spine and compelled her to face him. Her breath caught. Silhouetted in the doorway of his study, his powerful body was a study in masculine beauty. "Time got away from me."

"Was there a problem?"

"No. Things couldn't have gone better. The people I saw gave me as much as I gave them. I'd forgotten how older people have a certain way of looking at things, of expressing themselves that is practical and thought-provoking at the same time."

He stepped closer, his eyes searching hers. "Why do you keep rubbing your neck?"

She snatched her hand away. "Stiff muscles. I wish Melanie was here to give me a massage."

"Isn't she the one you wanted to send a picture to?"

Shannon lifted a delicate brow. She had no doubt Matt remembered Melanie from the night James called as well. "Yes. She's my best friend and the head of the PT department at Memorial." Shannon smiled in remembered pleasure. "She can give you a massage that will make you curl up and purr."

A strange expression crossed his face. He took another step. "I don't know about making you purr, but I can give it a try."

Shannon felt hot all over, her knees weak. "I—I wouldn't want you to go to any trouble. A good soak will do just as well."

"A massage would feel better," he said, his voice as dark and compelling as his eyes.

"W-we couldn't do it properly." She forced the words past her dry throat. His heavy brow quirked as his searing gaze ran the length of her. She gripped the banister for needed equilibrium. "T-there's no hard surface to lay on."

"You can sit in a chair and I can do it from behind."

Images immediately formed in her mind. Matt, barechested with a carelessly wrapped white towel around his lean waist, standing behind her as she sat on a backless chair. The heat and hardness of muscular thighs pressing firmly against her back while callused hands caressed her bare shoulders, then slid with aching slowness to gently close over her breasts.

She plopped on the step, her breathing erratic. Her entire body tingled in hopeless disappointment and growing need.

Instantly, he was there kneeling in front of her. "I told you you couldn't do all this."

"I . . . I . . ." She fumbled for words. She couldn't very well tell him it wasn't her work schedule but the passionate promise in his midnight eyes and velvet voice that caused her weakness. Her mind frantically sought a way out of her predicament.

"I don't want an escort."

"He stays," he told her, thrown not at all off balance by the change in topic.

His warm, minty breath bathed her face. It took all her willpower to stand instead of leaning closer to taste his mouth. "I can take care of myself."

Matt straightened. "If anything happens to you, Octavia would blame herself."

Why had she thought for a moment that he might care a little bit about her? "I've driven at night by myself before."

"The escort stays."

He was too close, her feelings too new. Turning away from the blazing intensity of his eyes, she fled up the stairs and to her room. Loving Matt was the easiest and the most difficult thing she had ever done.

Matt set a time record in removing his boots. Next came his shirt, followed closely by his pants and briefs. Stepping into the shower, he turned the water on full blast.

Shannon was killing him.

What the hell possessed him to offer her a massage? Stupid question. The opportunity to touch her soft skin without feeling guilty had been too much of a temptation. But something within him had also wanted to ease the lines of tension around her mouth.

He shouldn't care about easing her discomforts or seeing her smile. But he did. If he wasn't worried about her he was lusting after her or irritated with her. Somehow she had slipped past his ability to remain indifferent.

Throwing his head back, he let the blast of cold water hit him square in the face. This crazy wanting, this mind-

less need for her had to stop. She was not going to get
to him. He was not going to break his staunchest vow
of keeping his involvements casual. He was not going
to make love to her.

His head lifted. Water pelted the thick, corded muscles
of his arms, shoulders, chest. And it wasn't doing a bit
of good. He wanted Shannon, wished she were with him
now, sleek, wet, willing.

He tried to think of something else . . . the haying,
taking the cattle to auction, Sir Galahad's breeding
schedule. Matt groaned. This wasn't working. The only
thing that would work was the woman down the hall.

Only her.

Matt was avoiding her again. Shannon had hardly seen
him in the past three days. With the torrid dreams she
was having about him, perhaps that was for the best. Her
face heated just thinking about the lusty things he did
to her in those dreams. Sweet little Shannon Johnson
was turning into a wanton!

Shaking her head, she turned off the FM Road onto
the Badgets' driveway. Her car had barely straightened
when Mrs. Badget stepped out of the house, then came
down the flower-lined walk. Shannon frowned. The elderly woman had made a habit of meeting her at the front
door with a smile. Today, she was doing neither.

Unease swept through Shannon. She forced herself not
to slow the car to a crawl and put off whatever waited
for her. As she pulled to a stop and saw the lines of
strain bracketing Mrs. Badget's mouth, Shannon's dread
intensified.

Inside the tiny frame house, Shannon took one look
at Mr. Badget's flushed face, the subtle flaring of his
nostrils as he tried to draw more air into his lungs, and
knew she had been right.

She could not handle this.

"I'm so glad you're here, Shannon," Mrs. Badget said, the relief on her face easily discernible. "Henry hasn't been well since lunch."

"D-don't go worrying the girl," Henry admonished, and tried to rise from where he reclined on the couch.

Without thought, Shannon went to him. The uncertainty in his pain-filled gaze reached out to her. She was all he had. Once she had been the best. Gentle but firm hands kept him from rising. "Why don't you let me judge that? I want you to lie quietly while I take your blood pressure and vital signs."

"I'm fine," he said.

Shannon gave him a reassuring smile as she quickly wrapped the blood pressure cuff around his arm. "Then you shouldn't mind me taking a reading."

Henry nodded and relaxed.

Shannon quickly took the vital signs. They weren't good. "Let's prop you up a little so you can breathe better," she told him and did just that, all the time asking questions that required only a monosyllabic answer. Finished, she turned to Mrs. Badget. "I forgot to ask Octavia to take my things out of the dryer," she said to the elderly woman. "Can I use the phone?"

Mrs. Badget glanced sharply at the phone on the end table by the couch and began to tremble.

Shannon took the frightened woman to the kitchen. There was no time to pull punches. "I think your husband is having a heart attack. He needs immediate medical attention and he needs you to be strong." Reaching for the phone, she called the emergency medical service and Mr. Badget's doctor, all the time keeping an eye on the man through the open door.

As soon as she hung up the phone, Rose Badget clutched Shannon's arm. "I'm scared."

"I know and it's understandable, but you can't let your

husband know." Shannon closed her hand over the woman's frail hand and squeezed. She of all people knew what Mrs. Badget was going through, but this time Shannon was determined to win. "Help is on the way, and for what it's worth, I'm here."

"Thank God. I don't know what I would have done without you," Mrs. Badget said.

After another brief squeeze of Rose's hand, Shannon led her to the living room and urged her to take the seat by the couch. Shannon drew up the piano stool.

"Mr. Badget, I think you need to be seen by Dr. Gaines. The fastest way is by ambulance."

Fear and denial stared back at her. "I-I'm fine. Just indigestion."

"Then I'll feel foolish and you can have a good laugh on me."

"I . . . need to feed . . . the chickens," he told her, and once again tried to rise.

Again firm hands restrained him. "Please, I know this isn't easy, but I want you to lie back and try to relax. Don't talk."

"You listen to her, Henry. Be glad she's here."

His gaze found his wife's. She caught his left hand. Her eyes were suspiciously bright, but no tears fell. "Just be glad she's here."

Henry gave a half-nod, then his eyelids drifted shut. Mrs. Badget's worried gaze flew to Shannon, but Shannon assured her he was fine.

Mrs. Badget watched her husband for a few minutes, then looked at Shannon. "Nursing is clearly more than a job to you."

"Yes," Shannon answered.

"Wish I had some of your training. I thought it was indigestion from the red beans he talked me into cooking for lunch. He didn't start having trouble breathing until a few minutes before you arrived."

"Without training you couldn't be expected to know. Don't blame yourself for what you have no control over." As soon as the words were out of her mouth, Shannon felt them deep in her soul. That was exactly what she had done. Blamed herself for something beyond her control. Matt had been right on target. She could only help to the degree of her ability.

"I'm thankful you decided to come see Jackson Falls," Mrs. Badget said. "I'm glad you're here with us."

"I am, too," Shannon said, and meant it.

Matt walked into the ICCU waiting area, not knowing what to expect when he saw Shannon. Her call to Octavia from the Badgets' house had been brief. As soon as he received the emergency page he had known Shannon was involved. All the way to the hospital he had worried and wondered and prayed as much for Henry as for Shannon.

Her saw her immediately. Standing beside Mrs. Badget and Dr. Gaines, Shannon looked self-assured and competent. She hadn't buckled under pressure. Somehow she had found the strength and courage to face her fears. He didn't know why the knowledge both pleased and bothered him.

He watched Octavia rush over and hug Shannon, and wished he could do the same. She looked up and their eyes met. Shannon might have gained her peace, but she had taken his.

Matt was waiting in the kitchen early the next morning when Shannon walked in. Leaning negligently against the countertop, arms folded across his wide chest, he looked unbearably handsome. And utterly unobtainable.

Last night at the hospital, he had left her alone once she assured him she was fine. Dr. Gaines, Mrs. Badget, and others praising her only made Matt's aloofness more difficult to understand.

Although Henry Badget was resting comfortably and the preliminary tests results were good, her mood had grown somber. Before she knew it, she had been on the pay phone in the waiting area to her parents. Faced with the uncertainty of life, she wanted to see them. She hung up with a promise to be home for the weekend.

Gathering her courage, she walked over to the coffee-pot. "Good morning."

"I told you you didn't have to work today," Matt said, never taking his eyes from her.

"I couldn't sleep." He seemed more remote than ever.

"Probably a combination of last night and the prospect of going home." He picked up his cup of coffee. "Have you made your reservation yet?"

Hurt splintered through her, and her hands were unsteady as she poured her coffee. "I thought I'd make them this afternoon."

"I've got a better idea," Matt said. "If you leave now, you should be able to visit Mr. Badget and still get an earlier flight out to St. Louis."

Knowing her emotions were easily read, she kept her eyes averted. "I don't know if there's a flight then."

"There is. I called. Your parents will be happy to see you."

"Yes, they will." The pain deepened.

"If you get home and decide to stay, just contact Arthur," Matt told her. "I'm sure we can work out something about the meadow and see that your car gets to you."

Her head came up. "I'm coming back. I have a week left of my vacation." Her voice trembled with the effort to remain calm.

Hard black eyes impaled her. "Why? Jackson Falls

isn't what you're used to, and obviously you don't have any more doubts about what you want out of life."

"How do you know that? Before now you haven't said ten words to me in the past twenty-four hours. No, make that the last three days." The incriminating words were out before she could stop them.

He gripped the mug. "Last night you seemed totally in control. Mrs. Badget and everyone there looked to you for support and you gave it without a moment's hesitation."

Some of the anger left her. She didn't think he had noticed. "In caring for Mr. Badget last night and trying to help him and his wife deal with his illness, I finally accepted something you told me in the meadow was true. I had no control over what happened to my grandfather. My training has limits. Last night I realized how important just being there is."

She drew a hand through her hair. "I'll always feel empathy for the people I care for and their families, but it won't tear me up inside. It won't interfere with my effectiveness as a nurse."

"Then you've found what you came for, Shannon. Peace. There's no need to come back."

He didn't want her. She gripped her cup to fight against the crippling misery. "I haven't finished learning how to make rope."

A muscle clenched in his jaw. "I'm sure Cleve will understand if you didn't return."

"I'm coming back."

His face chilled her as much as his voice, "There's nothing for you here." Moments later he was out the door and striding toward the barn.

Her entire body shaking, Shannon watched Matt leave. He couldn't have made it any plainer. He didn't want her, didn't need her in his life. There was nothing for her to return for. Nothing except the anguish of seeing

him every day and knowing he'd never love her as she
loved him.

She hurt and it was her own fault. Melanie had tried
to warn Shannon, but she refused to listen.

Turning away, she went to her room to pack. She had
some pride left. He didn't have to toss her off the ranch.
Snatching up her overnight case, it opened. A can of
hairspray rolled across the room and came to rest below
the window. Stalking over, Shannon picked up the aero-
sol can. Blinking back tears, she looked out the curtained
window toward the barn.

A lone figure stood just inside the door. Although the
person was in the shadows, the fluttery sensation in the
pit of her stomach told her who it was.

Matt. His utter stillness was unnerving. What was he
watching? He seemed to be looking toward . . . Her
breath caught, hope blossomed. Tossing the spray can on
the bed, she rushed downstairs to Matt's study, grabbed
his binoculars and went around the side of the house.

Trembling hands lifted the glasses. She located Matt,
then followed his line of vision. Her room. The tremors
of her hands increased as she panned back to him.

He was gone. Slowly, she lowered the binoculars. His
face had been in the shadows, but the tautness of his
body had been obvious. It was almost as if he were preparing himself to receive an unexpected blow.

And he had been looking at her room.

Going back into the house, she returned the binoculars, went to her room and stared out the window again.
What if the idea forming in her head was wrong?

Leaning her head against the pane, Shannon closed
her eyes. She had barely gotten her life back together.
Why deliberately open herself up to more heartache?
Turning away, she began to pack.

* * *

Inside the barn, Matt's gloved hands clenched into fists. He had been careless. Light glinting off the binoculars had warned him a second too late. She knew he had been watching her window but not the reason why.

If they were both lucky she never would.

"Don't come back, Shannon. Just don't come back."

Seventeen

She wasn't coming back.

Matt glanced at the clock on the kitchen wall. It was five past eight. If she was going to return, she would be here by now. She wouldn't be late for work or to help Cleve.

From somewhere in the house he heard the distant hum of the vacuum cleaner. Octavia was getting an early start on her Monday morning house-cleaning. Everything was back to normal. It was almost as if Shannon had never been at the ranch.

Over the weekend, neither Octavia nor Cleve mentioned Shannon's name. Matt had thought she would have called one of them to let them know she had reached home safely. If she had, they didn't tell him. But why should they? He had assured them there was nothing between him and Shannon.

But the first night she was gone, it had taken a considerable amount of willpower to keep himself from going into her room to see if she had taken all her things. He had wanted her gone. He just hadn't known how . . .

His mind searched for a word other than the one hammering against his skull. Empty.

He did not feel empty! It was the quietness that made him so contemplative this morning. With Shannon around he never had a moment's peace. He settled more firmly in the ladder-back chair with the comforting assurance that he had figured out what was bothering him.

Suddenly the sound of an engine had him jumping up from the table. Instead of her car a blue-and-white motor home the size of a Greyhound bus pulled up. The tightness in his chest was not from disappointment; he probably needed to cut back on the caffeine.

Opening the kitchen door, Matt went to meet Daniel Falcon and his film crew. As expected, Daniel's custom-made red lizard boots were the first to hit the ground. Also as expected, he wore a smile on his honey-bronzed face.

Daniel smiled more than anyone Matt knew and meant it less. But when he stopped smiling it was time for the other person to start praying.

"You're right on time," Matt said, extending his hand. Daniel caught it in a firm grip and both men grinned.

"If not for the horse trails you call roads, I would have been here sooner," Daniel said, kicking back his pearl-gray Stetson.

"What's life without a little challenge?" Matt bantered, and for some odd reason thought of Shannon.

"Why the frown then?" Daniel asked, his black eyes probing.

Matt waved his question aside. Next to his brother Kane, Daniel was one of the most perceptive men Matt ever met. "You want some breakfast or coffee before you and your crew get started?"

One dimple winked in Daniel's cheek. "Now you're talking." He glanced around at the two men approaching. "Matt Taggart, meet Carter Simmons and Price Lofton, my cameraman and historian."

"Where's the woman? I thought you hired a woman to keep a daily record," Matt said after shaking the men's hands.

Daniel's smile slipped to half-wattage. "She found she

didn't like riding around the countryside as much as she thought."

"Meaning she discovered you're slippery even in a motor home," Matt said, laughing.

Carter and Price joined in.

"I don't notice *you* getting any closer to the altar," Daniel said teasingly.

Matt's smile died. "Nor will I ever."

Daniel arched a brow. "Never is a long time, friend."

"For some things, it's not long enough."

"Men, wait over there and I'll be with you in a minute," Daniel told the two men, then to Matt, "I thought you were through with the past."

Matt's face went blank. "I thought I taught you in Albuquerque to stay out of my business."

Crossing his arms over a chest as wide and muscular as Matt's, Daniel's smile was part taunt, part teasing. "A pity Kane had to intervene."

"Saved you from getting another broken nose," Matt said without heat.

"My nose has never been broken." He fingered the slight rise on the bridge of his elegant nose. "Nor have I met the man who can accomplish that feat."

Matt's smile grew slow and menacing. "We'll have to see about that once the filming's over."

Daniel's smile finally disappeared. "It's probably none of my business, but who the hell left you spoiling for a fight?"

His friend's statement was so on target, it caught Matt off guard and without a comeback. He and Daniel had half-heartedly thrown a few punches when they first met, but it was more roughhousing than anything else. Kane had ended it before it began. Matt couldn't even remember why or how it started.

"Your men are waiting," Matt finally said.

"I'd let them wait if I thought it would do any good."

"Come on, I'll introduce you to my housekeeper." Matt started for the house.

Daniel fell into step beside him. "That's why I like you, Matt. You're nearly as stubborn as I am."

They had gone only a few feet before the sound of a car caused both men to turn. A Cadillac convertible came to a screeching halt behind the small truck attached to the motor home.

Shannon jumped out on the driver's side, started for the front door, saw Matt and ran to him. She stopped a short distance away.

"Sorry, I'm late. I know I told you I'd be on time, but Mr. Hodges saw me when I passed and he waved me down. He had hurt his finger fixing his car and he wanted to know if I thought it was broken." She took a breath. "It wasn't, but I splinted it for him. I'm already dressed so as soon as you tell me what to do, I'll be on my horse and gone."

Joy.

Matt felt it in every fiber of his being. She had come back. Dressed in gently worn jeans, a chambray shirt with the collar turned up, new boots, and a hat with a daisy on the brim, Shannon looked more ready to go gardening than mend fences.

Her face danced with so many emotions he couldn't catch them all. Excitement, embarrassment, yearning. A gentle breeze brought to him the subtle scent of her perfume and he couldn't help inhaling deeper. The same breeze teased a lock of her silky hair.

Absently, she brushed it away from her cheek, her gaze still fixed on his. A wariness had entered her brown eyes, but her eyes still clung to him. Shannon had grit, just like Cleve said.

She was also wreaking havoc with his life.

"Aren't you going to introduce us, Matt?"

Matt glanced around at Daniel, but his friend was

looking at Shannon with a smile that made most females over six lose reason and follow him around like lost puppy dogs.

Matt jerked his gaze to Shannon. To his pleased amazement, she wasn't looking at Daniel any different than she had Matt's hands when she first met them.

"Shannon Johnson, Daniel Falcon."

"My pleasure, Shannon," Daniel said, grasping Shannon's hand in his. "I hope it's all right to call you Shannon."

"Hello. Only if I can call you Daniel."

"That will do for starters," Daniel said easily, still holding Shannon's hand.

She blinked, then laughed and pulled her hand free. "You're certainly not shy."

"But I'm very gentle," Daniel's deep voice dipped. "I'll let you pet me if you want."

"If you two are finished acting like teenagers, we have work to do," Matt barked.

One corner of Daniel's sensual mouth lifted. "Aren't we grouchy this morning. I wonder why?"

Matt damned the dentist's drill and gritted his teeth. He hadn't kept his hands off Shannon for Falcon to get her.

Grabbing her arm, he started for the kitchen. "Come on. Octavia will probably be thrilled to see you're back."

"I'm glad somebody will," she muttered.

"Shannon, you missed our lesson this morning."

She glanced over her shoulder and saw Cleve, hands on hips, scowling. Grinning, she ran and hugged him.

He patted her shoulder awkwardly. "That's enough of that."

"You didn't forget me," she said.

"You've only been gone a weekend," Cleve said, eyeing her critically.

"I missed you, too." She turned to the other three

ranch hands behind him and gave them all a hug. "I missed all of you."

The back screen door opened, then banged shut. Octavia joined the happy group as fast as her legs would cover the distance. Her arms went around Shannon's waist. She let out a holler and kept grinning.

Daniel leaned over and whispered to Matt, "Where's your hug?"

If looks could kill, Daniel would have keeled over on the spot. His pitiful attempt to smother his amusement set Matt's teeth on edge. By the time Shannon left he wouldn't have to worry about a dentist's drill because he wouldn't have a tooth in his head.

"You eat anything, child?" Octavia asked.

"No. They didn't serve anything on my flight and I didn't have time to stop," she said.

"Then come on inside," Octavia urged.

Warily, Shannon glanced at Matt. "It's after eight."

The hands, Cleve, and Octavia all turned in unison and glared at Matt. Yep. Toothless as a baby. "Since we're off schedule anyway, you might as well," Matt said and winced at the callousness of his words.

Daniel joined the others in glaring at his friend. "She'd eat if we had to wait all day."

"Shannon works for me, not you," Matt said.

"If you refuse to let her eat, perhaps she'd like a change of employment," Daniel said, his brown eyes narrowed.

"Thank you for your concern, Daniel, but not eating was my fault," Shannon explained. "I overslept, but Matt took it upon himself to bring something out to me."

"I don't need you to defend me," Matt snapped. How did she know he had brought her some food? One glance at a smirking Octavia and he had his answer.

"Matt, if you're gonna get anything done today, you need to let this child and your guests eat breakfast," Octavia said in a placating tone. "It wouldn't hurt to introduce everyone either."

Calling Daniel's crew over, Matt did just that. By the time hands had been shook all around, his temper had cooled considerably. "Cleve and Griff have the horses ready to leave in ten minutes. Does that meet with everyone's approval?"

Daniel was the only one brave enough to say yes.

Grabbing Shannon's arm, Matt went into the kitchen. Octavia, Daniel, and his two men followed. Daniel removed his hat.

Shannon gasped. A cascade of salt-and-pepper hair fell over his shoulders and down his back.

"Lord a mercy," Octavia breathed.

Daniel smiled his killer smile. His men exchanged long-suffering looks as if they'd been through this before.

Matt's jaw tightened. He had forgotten about Daniel's secret weapon.

Although he was only thirty-two it was lightly streaked with silver. His African-American mother had given him just enough curl in his hair to make it interesting. His Creek father had given him the pride to wear it stylishly cut in front and offer apologies to no one. In the summer months when he was traveling and doing African-American western heritage research, he usually let his incredible hair grow long.

"Your hair is beautiful," Shannon said. "You must create quite a stir."

Daniel took a seat beside Shannon. "Depends on who's in the room with me."

Octavia hooted and set a plate in front of Shannon. "A sweet-talking devil if I ever heard one. You watch this one, Shannon child. Slippery as they come."

"Don't worry. I'm on to Daniel."

"So, tell me Shannon. What leads a beautiful woman

like you racing back to work on a ranch?" Daniel asked mildly.

"It's a long story." She glanced sideways at Matt.

Thanking Octavia for the cup of coffee, Daniel leaned his muscular frame closer. "I've got time. Carter. Price. Finish your coffee and check to make sure everything is ready."

The two men were gone in seconds. It was all Matt could do to stop himself from telling Daniel he had seven minutes. Then, he heard Shannon repeating the same story she had to the church congregation. She ended by saying she had a week of vacation left.

"Earlier you said something about being ready to ride out. What exactly do you do on the ranch?" Daniel asked.

Shannon sipped her coffee. "Anything Matt asks me. Mucking stalls, riding fence, clearing brush."

"What a waste," Daniel said meaningfully and shook his mane of salt-and-pepper.

Shannon flushed and lowered her head.

"Daniel, remember your nose. Shannon, I thought you were hungry."

The other man smiled.

Shannon picked up her fork, then dug into her scrambled eggs. "Just like old times."

Matt was in a bad mood.

And it had worsened as the day progressed. Shannon looked at him through the fringes of her lashes as he stood off to the side of Wade's cabin with Daniel. Matt's jaw was so tight you could bounce a racquetball off it.

Sighing, she glanced around the flower-strewn meadow and tried to recapture the peace it once gave her. All she saw was Matt. Hard and unyielding. Her eyes briefly shut in misery.

Maybe she shouldn't have come back. Maybe she had misinterpreted what she saw with the binoculars. If having her here was making him be unhappy, she had to leave.

But how could she walk away from her heart again?

After all the mental acrobatics she had gone through to come back, he seemed more remote than ever. Although her parents and Melanie thought Shannon was crazy when she told them about Matt, she hadn't wanted to give up on him. Not even after she officially broke off with James were they willing to listen. Surprisingly he took the news better than her family or Melanie. He wanted a devoted, obedient wife. Shannon clearly was going to be neither.

Her mother and Melanie's conspiracy was the reason she was late this morning. First her tickets were misplaced, then Melanie called to say she had a flat on her car. Shannon had missed her flight.

She had made another reservation and taken a taxi to the airport. She had come back to try one last time to win Matt's love, only to discover despair greater than she had ever known.

She glanced down and saw an area where some of the flowers were bent and broken, and remembered sitting in the grass, Matt kneeling beside her, pushing her to face her fears and meet life head on. Out of nowhere she recalled her grandfather's telling her, if it wasn't worth fighting for, it wasn't worth having.

Her head came up and around until she saw Matt, one hand propped against an oak tree, his handsome brown face intent, the sleeves of his white shirt rolled back over his forearms, faded blue jeans taut over muscular thighs. The sight of him would always cause her heart to race faster, the air in her lungs to stall, but it was the man beneath who called to her, who she wanted to touch and love.

She had seen handsome men before. She had never met a man who called to her soul as Matt did. He needed love and laughter in his life and she had to be strong enough to risk giving it to him.

Taking a deep breath, she moved toward the men. Daniel's brow lifted questioningly, Matt's face remained implacable. "If you wanted history, Daniel, you couldn't ask for better than the original Taggart home."

"I couldn't agree more. I've decided to come out later this afternoon and film it against the setting sun," Daniel told her. "Then in the next frame get the ranch house. I can't think of anything stronger to show how one family kept and increased their heritage over four generations."

Matt sent Shannon an icy glare. "What belongs to a Taggart should stay that way."

"It will," she said with more calm than she felt.

"Black roots on the Texas plains goes back even further. A Spanish census in 1792 stated that it had two hundred and sixty-three black males and one hundred and eighty-six black females in its populations of sixteen hundred, yet to read some of the history accounts you'd never know it," Daniel said, the intensity clear in his voice. "They won't be able to ignore the films."

"How long do you plan to be here?" Matt asked.

"Think you can put up with me for a couple more days?" Daniel answered with a smile in his voice.

"No problem." Matt tugged his Stetson. "Come on, we better get back to where they're filming the men ride herd."

"I still think Shannon should have been in that shot. Women were and are just as important to our history as men," Daniel told him. "Don't you think so, Shannon?"

"I agree with you about the history, but the Circle T belongs to Matt. It's his call." Shannon stuck her hands in her pockets. "I just work here."

"You've done very little of that today," Matt said tersely.

Her hands whipped out of her pockets. "You're the one who wouldn't let me help repair the barbed-wire fence. And you're the one who said I couldn't help with the herd."

"With good reason," he roared. "You're also the one who banged her thumb. A two-year-old is more coordinated than you are."

"You should know about two-year-olds. You've been acting like one all day," she snapped.

Daniel roared. "She's got you there, man."

"Nobody asked your opinion," Matt snarled.

Palms up, Daniel tried to smother his laughter. "Leave my nose the way it is. I'm the narrator for this project. But if you insist, I'm sure Shannon will nurse me back to health."

"I'm going back to the herd." Matt mounted his horse and rode off.

Shannon shivered. She had only made things worse. "I didn't mean for you to get caught in the middle of our disagreement."

"Don't be. You're making progress with him."

She went still. "I—I don't know what you're talking about."

He studied her a long moment. "Are you going to deny you're in love with that stubborn cowboy who just left here?"

"Oh, no," she groaned in embarrassment. "If . . . if you guessed, then Matt surely knows."

"Your secret is safe with me." His led her to the trunk of a fallen tree and sat down beside her. "Besides, Matt's so busy trying to deny his own feelings he can't see anything else."

Her gaze clung to his. "You think so?"

"Trust me on this. I haven't seen Matt for about six

months, but I've been with him enough to know how he is around women." Daniel shook his head. "I've never seen him possessive before."

Shannon sighed and dropped her head in defeat. "For a while I thought you might know what you were talking about."

Strong fingers lifted her chin. "Matt watches you like a hawk. You're not riding with the herd because he's afraid you might accidentally get hurt, the same for the barbed-wire. It's wicked stuff."

Her smile grew until it reached her eyes. "You think so?"

"Positive. I've made a study of my friends who fell in love so I won't fall into the same trap."

"Love isn't a trap," Shannon said with feeling. "Love doesn't bind, it heals."

"For some people, but not for me." Daniel pulled her to her feet. "We better get going. I like the way my face is arranged."

Brushing off her jeans, she started to where their horses were tied to a scrub oak. "Matt's not the jealous type."

"You'd be surprised at what some people will do when they're pushed far enough." Daniel's face harshened. His eyes were as sharp and as piercing as talons. "Never underestimate your opponent."

"B-but Matt's not my opponent. He's the man I love."

"Anytime someone withholds something from you that you want, they become your opponent."

Shannon was not sure if she liked the hard-sounding man in front of her.

A shift of his mouth, a flash of strong white teeth, and the jovial Daniel reemerged. "Ready to go?"

"Matt was right. You can be ruthless."

"If I wanted you as much as Matt does, I wouldn't

deprive myself. I'd kidnap you like my father did my mother and damn the consequences."

She gasped.

"Just teasing."

Shannon got on her horse, then looked at Daniel. Something about the lingering glint in his eyes made her wonder if he had been telling the truth after all.

Eighteen

Matt's booted feet pounded out a steady but uneven beat as he stalked the length of his study from the heirloom rug in front of the massive stone fireplace to the hardwood floor that stretched to the door. With every step his fury grew. A fury so hot the air seemed to crackle around him and block out everything but the cause, his deplorable lack of control whenever he was around Shannon.

He couldn't deny he had been ridiculously pleased to see her drive up this morning. But his pleasure had quickly turned to unbridled jealousy when Daniel began paying attention to her.

Matt clenched his fists remembering his behavior when the three of them were at Wade's cabin. His crazy feelings for Shannon were hindering his ability to think clearly. He had been ready to punch Daniel out. He still might do it.

Ever since they joined him at the herd, she had been casting those comforting glances of hers at Daniel. Somehow he had managed to get to her. If Falcon touched her, he'd have more than a broken nose to worry about!

Shoulders sagging, he stopped in front of the fireplace and clamped his hand over the mahogany mantel. Shannon was making him crazy. She had to leave and soon,

8 Francis Ray

but the thought of never seeing her again made him just as crazy.

Emotions as confused as he'd ever known, he did the one thing he thought might help. He dialed his brother's number.

Kane never lost control. Well, except for the time Victoria, his wife, almost got hurt at the rodeo arena. Kane had lost it then, but good.

The phone clicked as someone picked up the receiver. Instead of a greeting, Matt heard the beckoning sound of a woman's laughter, the husky command of Kane's voice telling her to hang up.

The polite thing would have been for *him* to hang up. Matt leaned back against the corner of his desk. Come to think of it, there was another time Kane hadn't shown very much restraint. That time also concerned Victoria.

Two months after Kane and Victoria were married, Matt had entered the back door of their house without knocking and caught the two locked in a heavy-duty embrace. Kane's bare broad shoulders blocked his wife's body except for her slender arms clinging to her husband's neck.

When Kane turned to face him, Matt had been sure if he had been any other man seeing Victoria in only Kane's shirt, he would have been seeing the emergency room next.

Victoria's laughter abruptly ended and pulled Matt back into the present.

He grimaced. After three years of marriage and two kids you'd think they'd be used to each other. A picture of Shannon popped into his mind. His body hardened. Maybe a lifetime wasn't enough.

"Kane. Victoria. Cut it out. This could be Mama or Victoria's grandmother," he said into the receiver.

"Matt?" Victoria said breathlessly, "Is that you?"

"Good-bye, Matt," Kane growled.

"Kane, stop that," Victoria ordered. "Matt, is everything all right? It's after ten."

Too late Matt remembered that because of the twins, Kane and Victoria asked family members and friends not to call after nine unless it was important. "Yeah, I just need to talk to Kane."

"This better be important, Matt," Kane grumbled as he came on the line.

Matt smiled. "Hello to you, too, big brother. Catch you at a bad time?"

"It's a good thing I can't get my hands on you now."

"I had that same thought."

"I talked with Mama, Daddy and Addie this morning. Everything all right at the ranch?"

"Yeah."

"You're sick?"

"Nope."

A loud sigh came through the phone. "Did you have a reason for calling?"

"At the time I called I did," Matt said, unable to keep his uncertainty out of his voice.

"You all right?" Kane asked sharply, his irritation gone.

How do you tell a man you've looked up to all your life that a woman has scared the hell out of you? "I guess. I don't know."

"I can have Howard ready the plane and be there in three hours."

"Aren't you in the middle of a major marketing campaign with your company?"

"You're my brother."

Matt's chest felt tight. Those three words had carried him through some hard times. He felt the same.

"Matt?"

"I'm here. How are the twins?"

"Ruling the house as usual. They'd love to see their favorite uncle."

"Their only uncle."

"They couldn't have better."

"Glad you think so." Lights passed his window. Shannon was home. "I gotta go."

"Matt?"

"Yeah."

"I'm here. Whenever you need me."

"I know. Good night. Sorry for the interruption." He dropped the receiver back into the cradle. Talking with his brother only confirmed what Matt already knew: women sure changed a man's life.

He glanced over his shoulder at the account book and grimaced. If he didn't get to it soon, he'd never get caught up.

There was a brief knock on his door before it opened. Daniel, his eyes glowing with excitement, entered with Shannon next to him. "You won't believe what just happened."

Shannon had yet to look at Matt. "Perhaps you'd like to tell me."

"I just got a call from Bracketville. If I can get there by Wednesday afternoon I can meet with two of the descendants of black Seminoles whose ancestors were scouts." Daniel was almost dancing.

"I guess they finally forgave you for being part Creek," Matt said absently, his gaze on Shannon.

Her head came up. "What has that to do with anything?"

Daniel grinned. "Seminoles and Creeks were bitter enemies. One of the reasons the Seminoles resented being on the reservation so strongly was probably their placement next to the Creeks. That and the government's refusal to recognize the black Seminoles as part of their tribe," Daniel explained. "Their resistance in the Florida swamps lasted eight years. The black Seminoles fought bravely and led beside their Indian brothers in the Seminole War."

"I read about the black or Negro Seminoles in a couple of Wade's books on blacks in the West," Shannon said. "Black men and women fled to Florida for freedom, then eventually came to Texas after the government tried to force them on reservations. They came by way of Mexico in the 1850s?"

Matt nodded. "They were intelligent and fearless. Because of their knowledge of the Indians, firearms, and horses, it was natural for some of them to become scouts for the Army. The Commanches were a fierce group in Texas, but the black Seminoles met them head on. Three of the scouts received the Medal of Honor, the highest for combat bravery."

"That's why it's such a shame that many of them have become mainstreamed into society. Much of their culture and their unique language of African-rooted Gullah dialect mixed with Seminole, Spanish, English and French Creole is in danger of being lost forever. I'd like to capture it before that happens," Daniel said with fierce determination.

"You will. We'll be ready to ride out at eight sharp and work straight through to get you finished," Matt told him. "You can pull out Wednesday morning."

"I knew I could count on you. Thanks." Daniel left and closed the door behind him.

Shannon took a step toward the door. "I'll be going. Oh, Daniel was on his way to see you when I pulled up and insisted I come with him to see you. I guess he wanted me to hear his good news, too."

"You two seem to have developed quite a friendship," Matt's tone sounded accusatory instead of casual as he had intended.

"Daniel is a complex man," she answered.

Her answer told him nothing and keeping her there was too dangerous. She looked too tempting and he was too hungry for her. "I'll see you in the morning," he said dismissively.

"Good night."

"Night," Matt muttered, and watched her close the door.

The way he saw it, he had two choices, make love to Shannon and hope once was enough or keep on fighting the urge and let the ranch go to pot because he couldn't think of anything else. Slowly the tension in his body eased. He owed it to four generations of Taggarts to see that it didn't happen.

There was something different about Matt. It wasn't that he wasn't ignoring her or that he and Daniel were acting like Monday had never happened, it was something more subtle. Once he caught her watching him at the breakfast table and the look he gave her all but melted her into a puddle.

Shannon was still trying to figure Matt out when she followed him to the barn for her orders. Remembering the day before, she was sure she'd be left behind to clean the stalls. Seeing Cleve sitting tall in the saddle surprised and pleased her. Matt hadn't forgotten about the proud, older man.

"Mount up, Shannon."

Her lower jaw became unhinged as she turned to Matt, but he was getting on his horse. She glanced at Daniel for a possible explanation and found herself staring into the lens of a camera. Praying her sudden nervousness didn't cause her to mess up, she swung up into the saddle.

Beside her, Cleve nodded his approval.

"I've got the best crew in Texas. Let's show people

what ranch life is all about," Matt said, meeting the eyes of each hand, then Shannon's. In the next moment he was riding off. She felt so proud of him, tears pricked her eyes. He deserved to be loved.

Daniel or his cameraman kept one or both of the cameras going all day. Everyone on the ranch was captured on film. Whether the cameras were stationary or shoulder-held, they were constantly rolling. Even their short lunch break under an oak tree was recorded. After they had eaten, Matt had sent her back to the ranch. She hadn't minded. She had her own agenda for the rest of the day.

Once she learned Octavia didn't need her, Shannon drove into town for some shopping, then headed back to the cabin. Near sundown, she surveyed the room with a pleased smile.

The three-legged chair had been replaced with a new one, which had a peach throw pillow for a cushion. The table remained, but its scarred surface was covered by a peach-colored twin sheet overlaid with one panel of a lace curtain. All the material pooled on the freshly scrubbed floor. On the table next to a bouquet of wildflowers in a clear vase was, according to the hardware salesman, the strongest battery-powered light made.

Her gaze strayed to the bed that now had enough nails to attract a magnet from fifty yards away. But it was sturdy enough to withstand Shannon bouncing up and down on its new six-inch-thick layer of comfort. Draped over the newly screened window was the other panel of her lace curtain. More nails on either side of the window anchored the swagged material.

She had left the stove and apple crate filled with wood once she cautiously checked both to make sure no ver-

min had found a home there. In the corner sat her most
inspirational idea. An ice cooler, filled and waiting.

Everything was ready to carry out her plan:

After one last look, she closed the door and got in her
car. A distant rumble of thunder sounded overhead. She
eyed the sky apprehensively. Rain wasn't going to make
things easy for her.

When she got back to the ranch Matt and Daniel were
sitting at the kitchen table. Afraid Matt might be able to
read her as easily as Daniel, she concentrated on his
friend. "How did everything go?"

"Fantastic. The shooting is a wrap," Daniel said.
"We're all going out to celebrate. Including you."

"I can't. I have to see a couple of patients," Shannon
told him, unable to keep the disappointment out of her
voice.

Daniel stood and draped both arms over her shoulders.
"I won't take no for an answer. Matt and Octavia have
already cleared things for you." Dropping one arm, he
turned her toward Matt. "Tell her she has to come or
our celebration won't be complete."

The tentative smile on her lips died. Matt's face held
a furious expression.

"You seem to have more influence over her than I do."
Matt stood and left the room.

"If I thought you did that on purpose, I'd hate you,"
she told Daniel, her voice and body shaking.

Daniel's eyes narrowed. "Go get dressed. Wear something that will put a smile on Matt's face."

She didn't move. "Don't ruin this for me just because
you don't believe in love."

He drew in a sharp breath. "You learn fast, Shannon.
Never let anyone stand in your way. Matt is a lucky man
to have a woman who will fight for him."

"One day you'll be just as lucky."

His smile was as cold as his eyes. "Luck won't have

anything to do with it. Now, if you'll excuse me. I'll go change. And I promise to stay out of your and Matt's way."

Shannon's facial muscles ached from her forced smile.

A woman's high peal of laughter rang out in the quiet family restaurant. Shannon flinched as if the sound were a lash across her back. Heads turned toward Shannon, not the woman. Shannon felt the pitying gaze of every person at her table. They were all witnesses to her humiliation.

She felt conspicuous in her peach-colored slip dress, auburn curls cascading from the crown of her head. She had wanted to look beautiful, wanted Matt to notice her. Instead, people had only noticed how foolish she was. Hands clenched beneath the table, Shannon blinked her eyes to keep the stinging moisture at bay.

"If I thought it would do any good, I've give him the fight he's asking for," Daniel said tightly. "I'm sorry."

Shannon gave a slight nod to indicate she'd heard the comment. If she opened her mouth she couldn't vouch for her control. Dessert had been served; all she had to do was hold on a little longer.

"Thank you for the party, Mr. Falcon, but I think I'll call it a night." Cleve tossed his napkin on his plate and stood. One by one he was joined by the other men. Their dessert was barely touched.

"Let's go, child," Octavia said.

Shannon didn't move until Daniel's hand grasped her by the elbow and pulled her upright. She swayed. His arm circled her waist. She jerked away.

"Would you rather crumple in front of him and that bitch who's crawling all over him?" Daniel hissed.

Shannon leaned against Daniel. Somehow she made her feet move past Matt and the woman he had gone to sit with a short time after their party was seated. He had remained there for the rest of the evening. That was the cause of her humiliation.

Outside, Daniel led her to her car. "Give me your keys."

"N-no, I—"

"I'll get them." Octavia took Shannon's purse, located the keys and handed them to Daniel. "I'll ride back with Cleve. Don't you worry about a thing."

Opening the passenger door, Daniel helped Shannon inside, then went around and got in. He started the engine and took off. "I'll say this once. I'd take you with me, but I don't think you'd enjoy living with three men. But I have several homes around the country and friends with more property in and out of the country. In the morning tell me where you want to go and one of my jets will get you there. No strings for as long as you like."

Shannon said nothing. It wouldn't matter where she was, the pain would follow her, ripping her apart, killing her. She had gambled and lost.

Once at the ranch house, she went upstairs to her room, grabbed a few things, then came back downstairs. Cleve, Daniel, and Octavia were still in the living room talking softly.

"I can't stay here."

Cleve stepped toward her. "I'll drive you wherever you want to go."

Shannon fought tears. "I . . . I'm going to the cabin."

All three protested.

"Please. I can't be here when he returns." She took a steadying breath and tightened her hold on her blanket roll. "I've worked on it all afternoon."

"Shannon, there's a storm coming," Octavia said.

"I'll be fine." She walked past them; no one tried to stop her. She wasn't surprised to see headlights in her rearview window as she drove to the cabin. Either Cleve or Daniel or perhaps both wanted to make sure she reached the place safely.

She had friends and family who loved her. She was grateful, but at the moment it couldn't stop the pain.

He had shown Shannon he didn't care about her, so why did he feel like someone had kicked him in the gut? Matt's hands clamped and unclamped on the steering wheel as he pulled over the cattle guard to his ranch and stopped.

Because you sent her straight into Daniel's arms.

Matt hadn't missed how closely Daniel held Shannon or how she leaned into him. They could be in Daniel's motor home now. Rage swept through Matt as he pressed on the gas and took the road to the left.

He couldn't see the two of them together. Daniel wasn't the type to trespass on another man's territory. Matt could have set Daniel straight, but pride and uncertainty had kept him quiet.

Now Shannon was in the arms of another man.

And Matt felt like someone was tearing out his insides. He hit a rut without slowing. When the truck stopped bouncing, he noticed a light where there shouldn't have been one. He frowned. Where could the light be coming— The cabin.

His frown deepened as he saw Shannon's car reflected in his headlights. She didn't like the darkness. She hadn't mentioned sleeping in the cabin since Sunday before last. Why would she suddenly decide to come up here at night?

Only one answer came to him. The same reason his wife had gone to motels. Rage swept through him. Matt stopped in front of the cabin and slammed out of the truck.

The pounding of the door mixed with the rumble of thunder. "Daniel, you have five seconds to get out here or I'm coming inside."

"Go away" came the shaky sound of Shannon's voice.

"I'm not leaving until I see Daniel."

"Daniel isn't here."

"Then you won't mind opening the door."

"Go back to that woman in the restaurant and leave me alone," Shannon told him, her voice oddly muffled.

"I'm not going to ask you again."

The door jerked open. Shannon, her quilt wrapped around her shoulders, stood in the doorway, tears glistening in her eyes. "All right, come in and look, then get out."

Matt's gaze never left Shannon's. "I thought you were through crying."

Shannon looked away. "Leave."

"Not until you tell me why you're crying." Automatically he dug his handkerchief out of his back pocket and handed it to her.

She flinched from the white cotton square as if it were a snake. "I want nothing else from you."

The words sliced him to his very soul. "Shannon, talk to me. Is . . . is it Daniel? Are you crying because of him? I saw you two leaving the restaurant?"

Fire flashed into her eyes. "So naturally you assumed we'd run to the nearest bed."

"Shan—"

"Don't touch me," she shouted, jerking away from him. Tears streamed down her cheeks. "Not after you let that woman touch you. Did you enjoy humiliating me?"

"Shan—"

"Did you?" she interrupted sharply. "If you had really wanted her, you wouldn't have stayed in the restaurant. I finally figured that out. You stayed to punish me because you thought I liked Daniel." She shook her head.

"Didn't you realize you could hurt me only if I cared about you?"

Stunned, Matt tried to understand what Shannon was saying.

"Somehow, someway, I'll get over it, though. That's a promise. I'm leaving in the morning and I never want to see you again." She shoved the door closed.

Nineteen

The flat of Matt's hand kept the door from closing. "You've had your say, it's time for me to have mine."

"What could you possibly have to say that I'd want to hear?" she cried, her eyes blazing again.

"I don't want you to leave."

Shannon went still.

Matt closed the door. "I didn't mean to hurt you. I didn't even know I could. I was trying to protect myself, not hurt you."

"Protect yourself from what?"

"From you, what else," Matt shouted and yanked off his hat. "You started to disrupt my life the moment I found you asleep in the meadow looking so damned innocent and beautiful."

"You really think I'm beautiful?"

He meant to glare at her idiotic question, but she looked so unsure of herself it was all he could do not to drag her into his arms. "I can't think of anything more beautiful."

"Matt," she whispered.

Unable to resist he took her into his arms. His lips found hers, and her mouth opened, welcoming him. Her arms slid around his neck. The quilt fell to the floor.

Faintly, he heard the patter of rain against the asphalt roof, felt the rain-cooled air coming through the open window. His arms tightened as he drew her closer, his lips moving to the curve of her cheek, her slender neck. He couldn't seem to get enough of her, he wanted to fulfill his fantasy and taste her everywhere. Before the night was over, he promised himself he would.

Shannon couldn't get close enough. He had come to her. He really cared— She sniffed and almost choked at the cloying perfume. She stiffened. He had come straight from that woman!

"Let go of me!"

"What?" The haze cleared and he stared down into Shannon's angry face. "What's the matter?"

"You lied to me." She pushed out of his arms.

"I told you, I don't lie." Arms folded, she looked sultry and beyond beautiful in her long white nightgown. He wondered if she knew the diaphanous material revealed the curves and shadows of her body.

"What you care for is the meadow," she finally said.

"I wouldn't sleep with you to get the meadow."

She snatched her arms to her side. "Don't flatter yourself. I'm not as easy as the woman you obviously just left. Her perfume is all over you. Go back to her."

"I didn't go to bed with her."

Shannon's chin lifted. "Who you sleep with is no concern of mine."

"Who *you* sleep with is damn sure my concern. If the scent on the shirt is bothering you, I'll get rid of it."

Pulling the shirt out of his pants, he unsnapped the fasteners in front, stalked to the door and tossed the shirt into the rain. When he turned, Shannon was watching him with wide, uncertain eyes.

Her gaze roamed across his chest, then lower where hair thickened and disappeared into his jeans. Lower still to his obvious arousal. She snapped her head up. She swallowed. Any other man she would have shown the door. Matt was too sensually masculine, too handsome . . . and she loved him too much. She shook her head in silent defeat.

"You're right about one thing, if I really wanted Irene I would have left. I used her as an excuse to get away from the table. For the first time in my life I was jealous of another man. I wanted to punch Daniel out and take you to the nearest bed."

Her sharp intake of breath cut across the room.

"You scared me as much as you drew me to you. My ex-wife soured me on women. I was foolish enough to believe in everlasting love and fidelity. She taught me differently with any man who could buy her more than I could."

"Matt, don't."

The words had been held in too long to be contained. "I was so blinded by lust, I would have done anything to make her happy. Working two jobs and riding the rodeo circuit on the weekends was worth it as long as she was happy." His face and tone harshened. "I bragged to anyone and everyone what a wonderful, loving wife I had. Then I caught her with her boss at a bar next door to a motel I learned she frequented."

Shannon went to him, her arms going around his waist, hugging him tightly. His hand brushed a lingering tear from her cheek. "She was a stupid, vain, petty woman."

"And she fooled me completely."

Hearing the contempt and bitterness in his voice she leaned back and looked into his set features. His ex-wife had done more than make him mistrust women, she had made him doubt himself. "Her mistake, not yours. You don't expect lies and deceit when you give love. She tried to ruin your life. Don't let her succeed. I'd never use you."

"Not intentionally."

She frowned at his phrasing. "I wouldn't hurt you at all."

"I don't want to talk about it." His head dipped, his lips finding the sensitive hollow in the curve of her neck.

Shannon shivered. "Matt, we need to talk."

He nibbled the lobe of her ear. "Later."

"No, now." Using the last of her strength she pushed him away. Ebony eyes blazed down at her. "I need for you to believe me."

"Shannon," he said tightly.

"I need to hear you say it."

"You won't hurt me," he said, his lips taking hers.

Shannon's thoughts stumbled and fell. Matt's arms went around her, she felt the softness of the bed against her back, the hardness of Matt above her, pressing her down.

Before she had time to be nervous, their clothes were gone and he was kissing her as if he'd never get enough of her. His mouth left hers and she whimpered at the loss. Then, his avid lips closed around her nipple and sucked. Shannon arched off the bed, a low moan coming from the back of her throat.

All her senses were alive to the touch, the lingering taste of him on her lips. Sweat beaded on her brow. There was something she had to tell him.

"Matt, I . . . I . . ."

"Shh. I want you to want me as much as I want you."

"If . . . if you did, you wouldn't torture me this way."

He laughed, a deep, husky sound that teased her heated flesh. He feasted on her lips again. When she thought she could endure the aching hungriness no longer, his mouth came back to hers and at the same time his hips thrust once, sharply.

The ache became pain. Her body tautened, her fingers flexed, then closed. Nails bit into his muscled shoulders.

His body stiffened. He stared down at her with a mixture of wonder, amazement, and joy. "Why?"

Shannon's hands trembled as she touched his lips, the

curve of his jaw. "Because I was waiting for you." The same wonder, amazement and joy were echoed in her words.

He tenderly smoothed the hair from her sweat-dampened face with a hand that trembled. "I waited just as long."

Before she had time to decipher his words, he moved again, pulling away from her quivering warmth only to return, each slow thrust longer and deeper. Again and again he measured the velvet length of her, driving her to sweet madness, driving her closer to something she had never experienced before.

Her legs locked around his hips. Soon she felt her entire body tense, gathering like a giant storm cloud. When her release came it rocked her. A scream tore from her throat. Moments later Matt found his own release.

Shannon slowly surfaced from her haze. She opened her eyes to see Matt's intent gaze on her. She shyly lowered her gaze.

"You all right?"

She nodded.

"You mind looking at me?"

Her eyelashes lifted. He was frowning. Her heart twisted. "I disappointed you."

"If you had disappointed me any more, I'd have had a coronary," he replied, a slow smile spreading across his face.

She threw her arms around his neck. He let her pull him down on top of her, their laughter filling the small room. She shoved him away again, her eyes shining.

"What's the matter?"

"You never laughed with me before," she confessed. "I can't believe it. I wanted your smile and your laughter, now I have them."

His brow quirked as if to say that wasn't all she had.

Shannon ducked her head. "W-would you like something to drink?"

"Not if it means I have to let go of you to get it."

"I'll get it," she offered.

His thumb brushed across her lower lip. "You'd still be out of my arms."

"I didn't think of that."

"Wonder what was on your mind?"

Her hips moved against his burgeoning arousal. "Same thing that's on yours."

He blinked, then laughed out loud. "You're right, but that's about as far as it's going to go. My mind. I don't have a way of protecting you again."

Puzzlement turned to a smile. Once again, she was pushing on his chest. Matt moved off her. She picked her purse off the floor, rummaged inside, then without looking at Matt, handed him something.

Matt glanced down at the two small foil-wrapped packets in the palm of her hand and picked them up. Shannon plopped down on the bed, dragging the comforter with her, her gaze fixed on the flower arrangement.

His gaze followed. Shannon had turned the dingy cabin into a cozy room. His hand fisted. "You planned to move out of the house."

"I planned to kidnap you," she said quietly.

"What?" Thumb and forefinger turned her face to his. "Repeat that."

"I figured if I could get you alone, you might forget you didn't quite trust me."

The foil crackled. "And these?"

"You never know what might happen."

"Shannon?"

"Yes?"

"How many times can this happen?"

Grinning, she reached under the bed for a paper sack,

then emptied the contents on the bed. Five boxes of con-
doms tumbled out.

Matt laughed and drew her down on the bed. "That'll
do . . . for a start."

"No."

"Come on, Shannon, it won't be so bad."

"How do you know? Have you ever done something
like this before?"

"Of course not, but—"

"I can't."

Sighing deeply, Matt held Shannon in his lap, her head
beneath his chin. She was the most stubborn woman he
had ever met . . . and he cared for her more than he ever
thought possible. "I'm not leaving you here alone."

"You could stay with me."

"If I stayed, we'd be in bed and I'd be loving you most
of the night."

Warm brown eyes stared up into his face. "Would that
be so bad?"

Somehow he resisted the urge to kiss her. "Honey,
I've been at you for most of the night. You need a warm
soak and a soft bed. If we stay here, we'll be back in
bed with me inside you in no time."

She wound her arms around his neck and kissed it.
"I'm not complaining."

"Shannon, stop that." His tone brooked no nonsense.
"You have your gown back on and we're having this talk
in this chair instead of bed, because my control is being
held by a thin thread as it is. I'm taking you back to the
ranch house."

"I couldn't face Octavia." Snatching her arms down,
Shannon stood. "She'd know, and so would everyone
else."

Standing, Matt pulled her into his arms. "No, they wouldn't."

"They'd have to be blind not to see when I look at you my legs get weak and I go limp all over."

"Fortunately you have the opposite effect on me."

"Matt, be serious."

He kissed the top of her head. She fit perfectly against him. He felt protective and possessive. His woman. Only his.

"Once we get to the ranch house you'll go straight to your room. In the morning I'll tell everyone I went to your room to apologize for last night and discovered you weren't feeling well. In light of how I acted, I insisted you stay in bed the rest of the day."

"I can rest here."

"And everyone will be worried. Octavia and Cleve are probably tossing in their beds worrying about you," he reasoned. "If they see your car in the morning that will put their mind at ease. Think of them."

She bit her lower lip. "They were worried and so was Daniel."

Matt hadn't wanted to include Daniel. Matt took her dress from a nail hook and handed it to her. "Hurry up. I'll tidy up the place."

She gathered the light rayon dress to her chest, but made no move to take off her nightgown and put it on. "I couldn't stand it if they looked at me any differently."

The uncertainty in her face tore at his heart. "That won't happen."

Still clutching the dress, Shannon walked to the bed and slipped off one shoulder of her nightgown.

Temptation was a woman called Shannon.

Clutching Matt's hand, Shannon followed him through the front door of the ranch house and up the stairs. With every step she expected Octavia to appear and ask where they had been. Or more to the point, what they had been doing.

To make matters worse, she had been so worried and distracted, she didn't realize she hadn't put back on her panties and strapless bra until they were outside the cabin and the rain-scented air touched her skin. She had been nervous all the way to the ranch house, and her nervousness increased with each beat of her heart until they were in front of her room and Matt opened her door.

"See. No problems." He handed over her quilt. "Rest and sleep late. That's an order."

Shannon watched Matt turn away without so much as a kiss on the cheek. She needed his kiss, his touch, to reassure her things would work out for them.

Halfway down the hall, he glanced over his shoulder. In several long strides he was back by her side. "Stop looking at me that way."

She dropped her gaze and heard him swear. She flinched at the harsh sound.

"If I kiss you, we're going to be in your room and in your bed and I won't care if the entire county comes banging on your door. Do you understand?"

She did. She felt the same way when he touched her, out of control and loving every second of it. "Yes."

"I can see I'll have to do this myself. Come on."

Shannon followed him into her bathroom. Hunkering down, he turned on the faucet over the tub, then dumped in a generous portion of bath salts. Foaming bubbles immediately formed, but Shannon was more interested in the play of muscles on Matt's shoulders and the loving way his jeans cupped his hips.

Matt dipped his hand in the water, then held the fading bubbles to his nose. "My tub is bigger. We'll have to use it sometime."

The picture of them naked in the tub weakened Shannon's legs and sent desire racing through her. Her hand gripped the corner of the built-in wash basin to keep upright.

Swiping his damp hand on his jeans, he came to his feet. "Do I need to make sure you get in?"

"No," she choked out. "Thank you."

"Good night." He brushed past her.

The bedroom door closed. Shannon released her grip on the quilt, slipped off her dress, and stepped into the scented water. She'd never understand Matt's mood changes. He went so quickly from caring and gentle to gruff and distant.

Some time later, Shannon climbed out of the tub and dried off. Putting her clothes away, she slipped into a white satin nightshirt. Although she was tired, she didn't want to go to bed. Walking over to the window, she stared out. Except for the single light in her room, darkness surrounded her.

She had never felt so alone and lonely in her life, not even when her grandfather died. Tears stung her eyes, but she told herself she wouldn't cry. Matt did care for her. Letting her rest made perfect sense; she just wished leaving her hadn't appeared so easy for him. Eyes closed, she fought the tears and loneliness.

The creak of her door opening snapped them open. *Please don't let it be Octavia.* She couldn't stand— "Matt."

His gaze captured hers and they simply stared at each other. Wearing only black pajama bottoms, his hair damp from the shower, he looked as uncertain as she felt. That small hint of vulnerability touched her as nothing else could.

The tears she had been trying to contain slipped from her eyes and rolled down her cheek. Closing the door, he was across the room in seconds, holding her securely against his bare chest.

"Shh. Don't cry." His broad hand swept up and down her back. "I don't have a handkerchief, so stop that."

Nodding, Shannon inhaled his clean scent and clung to him. No matter how he pretended otherwise, he was as unsure as she.

"Knowing how new you are to this, I thought you might feel abandoned." He pushed her gently away. "I'm going to stay with you, but that's all. Tomorrow you're going to stay in bed and rest."

She nodded again. He looked so stern and held her so gently.

He led her over to the bed and pulled the covers back. "Get in."

He didn't have to tell her twice. The light on the nightstand went off, throwing the room into complete darkness. The mattress dipped, his arm loosely circled her waist. Taking his hand in hers, Shannon scooted backward until the solid warmth of his body stopped her.

"Shannon, cut that out."

She settled against him with a contented sigh. "Good night, Matt."

Early the next morning, Matt carefully withdrew his arm and his body from Shannon's sleeping warmth and slipped from her bed. He hadn't slept a solid thirty minutes the entire night. Every time he moved, she moved with him, wiggling her hips against him until he was as hard as a rock. The only thing that kept him from burying himself deep inside her was the knowledge that she was asleep and didn't know how she affected him.

And she wasn't going to know.

Without looking back, Matt quietly let himself out and went to his room to dress. Shannon made him feel too much. He'd known from seeing her face when he left the bathroom, she felt deserted. He'd lain in bed staring at the ceiling for as long as he could.

Except for his ex-wife he'd never spent the entire night with a woman, preferring to wake up by himself. He'd gone to Shannon because of a desire to comfort her that was too strong to deny.

Shoving open the swinging door to the kitchen, he went straight to the automatic coffeepot. He grimaced. No coffee. Looking through the cabinets didn't yield any, either.

Matt had a hunch it was more than an oversight on Octavia's part. After last night, he'd be lucky if she fixed anything for the next month. That might work to Shannon's advantage. As long as Octavia was upset with him, she'd have less time to notice Shannon. He didn't want her upset. He scowled at the protective, instinctive thought and opened the back door, then abruptly pulled it closed.

Going to the window, he watched Shannon pause near the back of Daniel's motor home. Equal parts of jealousy and annoyance swept through him. She was supposed to be resting, not going anywhere near Daniel. Matt didn't know he had held his breath until she passed the hood and kept going. Air gushed over his lips as he watched her.

The saucy spring in her walk was gone. Instead, her movements were more deliberate. He remembered the reason, the open generosity of her body. She had touched him as no other woman ever had and her stubbornness set his teeth on edge.

Seeing Shannon disappear behind the barn, Matt headed out the door. She was going to rest if he had to tie her in bed. His gaze on the spot where Shannon had disappeared, he didn't hear Daniel until the other man spoke.

"You look like you're in a big hurry."

Matt never slackened his pace. "I am."

"When you catch up with Shannon don't make her cry again," Daniel told him, a slight edge to his voice.

Hands fisted, Matt spun to face Daniel, who was leaning against the front of the motor home. "Stay out of something that's none of your concern," he ordered.

"I was worried about her last night, so I drove up to the cabin and saw your truck. You two didn't come back until hours later."

Matt went still. "Mention one word of this to Shannon and I'll tear you apart."

"Do you really think I'd do that?"

"No," Matt clipped out.

Daniel studied his manicured nail, then glanced up. "So when's the wedding?"

"I'm never getting married again."

"Does Shannon know that?" he asked mildly.

"Daniel, you don't want to push me this morning."

"I saw her face last night when you were with that other woman. Shannon doesn't understand how the game is played. She's too honest to use subterfuge, too good to hurt someone intentionally." Daniel laid his hand on Matt's tense shoulder. "This could blow up in your face."

"I know what I'm doing."

"I really hope you do. For some men there's only one woman." His expression hard, Daniel walked into the motor home.

Matt shrugged off Daniel's warning and started after Shannon. He had made no promises and Shannon hadn't asked for any. It was easy to confuse love with lust. He knew.

He took the steps two at a time at the bunkhouse, then knocked on the door. "Cleve, it's Matt. I'm looking for Shannon."

"Just a second," Shannon called, but it was more like sixty before she answered the door. "Good morning, Matt."

Her gaze was centered on his chest. Cleve remained at the table, a cup of coffee in his hands. Matt glanced down at the top of Shannon's head. "I thought we agreed you were going to rest."

"I'm resting sitting down."

She thought of others before she thought of the consequences to herself. But she had given him her word. "I won't argue semantics with you, Shannon. Can I trust you to keep your word or not?"

Her head lifted. "After I leave here I was going back to my room."

"Yes or no?"

Hurt flashed into her eyes before she glanced over her shoulder. "I'm not feeling as well as I thought, Cleve. Do you mind if we put the lesson off?"

"Don't worry about me, Miss Shannon. You go on back to the house."

Stepping around Matt, she went down the steps. His gaze followed. He noticed everything about her, particularly the slight droop of her shoulders. He had meant to push her into going to bed, not hurt her.

"Pretty hard on her, weren't you?"

Matt sighed. Another of Shannon's champions. He had had enough, but when he saw the censure in the eyes of the man he respected and loved, all Matt said was, "She takes too much on herself sometimes."

"That's the kind of woman she is."

"Today she rests."

"Glad to hear your concern. I took a drive out to the cabin last night to check on her."

Knowing what was coming, Matt groaned. At least Octavia wasn't wit— "Were you alone?"

"Yep. Good thing I was, too." Cleve's eyes were as hard as jagged glass. "A man has certain responsibilities. Don't you go forgettin'."

Matt's ears and face grew warm. With unnecessary haste he went back down the steps. And Shannon had worried about them seeing *her* face.

Twenty

Shannon heard Matt's footsteps behind her and paused in front of the kitchen door. She hadn't meant to break her promise, she had only wanted to help Cleve. Somehow, Matt had to understand.

A hand reached around her and opened the door. "Go on inside."

She faced him. Dread pounded through her as she saw his harsh expression. "I know how important trust is to you. I don't want you angry with me."

"You were supposed to stay in bed."

"Matt, I admit I'm a little sore, but that's no reason to become an invalid," she told him. "Frankly, you look more in need of rest than I do."

His eyes narrowed. "Something kept me awake last night."

"What?"

"You using me as a back warmer."

Shannon flushed, her gaze lowering. "Oh. I didn't . . . er, realize. I'll be more careful tonight—" She laced her trembling hands together.

"If you rest today, you won't have to."

Her lashes lifted. What she saw caused her breath to catch. In Matt's hot gaze was a desire barely held in check, a hunger that matched her own. Her fingertips lifted to press against his lips.

"Not if you don't want to shock Octavia and everybody else within sight," he said roughly.

"Can I touch you tonight?"

"Anywhere and everywhere."

Shannon shivered and withdrew her hand. Silently she entered the kitchen and tried to calm the wild cadence of her heart, the need churning through her body. Not wanting to leave him, she started for the coffeepot. "No wonder you're so grouchy. I'll fix you some coffee."

"I couldn't find any. We must be out."

"That's impossible, I opened a fresh bag yesterday." Looking in the usual spot where the coffee was kept revealed nothing. Undeterred, Shannon opened the cabinet over the refrigerator. "Eureka."

Matt plucked the can off the shelf. "I can handle it from here."

He was certainly being protective and stubborn. She worked hard to keep from grinning. She took the coffee. "I'd like a cup myself. I'm also hungry."

"I cook worse than Cleve."

Shannon laughed at his disgruntled expression. "I heard. Now sit down and stay out of my way." After preparing the coffee, she took out two big skillets. "I'm sure Daniel and his men would like breakfast before they leave," she explained. Opening the refrigerator, she removed a package of butter, a can of biscuits, rolled sausage, and some bacon.

"I can cook for them," he said, a smile in his voice.

"If you don't mind, I'd rather not have to use my nursing skills this early in the morning," she said drolly. "I wouldn't want to tax myself unnecessarily."

Black eyes narrowed. "You'll pay for that."

She laughed. "Oh, Matt. Where's your sense of humor?"

"Gone South."

She laughed so hard her stomach hurt. Who would

have thought Matt had a sense of humor? She leaned her head against his chest and felt his body shaking with his own laughter.

"Don't you dare forgive that scoundrel."

Shannon whirled to see Octavia, hands on ample hips, glaring over Shannon's shoulder at Matt. "G-good morning."

The housekeeper advanced on them with firm steps. "If I had my broomstick handy, I'd teach you a lesson about respecting women."

Shannon held her breath. Octavia knew.

"Shannon forgave me for my bad manners in the restaurant, why can't you?" Matt said.

"I'm immune to that smile of yours." She looked around the room. "That skillet will do just as good."

"Octavia, no," Shannon yelled and caught the other woman by the arm. "He apologized, really he did. He even gave me the day off because I'm not feeling well."

The housekeeper looked back at Matt. He hadn't moved. "See what you did."

"I know. That's why I'm not trying to stop you," Matt said calmly.

"Please," Shannon pleaded. "He apologized and just offered to cook breakfast."

"He did?" the older woman questioned, surprise in her voice.

"He did."

The expression on Octavia's face went from censure to approval. "It's about time you came to your senses."

Shannon didn't like the sound of that and from the way Matt's brows bunched, he didn't, either. She flicked on the gas burner under the skillet. "Octavia, do you think a pound of bacon is enough?"

"Better cook two." She beamed at Matt. "We don't want our men going hungry."

Rolling her eyes, Shannon began placing the strips of

bacon in the hot skillet. Talk about jumping from the frying pan into the fire.

Matt unsaddled his horse and headed for the house. He tried to tell himself the account book was the reason he had stopped work so early in the day. He wasn't quite able to convince himself. Ever since Daniel left and Octavia mentioned Cleve was taking her into town to do some shopping after lunch, the thought of coming home and just holding Shannon had never been far from Matt's mind.

It was going to be dangerous as hell to hold her and not make love to her, but worth every nerve-wracking moment. He was crossing the den when he noticed the door to his study ajar.

Shannon. She was probably searching for something to read.

Opening the door, he saw her lying on her stomach on the couch, a pencil poised in her hand, staring at his account book. He had let his body rule his mind. Look where that had gotten him. Now she knew everything about the ranch's finances.

"Looking for anything in particular?" he asked.

She jumped and almost fell onto the floor. Eyeing him warily, she sat up. "I was hoping to have this finished before you came home."

"I don't like anyone working on the accounts except me." The door snapped shut.

Anguish flashed across her face. "I should have asked if you wanted my help." Picking up the hand-held calculator and the account book, she placed them back on his desk.

He stepped in front of her when she would have left the room without speaking again. "Where're you going?"

"My room," she said softly, her gaze meeting his squarely.

"Sulk all you want, but I haven't changed my mind about tonight."

"I don't remember asking you to. At least when you make love to me I don't have to see the mistrust in your face," she told him.

The anger left as swiftly as it had come. He didn't understand her. He had offended her, but she was staring at him as if he was all in the world that mattered to her. His hand curved around her neck, anchoring her, searching for deception in the depth of her eyes, hating the thought of finding it.

"A woman's body doesn't lie as easily as her tongue."

"Let me go."

When he did, Shannon picked up his hands and placed them over her breasts. Never taking her eyes from his she curved her arms around his neck and pressed her lower body against his. "I'm ready to take a lie detector test."

Before he had a chance to reason, to think, his hands closed around the soft mounds, his thumbs stroked over her nipples. Her breasts blossomed in his hands, the tight bud of each nipple straining toward his hand, seeking. Some force compelled him to look down to where he held her.

The erotic sight of his hands on her made him feel humble and tender. A desire so strong it shook him to the deepest level of his soul coursed through him. She wore another of those loose-fitting blouses. This one was made of some kind of turquoise clingy material that hung off the shoulder. All he had to do was . . .

His hand opened, then he hooked one finger over the top of the scooped neck and tugged. The blouse slid down revealing the lush swell of her naked breast.

"Y-you better ask your questions while I'm still able to think."

"I thought I was." One arm slid around her waist as his tongue stroked across her nipple. Then he sucked long and hard.

"M-Matt!" He caught her in his arms as her legs went out from under her. "M-maybe we should do this sitting down."

"You want to continue?" He couldn't keep the surprise out of his voice.

Her arms tightened around his neck. "Whatever it takes. Besides, you may look ready to shake my teeth out, but you only touch me with gentleness."

"Why would you say something like that?" he yelled, fighting the tender warmth of her words.

She kissed his cheek. "Because it's true. Even with the test, you didn't grab and take, you gave to both of us."

"You confuse the hell out of me," he admitted grudgingly.

"You're not so easy to understand yourself."

He eyed her. "I'm a reasonable man, and if you don't stop smiling I'll drop you."

"I'm going to give you a chance to prove it. But first I think you better put me down," she requested.

He put her down. She drew her blouse up on her shoulder and backed away a couple of steps. "That bad?" he asked.

"Not if you're going to be reasonable, and I hope you are because what I'm about to say also concerns me." She took a deep breath. "I couldn't help but notice that buying the bull almost depleted your operating expenses for next month. Since the meadow is a part of the ranch—"

"Name your price for the meadow and I'll get it," he cut off, his voice cold and curt.

She continued as if he hadn't spoken. "I think it's only fair that I pay my share of the operating expenses. I didn't get a chance to figure out the percentage, but you and I could come up with a figure. Of course, I also insist on helping with the taxes."

Stunned. When he opened his mouth, nothing came out.

"I am a junior partner and you're the one who told me how integral one part of the ranch is to the other." She fidgeted when he continued to remain silent.

"You want to give me money?" he finally got out.

"It seems only fair."

"It also doesn't make sense. Unless you plan on keeping the meadow."

She clasped her hands in front of her. "My vacation is over at the end of the week. When I leave, the meadow is yours."

"Where had you planned on getting the money? Daniel?" He didn't wait for an answer. His face became harsher with each word he uttered. "I don't need any help taking care of the ranch. That's not what I want or need from you."

She flinched, but her eyes flared. "No, you don't want any woman's help. You want an obedient bedmate. Shall I lie on the desk or on the couch?"

The torment of her words, the sparkle of tears in her eyes, lanced through him. He handed her his handkerchief and she snatched it out of his hands. Why did her tears always get to him? "I didn't mean that the way it sounded."

She sniffed. He touched her and she moved away.

"You want to give me a lie detector test?" he asked.

"I'd rather punch you in the nose."

"Then you'd go get me an ice pack and defeat the whole purpose." When she didn't bother to deny it, Matt shook his head. Shannon was generous, kind, and easily hurt. Too soft for a hard man.

"Maybe we shouldn't discuss the ranch or the meadow for the time being," she suggested, removing the last traces of tears with his handkerchief.

"Maybe not."

She bit her lip, her face solemn. "Would you like some lunch?"

She was also polite, kind, willing to forget, to forgive. She was too soft-hearted for her own good. It was about time someone tore those rose-colored glasses off her eyes.

The world was cruel and life sure as hell wasn't fair. And most men were heartless bastards when it came to getting a woman into bed. He stood at the head of the line.

"I've got a better idea." He picked her up, laid her on the couch and followed her down, planting soft, fleeting kisses on her lips, her cheek, the curve of her cheek. Nearing her mouth, but never fully joining their lips.

With a little whimper Shannon arched against him and tightened her arms around his neck, trying to bring his mouth to hers.

The honest need in that sound rocked his body and made a liar out of him. He wasn't teaching *her* a lesson, she had taught *him* one. Even heartless bastards had a conscience with the right woman.

Lifting his head, he stared into her eyes. "Do you know why they call me Hardcase?"

"What has th—"

"Do you?"

"Wade said it was because nothing affected you. That your emotions were encased in ice."

"You should have listened. I kissed you just now to teach you a lesson that men and life aren't going to play fair. Hell, I sure didn't. Last night I wanted you and I took you," he said tightly.

She punched him as hard as she could on the shoulder. To her increased anger, he didn't even grunt. "Of all the arrogant braggarts. You didn't take anything. I *gave*. I am sick and tired of people thinking I'm some kind of nitwit because I try to be nice. Get off me!"

"Shan— Ohhh" From his sprawled position, Matt watched Shannon head for the door.

He reached it before she did. For some reason, he couldn't stop grinning. "Now, honey, don't get so upset."

"I'm not your honey and that smile is wasted on me."

"I was only trying to protect you."

Her arms crossed over her chest. "By insulting me. Get real."

He looked uncertain. "It sounds kind of strange I guess, but I was angry that you forgave me so easily after I hurt you. I was trying to teach you to be less forgiving, but when you made that little sound in the back of your throat, I couldn't go through with it."

Smiling, Shannon launched herself into his arms. "Matt, that's the nicest compliment anyone ever gave me."

"Trusting isn't easy for me, Shannon."

"I know." Her tongue stroked across his lower lip. "So we'll work on something we both enjoy and go from there."

His mouth sought hers, his lips molding against hers with gentle pressure in a kiss as slow as it was deep. With a little sigh, she opened to him, luring him deeper to explore at his leisure the taste and texture of her mouth's sweetness.

He couldn't seem to get enough. Then it was her turn to savor him. The tentative glides and strokes of her tongue became more aggressive, more demanding.

His hands in her hair, he gave her all she asked for

and more. When he finally lifted his head they were both breathing hard. He stared into her passion-filled eyes and pressed his forehead to hers.

"You go straight to my head, among other places."

Shannon stroked his back. "You seem to have the same effect on me."

Sighing, he reluctantly opened the study door, the other hand draped loosely around her waist. "Will you come to the cabin with me tonight?"

"Yes."

He kissed her. Shannon was nobody's pushover, and for the time being she was only his.

Shannon was nervous. With each rotation of the truck's tires taking them closer to the cabin, her agitation mounted. It was one thing to agree to a rendezvous but quite another to deliberately carry it out under the nose of people you respected. She had never snuck around like this in her life. Although she wanted to be with Matt, she wished it could be different.

His continued silence wasn't helping.

She cast a glance at the shadowed profile of the man sitting next to her. He'd only spoken two words to her since she arrived back at the ranch tonight: "You're late." He had proceeded to put her in the truck parked a little ways from the house and drive off.

The truck came to a halt. Matt cut the motor. "I'll see about some light."

Without waiting for an answer, he got out and went inside. After what seemed like forever, he came back and opened her door. The light coming through the window was barely discernible. She started to ask him about her lantern, then decided perhaps it was best they couldn't see each other clearly. Whatever closeness they had shared earlier was gone.

Head down, she let him lead her to the cabin door, praying, hoping, when he took her into his arms, the power and passion of his touch would make everything all right.

Two steps inside the cabin, she came to a dead halt. Her mouth formed a silent O of wonder. She couldn't believe it. Scattered around the cabin were more than a dozen large candles. Peach fragrance permeated the air. On the table was a bottle of wine in an ice bucket and two long-stemmed glasses.

"Say something," Matt demanded.

"I—it's beautiful."

"If you cry, I'm going to blow out all these candles and keep my surprise," he told her.

Shannon brushed the moisture from her eyes and gave him a watery smile. "Thank you."

Going to the ice chest in the corner, he lifted the lid, came back, and shoved a bouquet of spring flowers at her. "Here."

Shannon glanced at the bouquet, then at Matt's stern expression. Her brows furrowed. Matt didn't do anything he didn't want to. Yet, he acted as if he had been dragged kicking and screaming all the way. The reason hit her all at once.

He was as nervous as she was. Not about coming here, but about how she would react to his gifts of tenderness when he wanted her to think he was incapable of such acts.

More than anyone she knew he needed and deserved love, but he would deny it with his last breath. His willingness to be vulnerable to please her calmed her fears and strengthened her love.

"Matt. How did you know?"

"The more Octavia dropped hints about us during dinner, the more subdued you became. By the time you left tonight, your chin was dragging the floor." His shoulders hunched. "You looked like you could use some cheering up."

She wanted to know how he'd thought of the scented candles, but most of all she wanted to be in his arms, his lips on hers. She lifted her face to his.

His mouth was hot and soft and utterly intoxicating. She could kiss him forever. The taste, the feel of him curled through her body as much as the slow building of heat.

He lifted his mouth enough to mutter, "What about the wine?"

"I'd rather taste you."

His eyes narrowed and darkened. "We'll take turns."

"Anywhere and everywhere," she breathed softly.

Matt's entire body went still, then he repeated her words: "Anywhere and everywhere."

His lips took hers and it was a long time before either thought of anything, but each other.

Twenty-one

I'm in trouble.

And Matt didn't have the foggiest notion of how to get out. He had come up against unpredictable calves, killer broncs, blind judges, bad weather, failed crops, deceitful people, but nothing had prepared him for Shannon.

In the four days since they had become lovers she had gotten under his skin but good. It wasn't just the sex, though Lord knew it was hot enough sometimes to blow his mind, it was Shannon herself. He had never met a woman more open, more generous, more compassionate, or more attuned to his needs. A lot of time, he lay awake just holding her, listening to the even sound of her breathing, feeling oddly content.

But then there were times he was as greedy for her body as he was for her teasing smile, her disarming laughter. The shape of his jeans changed just looking at her. He worried about her when she was out of his sight. Like now.

He'd been pacing the porch for the last fifteen minutes waiting to catch a glimpse of Shannon's headlights. Last night she'd flatly refused the escort any longer. At the time she'd presented her argument, he was on his back in the hay. She was straddling him, her blouse hanging open with nothing underneath except temptation, her lips working their way down his chest. He'd agreed before she reached his navel.

He had taken her to the hayloft instead of the cabin because he remembered her comment about not understanding how people could make love in the hay. He had planned to show her. Instead, they had ended up showing each other.

Her vacation would be over this weekend and she'd be gone. The thought of her leaving filled him with an anger which made no sense. He refused to dwell on it. The ranch was what mattered. In the distance he saw a flash of light. Excitement and anticipation drummed through him.

He took a step off the porch before he realized it. He paused, only then measuring the undeniable response of his body to a woman he didn't completely trust. How had he forgotten the lesson his ex-wife taught him?

Letting another person have control over your emotions was asking for a kick in the teeth. He had to remember that. Stepping back up on the porch, he turned to go into the house, then noticed the headlights were different.

The late-model sedan stopped directly in front of the house. The door on the driver's side opened and out stepped a broad-shouldered man a good three inches taller than Matt.

"Gazing at the stars or wishing on one?" drawled a deep, velvety voice.

"Kane." The brothers met halfway, hugged unashamedly, smiling at each other. "What are you doing here this time of night?"

"Visiting my brother," he answered.

Matt's eyebrow lifted. "If it's about the call, I have everything worked out."

"Glad to hear it." Kane reached into the front seat and

drew out a small suitcase. "That'll give us more time to catch up."

Matt, who knew how stubborn his older brother could be, turned toward the house. "Come on inside."

"Looks like you've got more company."

Those headlights Matt recognized. Shannon. He cast a quick glance at his brother. This was going to be as tricky as hell. "She works here."

"What is she doing here so late?"

"She happens to live in the ranch house," Matt explained. Although Kane didn't say anything, Matt felt the weight of his stare.

Shannon stopped behind Kane's car and got out, her smile tentative, her lower lip tucked between her teeth. Kane, used to people being fascinated or intimidated by his size, backed up closer to Matt. Her gaze widened, slid to Matt, then away.

Matt realized their relationship, not Kane's size, was causing Shannon to chew on her lip. When they were alone, she held nothing back, but around other people he often caught the dread in her eyes that someone would find out they were lovers. No matter how much he told her they had nothing to be ashamed of, he wasn't able to convince her.

From the suitcase in Kane's hand, it was obvious he was staying. As much as Matt loved his brother, he wasn't going to let her get all tense. He might not completely trust her, but no one was going to cause her be uneasy, not even Kane.

Stepping forward, Matt gave her a smile hot enough to melt steel. The change in Shannon was instant. Her eyes softened, her lips parted.

"Keep that thought and you'll be all right," he whispered.

"If I don't melt first."

He grinned and brought her to where Kane was standing. "Shannon Johnson, Kane Taggart, my brother."

Shannon extended her hand first, her smile open and warm. "Hello, Kane. I've heard a lot of good things about you."

His large hand completely enclosed her smaller one. "Hello. Apparently you weren't talking to my brother."

Matt noticed the way Shannon's eyes widened, her head tilted to one side as Kane spoke. His voice and his size always demanded a second look. It annoyed him a little to know Shannon was affected, too.

"Octavia," she finally admitted.

"Come on, let's go inside." Matt's hand still in the small of Shannon's back, he led the way into the house.

Shannon stepped away from Matt as soon as Kane closed the front door. "Good night. I know you two must have a lot to talk about. I'll just let Octavia know I'm back."

"She adopted you, too," Kane said with a smile.

"Yes. Good night again."

As soon as she disappeared through the swinging doors, Kane started for the study. "I need to call Tory and see how she and the twins are doing."

"How long have they been out of your sight? Three hours?" Matt said drolly and followed his brother inside.

"Laugh all you want. Your turn is coming." Kane picked up the phone. "Real soon, it seems."

Matt tensed. "What do you mean?"

"Shannon is a beautiful woman."

"She's okay, I guess."

Kane replaced the phone without dialing, his laughter booming around the room. "Matt, your eyes were following her like a homing device. And she was trying so hard to keep from looking at you, I kind of felt sorry for her."

"You must be really tired to make you see things." Matt flung himself into the chair behind the desk.

"Daniel said you were in trouble, but I never thought it had anything to do with a woman."

Matt came out of his chair and around the desk in a flash. "Daniel needs to keep his mouth shut and stay out of my business."

"Since he usually does, his call this morning concerned me a great deal." Kane folded his arms and leaned against the desk. "He was worried that you were going to mess up somehow. He wouldn't be specific. Now I understand what he meant."

"The only reason he's meddling is because he wants Shannon for himself," Matt blurted, then scowled at his admission.

"From the little I saw, it's *you* Shannon wants. And for her to be staying here with Octavia's obvious approval, she must be a nice young woman."

"That nice young woman wants to steal my land!"

Kane straightened. "What?"

"She was Wade's nurse when he was in the hospital in St. Louis. He left her the meadow. All she came here for was the land."

"Is she going to sell it back to you?"

"She claims Wade left it to her to help her get her life back together and once her vacation is over the end of this week, she's going to just sign it over to me." He stalked across the room. "I'm not that big of a fool."

"I don't know, Matt. Wade was a pretty good judge of character."

"Not when it came to women. Shannon can twist men around her little finger without trying. You see how quickly you jumped to her defense," Matt accused tightly.

Kane studied his younger brother intently. "Are you

angry because you're scared you love her or angry because she has a claim to part of the ranch?"

"I'd rather be kicked in the head by a bronc than let another woman tear my heart out. Shannon can leave tonight for all I care. The only thing I care about is keeping the ranch intact," Matt hurled.

A small gasp had him turning toward the sound. Shannon stood in the doorway, a tray of sandwiches and iced drinks in her hands. Anguish bracketed her tightly compressed lips. She stared mutely at Matt. He sensed she wanted— needed—him to deny his words, but he couldn't.

"Matt," Kane said. "Don't let the past ruin this for you."

Matt walked to Shannon. He had tried to warn her. "I'm too hard to care for anyone. The ranch is the only thing I need."

With a whimper of pain, she thrust the tray at him and fled up the stairs.

Matt's hands clenched the wooden tray. His chest felt tight.

"You're a fool if you don't go after her."

"Just let it go." Matt placed the food on the coffee table. "The bedroom across from mine is empty. I'll be back in a little bit."

"Need some company?"

"No thanks." The tightness of his chest increasing with each breath, each step farther away from Shannon. Finally he reached the front door and opened it. Surprise widened his eyes.

Victoria Taggart gasped, then smiled on seeing her brother-in-law. "Hello, Matt. I didn't know the twins and I were making that much noise coming up the steps."

A stunned Matt barely had time to glance down at the sleepy-looking toddlers leaning against their mother's legs, before he was brushed aside.

Kane scooped up a child in each arm. Their drooping

lids drifted closed as they settled against the familiar muscular warmth of their father. "Tory. I thought we agreed you were going to stay home."

Victoria, stunning in a white linen suit accented by gold jewelry, smiled into the scowling face of her husband. "It's a woman's privilege to change her mind. Give me a kiss before I start thinking you aren't just as happy to see me as I am to see you." Catching him by the narrow space of shirtfront between the twins, she pulled his head down to hers.

When she released Kane, he reluctantly lifted his head. "That wasn't fair."

She smiled ruefully. "It wasn't meant to be. We've never spent the night apart and the more I thought about it, the more I knew I didn't ever want to."

"I wasn't looking forward to it, either," he confessed.

"Then it's a good idea I had the foresight to expect such an occurrence and get flight reservations and rent a car to get me and the children from the airport," she told him.

Kane chuckled and kissed her on the nose. "This is what I get from being married to a businesswoman. Sassy and smart. Don't ever change."

"Hello, Victoria. Excuse me and make yourself at home." Matt stepped around the happy couple. It wasn't envy he felt. He didn't need a woman's love.

"Is he all right?" Victoria whispered.

"No, and he's too stubborn to admit it."

Matt walked faster. It was best, safest, to be alone. All he needed was the ranch. Getting in his truck, he drove off. The strange tightness in his chest somehow had moved to his throat.

With trembling hands, Shannon threw her possessions into her suitcase. She had to get away before she completely broke down. If she let the tears start, she didn't know if she'd be able to control them. The only person who could help was the man who had caused them.

The searing knowledge eclipsed everything else. Her love hadn't been enough to heal his heart as he had helped to heal hers. If she thought there was a chance, she'd stay. If only they had more time, if only the meadow wasn't between them, if only his first wife hadn't scared him so badly. If only . . .

Snapping shut the overstuffed suitcase, she groaned under its weight as she picked it up. She'd have to come back for the rest of her things. Closing her door softly, she made her way quietly past Matt's room and his study.

Outside, she breathed easier, but the tension returned when she saw Matt's truck missing and a car parked behind hers. Getting her car out would be a tight squeeze. She had no choice, though. The alternative of facing Matt was too painful. Putting her luggage inside the trunk, she went back upstairs for her overnight case and her quilt.

She was on her way back downstairs when the door across from Matt's room opened. Kane. She wanted even less to see the man who had witnessed her embarrassment.

He stepped into the hallway. Shannon was sure she didn't make a sound, but he suddenly looked over his shoulder and saw her. His gaze immediately went to the case in her hand. Softly he closed the door.

"I don't guess I can get you to reconsider."

Trembling fingers tightened on her luggage. "No."

"Where do you plan to spend the night?"

"One of the hotels on the interstate."

"What if there aren't any vacancies?"

Shannon stared straight ahead. "I'll manage . . . be fine."

"That may be, but I can't let you leave."

"What!"

"Running away is not going to solve things between you and Matt," he said bluntly.

"You heard him yourself, he doesn't want me," she whispered, the words making her ache.

"He wants you too much. That's the problem."

Shannon refused to let herself hope he was telling the truth. The bedroom door Kane just closed opened. He turned in that direction.

She started for the stairs. Out of the corner of her eyes she caught a glimpse of a woman, then she heard Kane call her name. Her speed increased. She had to get away.

"Shannon. Stop!"

She swung around, the case banging against her leg and throwing her off balance. She was too close to the landing. Her eyes widened as she dropped the things in her hand, her arms windmilling to keep her balance.

Kane's hand shot out to grab her a second too late. She felt herself falling backward. A scream tore through her throat.

Her body hit something hard but yielding. She heard a muffled sound and felt the shock of landing. Her body trembling, she shut her eyes.

"Say something," demanded Kane.

Shannon opened her eyes to see Kane and a beautiful woman kneeling by her side. Both of their faces were filled with concern. "I . . . I'm only winded."

"How about you, Matt?"

"I'll live."

Shannon tensed. The sound had come directly behind her. Rather beneath her. The warmth and hardness of a man's chest, Matt's chest, came through her clothes. She had fallen on top of him.

She scrambled to her knees beside him. Her hands ran over his chest, his arms. "Do you have any trouble breathing? Does anything hurt? Dizziness?"

"Yeah," Matt said.

"Where?"

"Here." He laid his hand over his heart.

Shannon hadn't dared let herself look at his face. Now she slowly allowed herself to do so. In his eyes she saw a tenderness he made no attempt to conceal.

"You . . . you must have bumped your head."

Matt sat up, his arm going around her waist. "For once I'm thinking straight. You can take those things back upstairs."

"So that's all you want." She pushed out of his arms and reached for her overnight case. Matt pulled her back in his arms, and before she could do more than gasp, he held her down with his body. "Let me go."

His grin infuriated her. "I'm not that big of a fool."

"Matt, are you all right?" Victoria asked.

"Never better. If I'm not, Shannon can take care of me. She's a nurse."

"Couldn't you tell from the way she was so, ah . . . thorough in checking him over," Kane said with a smile in his deep voice.

Shannon groaned. She wanted to disappear through the floor. It wasn't fair that they could laugh at this any more than it was right for her body to betray her. Her nipples had hardened and she had to grit her teeth to keep from arching her hips toward his.

"You want me to use my broomstick, child?" Octavia asked. "I heard all the commotion in here and grabbed it just in case."

"Told you twern't necessary," Cleve pointed out.

"Why are you here then?" the housekeeper questioned.

" 'Cause I saw all them cars, and then after the boss left I got to thinkin' somebody might be sick or something," the ranch hand answered.

Matt glanced around to see Octavia in her robe and

Cleve by her side. He felt Shannon tense, then wiggle her body trying to hide under him. He wished she'd stop that. He wanted her bad enough as it was, and if he stood up everyone would know it.

"If you don't mind, Shannon and I would like some privacy," he finally said.

"Matt's right," Victoria agreed. "Octavia, Cleve, good night. We'll talk in the morning."

After exchanges of good nights, there was silence.

"Get off me!" she hissed.

Matt came to his feet and immediately swept Shannon into his arms and held her securely against his chest.

She glared at him. "I'm leaving no matter what you say."

"If I can find the right words, I don't think you'll want to."

Shannon was so surprised by what he said that she didn't resist when he carried her into the den and sat in his desk chair with her in his lap. Opening the drawer, he took out the account book, a second larger thin blue leather-bound book, and a brown folder.

"The ranch is the only thing I ever owned that gave back. Even when I'm working sixteen hour days, the ranch brings me a sort of peacefulness I've never known before. I never thought I'd need or want anything more until I saw you asleep in the meadow." His hand stroked her from hip to shoulder and she was powerless to withhold a shiver of response.

"I tried to control my feelings, but it was as useless as trying to hold the wind. I didn't want to believe your kindness didn't have a price. Even when we made love, I refused to believe you just wanted me. It was easier to look for deceit in you than face my own feelings. Diana, my ex-wife, had taught me too well. Before tonight I didn't even want to say her name and I became enraged if anyone else did."

So that's why everyone referred to her as "that woman." Shannon turned in his arms. "I understand, Matt. You don't have to explain. I know you gave me all you could. You can't love me the way I love you."

His hand paused, then began the slow steady glide again. "When you ran up those stairs, I felt like a vise had clamped around my chest. I didn't know what it was until I drove to the cabin, walked through the door and realized we'd never be there together again."

He set her away, his hands cupping her face, a tender smile on his. "Do you know what it was, Shannon?"

Too full to speak, she shook her head.

"It was my heart breaking free. Diana doesn't have any power over me any longer because you banished all the anguish with your unconditional love. Daniel was right when he said for some men there is only one woman. For me, you're that woman." His knuckles gently brushed across Shannon's damp cheek. "I finally figured out it wasn't you who I didn't trust, but myself. I love you, Shannon. Only you. With nothing held back, no reservations."

"Oh, Matt, I hoped, I prayed. I love you, I love you," she repeated, overjoyed to finally be able to say those precious words aloud to him. The flow only stopped when his mouth covered hers hungrily.

After a long time he finally lifted his head. With one hand, he pulled the books closer. "Nothing I own will ever be off limits to you again. My checking account should reassure you that I can take care of the ranch in a crunch, and if not, my investment portfolio can. It's just that I want the ranch to be self-sufficient."

She never took her eyes from his. "Then I guess I'll have to come clean, too."

A moment of wariness flickered in his dark gaze, then it was gone. "Shoot."

"My great-grandfather and Granddaddy Rhodes loved

land also. In fact, they sort of collected it. Some of it turned out to be very valuable. When Granddaddy died, he left a large chunk of his estate to me."

"You're rich," he almost shouted.

"Like Octavia once told me, rich is relative."

"So you bought the Cadillac and diamond earrings for yourself."

"Graduation presents. The car came from my parents, the earrings from Granddaddy," she told him. "I'm really conservative with my money. You needn't worry that I'm going to waste yours, either. I'm not like my mother who spends hundreds of dollars on clothes and lingerie."

"Don't let Victoria hear you say that. At least not about the lingerie."

"Why?"

"She owns several lingerie boutiques, and from what Kane tells me, the prices are as high as a cat's back."

Shannon laughed at the dismay on Matt's face. "Don't worry, if I want something, I'll pay for it myself."

"You'll do no such thing," he told her sternly. "I can buy you whatever you need. In fact, I'm looking forward to it."

"Matt—"

"I mean it, Shannon, I can buy my wife her clothes and nightgowns. Not that you'll keep a nightgown on very long."

Her face glowed. "Your wife?"

"Yeah, and that's final. But I might as well tell you that I don't plan to sleep single until we're married. So we better have a short engagement."

"Anything else?" she asked, wanting to sound stern, but knowing she was too happy to hide her excitement. She had a very good idea how to get around any objections he might have.

"Yes, there is. This going around at night is going to

stop. I know you love nursing, so you and the families will have to work something else out."

She kissed the frown from his face. "I think that can be arranged."

"We'll call my parents and yours in the morning." He looked thoughtful. "I better warn you. Before Kane and Victoria eloped, my mother and her grandmother were trying to plan their wedding for them."

"My mother will be just as bad." She smiled down at him. "I'd opt for eloping, but she'd never forgive me. She's waited too long for someone to put a Mrs. in front of my name."

He turned serious. "I'm glad you waited for me."

"So am I." Beguilingly, Shannon looked up at him through a sweep of lush lashes. "I know it's rude to leave house guests, but could we go to the cabin?"

Abruptly, Matt stood with her still in his arms and headed for the front door. "All you ever have to do is ask."

Epilogue

The bride was breathtakingly radiant in white silk satin and French alençon lace. And the groom was devastatingly handsome in a morning coat.

The mother of the bride and the mother of the groom cried through the entire candlelit ceremony. Everyone agreed it was the most romantic and beautiful wedding they had ever seen. No one remembered such a splendid array of flowers. The scented peach candles added a nice touch. And weren't the Taggart twins precious.

Kane Jr. refused to give the ring to his uncle and instead presented it to the best man, his father. That brought a chuckle from the father and a groan from the mother. Not to be outdone, his sister, Chandler, left the other bridesmaids and handed her father her empty flower basket.

The father had squatted down, thanked each child, then plucked the ring from the pillow and handed it to his brother. When Kane stood, both children were standing dutifully in front of their father, who somehow managed not to look awkward with a tiny flower basket in his powerful hand.

The two busloads of guests from Jackson Falls and the three from Tyler would certainly have a lot to talk about on their trip home from St. Louis. Imagine, three ministers had officiated. One from each of their respective towns and the bride's minister.

But the three ministers didn't stop the groom from giving his bride a kiss that was as boldly erotic as it was meltingly tender. No one expected them to stay long at the reception and they hadn't. Cleve Redmon, the groom's new foreman and groomsman, and Octavia Ralston, helped the newlyweds slip away. And didn't Cleve and Octavia look happy dancing and smiling up at each other. Could there be another wedding in the making? Time would tell.

While the wedding guests were downstairs in the Crystal Ballroom sipping on vintage French champagne, eating prime rib and lobster tail, and speculating on the absent newlyweds, the two in question were on the top floor of the five-star hotel in the honeymoon suite instead of the cabin the bride had requested. For once Matt had held firm.

Low, feminine laughter, followed by a deep masculine growl, came from the entwined couple in a tangle of sheets on the king-size bed. Bare skin touched bare skin. A kiss here, a nuzzle there. For once there was no rush to explore the other's body.

"I'm glad you talked me out of the cabin." Shannon nipped Matt's earlobe.

"No gladder than that you decided to wear one of the nightgowns from Victoria's shop. Once my heart slowed down, I enjoyed it on you. Brief as it was."

"You were quite demanding," she laughed.

The smile slipped from Matt's face. "For a while, I didn't think I'd make it."

"I'm sorry, Matt. My family descended on the ranch the day after you called and mother insisted I come home."

Some of Matt's good humor returned. "Smart lady. She took one look at me looking at you and hustled you away. I thought I had her when I insisted I drive back with you. She nipped that in the bud by telling your brother to drive your car and you to take his plane ticket."

"She's a lawyer," Shannon said by way of explanation. "By the time you came to St. Louis we could have been together."

Matt shook his head. "No way was I going to take you to my hotel room. I knew you wouldn't feel comfortable facing your parents afterward. Besides, you deserved better than that."

Shannon kissed him. "I have the best. I have you. You'll have to thank Daniel for getting the ballroom for the reception, and the suite. I still don't know how he pulled it off on just two months' notice. Too bad he couldn't be here."

"My sister was disappointed, too. She thought she was finally going to meet him. When Daniel and I talked this morning he said the suite was a wedding gift and to stay as long as we wanted. That reminds me, I have something for you." Getting up from the bed, Matt went to the suitcase and brought back a thick white envelope. Ferguson & Ferguson letterhead stood out in bold lettering.

"Oh, Matt, I already took care of it." Not as comfortable with her nudity as her husband, Shannon slipped on her peach-colored lace gown before going to her suitcase. "With the wedding preparations I forgot to tell you."

Locating what she wanted, she came back to the bed and handed Matt the envelope. The letterhead on the outside of the envelope was also Ferguson & Ferguson.

"Now, the ranch belongs only to you," she said with a smile.

He nodded toward the envelope in her hand. "I think you better open that."

Frowning at the strange expression on his face, she

opened the letter and gasped. Her startled gaze went to Matt. It couldn't be. It just couldn't be.

"It seems we've traded ownership. The ranch now belongs to you and I have the meadow."

Tears streamed down her cheek. "You can't do this."

"I already have."

"I won't have it. The ranch is yours. It belongs to you."

"It belongs to a Taggart and you're now a Taggart. You can pass the ranch down to our children just as well as I can." He kissed the tears from her cheeks. "It's still hard to believe Wade planned all this from reading one of Octavia's romance novels and that she and Ferguson were in on things from the start."

Shannon nodded and snuggled closer in his arms. "Octavia admitted she kept her romance books hidden because she was afraid you might find one, read the back, and figure things out. She certainly succeeded. I couldn't believe it when Mr. Ferguson gave us another letter from Wade after our engagement was announced. I hope he knows his plan worked and that we're so happy."

"I got a feeling he does, and your granddaddy, too."

"I never knew I could be this happy. I love you, Matt, but I'm signing the ranch back over as soon as we get home."

Grinning, he lay back on the bed and folded his hands behind his head. "I look forward to you trying to persuade me, Mrs. Taggart."

"So do I, Mr. Taggart." Coming to her knees, Shannon faced Matt. A sultry grin on her face, she began to slowly inch the lace nightgown over her thighs, past her waist, over her breasts. By the time the nightgown floated over her head to land on the plush carpeting, Matt knew he was in trouble. And he was going to enjoy every second of it.

The last coherent thought Matt had as Shannon staked

her claim to his willing body was eternity wouldn't be long enough to love this unique woman of his. He wondered if she knew how special she made him feel, how loved. As soon as he got enough breath back into his lungs he was going to tell her and keep telling her every day of their lives.

She was his woman and he was only hers.

Dear Readers:

After the publication of FOREVER YOURS I received numerous requests for Matt's story. Surely, the letters stated, there was a story there and a woman strong enough to heal his wounded soul. And, yes, his cynical heart. I hope you'll agree that Shannon Johnson touched Matt as no other woman could.

I'd like to thank you for your warm response to FOREVER YOURS, SARAH'S MIRACLE (a short story in SPIRIT OF THE SEASON), UNDENIABLE, and THE BARGAIN. DANGEROUS MASQUERADE is the working title for my next book due out early 1997.

If you wish to write you can do so at the address below. A business-size self-addressed, stamped envelope is appreciated.

P.O. Box 565872
Dallas, Texas 75207

All the best,

Francis Ray

Francis Ray

Francis Ray, the bestselling author of FOREVER YOURS and UNDENIABLE, is a native Texan and lives with her husband and daughter in Dallas. After publishing sixteen short stories, she decided to follow her love and write longer works which would show the healing power of love. She launched the Arabesque line with FOREVER YOURS and was included in the Arabesque December anthology, SPIRIT OF THE SEASON. A school nurse who cares for over 1,500 children, she is also a frequent speaker at writing workshops and is a member of Women Writers of Color and Romance Writers of America.

Look for these upcoming Arabesque titles:

May 1996

BETWEEN THE LINES by Angela Benson
MOONRISE by Roberta Gayle
A MOTHER'S LOVE, A Mother's Day romance
collection with Francine Craft, Bette Ford,
and Mildred Riley.

June 1996

SUDDENLY by Sandra Kitt
HOME SWEET HOME by Rochelle Alers
AFTER HOURS by Anna Larence

July 1996

DECEPTION by Donna Hill
INDISCRETION by Margie Walker
AFFAIR OF THE HEART by Janice Sims

FOR THE VERY BEST IN ROMANCE— DENISE LITTLE PRESENTS!

AMBER, SING SOFTLY (0038, $4.99)
by Joan Elliott Pickart

Astonished to find a wounded gun-slinger on her doorstep, Amber Prescott can't decide whether to take him in or put him out of his misery. Since this lonely frontierswoman can't deny her longing to have a man of her own, who nurses him back to health, while savoring the glorious possibilities of the situation. But what Amber doesn't realize is that this strong, handsome man is full of surprises!

A DEEPER MAGIC (0039, $4.99)
by Jillian Hunter

From the moment wealthy Margaret Rose and struggling physician Ian MacNeill meet, they are swept away in an adventure that takes them from the haunted land of Aberdeen to a primitive, faraway island—and into a world of danger and irresistible desire. Amid the clash of ancient magic and new science Margaret and Ian find themselves falling helplessly in love.

SWEET AMY JANE (0050, $4.99)
by Anna Eberhardt

Her horoscope warned her she'd be dealing with the wrong sort of man. And private eye Amy Jane Chadwick was used to dealing with the wrong kind of man, due to her profession. But nothing prepared her for the gorgeously handsome Max, a former professional athlete who is being stalked by an obsessive fan. And from the moment they meet, sparks fly and danger follows!

MORE THAN MAGIC (0049, $4.99)
by Olga Bicos

This classic romance is a thrilling tale of two adventurers who set out for the wilds of the Arizona territory in the year 1878. Seeking treasure, an archaeologist and an astronomer find the greatest prize of all—love.